I0739250

THE GENTLE KNIGHT

ASHLEY YORK

THE HARRYING OF THE NORTH

The King has stopped at nothing to hunt his enemies. He cut down many people and destroyed homes and land. Nowhere else had he shown such cruelty. This made a real change. To his shame, William made no effort to control his fury, punishing the innocent with the guilty. He ordered that crops and herds, tools and food be burned to ashes. More than 100,000 people perished of starvation. I have often praised William in this book, but I can say nothing good about this brutal slaughter. God will punish him.

as recorded by *Orderic Vitalis*

CHAPTER 1

The head of the once powerful MacNaughton Clan lay dying a slow, agonizing death. The great Padraig MacNaughton would be mourned by hundreds, some who knew him well, some who only knew of him, but none would miss him as much as his only daughter, Brighit. She stood beside the bed, willing him to open his eyes and acknowledge her presence.

The darkened room reeked of sickness and putrefaction, adding to the malevolent sense of death-come-too-soon. Brighit couldn't take a deep breath. Her lungs too tight with emotion, her senses clogged with noxious fumes.

She was desperate to speak to her father one more time. To convince him not to send her away from her home, her family, her security. She leaned in close to his ear.

"I love you, da." She strained her voice to keep the whisper unheard by Aunt Ruth. Her bent shape milled in the shadows about the far side of the bed, straightening the covers, adjusting his bed cap.

Idle hands.

The older woman's shoulders seemed to bend even more with the weight of caring for her last remaining brother. Her features froze into a permanent, disapproving scowl. Her eyes downcast as if always in a state of penance.

Brighit kneeled beside the bed. "Father?"

No response.

Auntie tucked the blanket tighter around his emaciated frame without so much as a glance her way.

Brighit felt certain she was being sent away out of fear. Fear of a forced marriage with the O'Brien. Her father had withdrawn his support, cut all ties, and broken the betrothal between Tisa O'Brien and Brighit's brother, Tadhg, earlier. All were shocked by the decision but no one would gainsay him. Even when it made things so much harder for the MacNaughton Clan to be without the support of their more powerful neighbor, no one had said a word.

Her mother might have been able to change his mind but she had just passed on. Brighit's eyes rimmed with tears. The shock of having lost her mother was still so fresh and now this. Her entire family was being ripped away from her and her heart squeezed with the pain of the loss.

At the recent suggestion of a new match between the two clans, her father had become incensed despite being given the pick of any one of the O'Brien's five strong sons. He had refused the new match as if he'd been offered a deal with the devil himself. It had inflamed the ongoing hostility between the two clans. Once very close, the cause for the rift was known only to her father and he held fast to his decision to separate from the larger, stronger clan.

The wind pressed against the thatched roof, shoving its way through the wooden shutters. The unrelenting desire to whip open the windows and let in the fresh air, the outside world, the life they used to have, clawed at her gut. She'd never have that life again.

Dread snaked its way through her bowels. Now father had asked for her, wanting to talk to her about her future. Make his decree. He didn't seem to even know she was there.

Da's chest rose with the sudden intake of air. Both women jumped at the sound of his raspy breathing.

"Auntie?" Brighit began to reach toward the stoic woman before thinking better of the gesture. Her pathetic plea for assistance reverberated in that one word.

Yes, her desperation had surely hit the lowest point of her life to seek the older woman's guidance.

Aunt Ruth's hand paused just above the blanket then gently squeezed his hand. She dropped close to his ear.

"Padraig? Brighit's come to see you." She finally looked at Brighit. "He hasn't awakened since he asked for you last night."

Auntie Ruth's voice was solemn and Brighit understood the implications. He might never awaken again.

He drew in another deep breath, shifting like one coming out of a deep sleep.

"Brighit?" He called her name, his eyes bare slits in his gaunt face, seeking her in the darkness. His clouded eyes probably saw very little so Brighit was quick to take his hand.

"Yes. I'm here." She regretted sounding so distraught.

Auntie Ruth returned to the other side of the bed, fluffed his pillow, and picked up her needlepoint. There wasn't much else for her to do, but she was determined to stay. She would stand as the only other witness to Padraig MacNaughton's dying wishes.

"Ah, Brighit, my lovely daughter." Her father brushed her chin with his fingertips before he found her cheek and cupped it with his cold, weathered hand. Perhaps he didn't notice the dampness from her tears.

He shook his head slowly. "Sorry I am that I've not been able to find a good husband for you, Daughter."

He was about to decree her future fate. She struggled to breathe as if she were being shoved under water. She knew in her heart he would be wrong in what he was about to tell her.

"Da, Sean would be a fine husband."

"That's not what you said when your mother and I approached you with the match."

Sean was more like a brother to her and she *had* rejected the very idea a year ago. She worried what her father was about to propose now was even more abhorrent.

"No, you can't wed Sean."

She scooted closer to his face, inwardly begging him to hear her. "But I will, Da. I will make him a good wife and give him many children."

"'Tis not to be."

Dread gripped her heart at the finality of the statement. She imagined herself fully submerged. Her body just floating in the water's current.

"Your mother wanted you to take your vows at the Priory. She wanted you to be a bride of Christ."

"You're not remembering it right." Her voice pitched slightly higher. She fought to stay calm. "Maw said it would be better to have me a nun if there were no one else. But Sean is here. So there is someone else."

Her father drew her to him with surprising strength, urging her head to his shoulder. She obliged.

"The decision has been made, lass. It won't be undone. I will keep my own from that whoreson O'Brien Clan."

She bit her bottom lip to cease its quivering.

"Your mother's brother, Ronan, will be here by nightfall and see you to the Priory at Tanshelf." His hold weakened. "He'll see you're met with no harm."

"On the other side of the water? To England? Please don't send me away."

"It's what your mother wanted." His arm fell slack and she sat up. His eyes were closed again. He'd already fallen into a deep sleep.

The tears washed over her face but she didn't care. She'd dreamed of having a love like her parents. They had encouraged that dream since she was a small girl. Even promising they'd give her time and allow her to find a man she could love. But when her mother took ill last spring and quickly died, that dream had died with her. Her father's despondency at the loss of his wife had sent the clan into turmoil. The unexpected break from the O'Brien Clan, and the turning out of his closest friend, Roland O'Brien, only added to their problems. Where they had once been their closest allies, they were apparently a threat to their well-being.

Aunt Ruth came to her side and Brighit fell into her stiff arms. After a moment's hesitation, the woman held her closer, caressing her long, brown hair down her back. "All will be well, love, wait and see."

"Please," Brighit brightened, pulling back to search her aunt's face, her voice imploring. "Can you say he offered me to Sean?"

Aunt Ruth went rigid. "Your father did not work out any betrothal but he did send word to your uncle to escort you to the Priory. He's already been sighted on MacNaughton land."

Brighit took a deep, shaky breath and turned to face the man she'd loved like none other. She'd wanted a husband as good and kind as her father. In her mind's eye, she saw him again as he'd been, happy and smiling. She bent and kissed him on the lips.

"Thank you for taking care of me, Da."

She turned toward the door without a backward glance.

"Well?"

Brighit turned quickly to see her brother Tadhg standing in the shadows farther down the hall. His tall figure easily filled the narrow space.

"Uncle Ronan is almost here, ready to take me to the Priory."

"Aye. He comes with a contingent bent on seeing you safely across the water."

Tadhg took a step closer, his arms crossed about his chest and studied her face.

She knew he'd be able to see every thought she had. He'd always been able to do that. It mattered little. He was not lord yet and couldn't gainsay their father.

"Will it be well with you?" His quiet voice intended to comfort but she rebelled against it.

She stepped closer, nose to nose with him. Her mouth tightened. "What do you think?"

He didn't step back but held her gaze, his intense brown eyes so like her own.

"You will make do as you always have." He expressed a confidence in her that she certainly did not feel.

She rolled her eyes and pulled away. "I will get by."

He took her arm with a gentle hand, forcing her to face him. The dark curls fell around his chiseled features, giving him the look of angel. "I'm sorry for this, Brighit. This is not what we had planned for you. All of us wanted to see you wed here, living close by. Now you must travel so far and me not able to accompany you."

"I know you have things to see to here." She placed her own small hand over his much larger, stronger one. "I know you would come but there's naught you could do."

"The O'Brien could take you, forcibly if need be, and we can't allow that to happen."

"That I know quite well." She fought to keep the bitterness out of her voice but failed. "Maw had never wanted that."

Tadhg's jaw dropped. "Would *you* have us marry you to that... that warmonger?"

"No!" A shiver of fear slithered down her spine. "That is *not* what I want."

Brighit had been warned about the treatment she could expect from the O'Briens. They no longer held the MacNaughtons in high regard. The bad blood had run deep since her mother's death. And though it made no sense, the O'Brien did covet their land now. Brighit would merely be a means to an end. Surely life as a bride of Christ was a better choice.

"Then you do understand?" His voice was hopeful but his gaze remained severe.

"I prayed as hard as I could that this would not come to pass, that I would not be sent away." She turned away before he noticed her quivering lip "God has other plans for me. I will get by. I never cared for children overmuch anyway."

"That's a lie." Tadhg's tone was reprimanding. "You can tell the truth and still do the right thing, Brighit."

She turned back to him. It wasn't easy for him either. He had been in love with Tisa O'Brien since they'd been very small, when the two clans had shared all things in common. After the troubles, he had to set aside his own desires for the sake of the clan. Out of respect for their father.

"Yet I don't hear you sharing the desires of your heart. Why shouldn't I put on a brave face as well?"

He tipped her chin with gentle fingers. "So long as you keep your heart pure. Don't be filling it up with lies. Be true to yourself. You're a gently-bred woman. You'll have the strength you need whatever happens... but don't have a false heart."

She swallowed the lump in her throat. "I won't have a false heart, Tadhg. I promise."

There really was no other choice for either of them. Their father was the seventh son of the seventh son and as such, had a special anointing that all Irishmen respected. But their fate had been foretold long ago. Tadhg would take over as leader at his father's death but being the sixth son, he'd have nothing but troubles. There had been no seventh son issued by their father. After Brighit, no more children came. The joy at having a girl soon faded by comparison to what power and favor the MacNaughtons would have received had she been born the seventh son. Better for them both to avoid any further duress by accepting the inevitable.

"Keep your deepest desires close. Be watchful and see what is planned for you."

"And you as well."

Tadhg's eyes rounded. He pulled her into a tight embrace. "I'll miss you, little sister."

She etched the feel of his embrace on her heart. It would give her comfort when she was alone in the Priory.

He released her suddenly. "Now go. Pack quickly."

He kissed her cheek and turned her from him, as if overcome with emotion.

"You're to leave at daybreak," he tossed at her.

She continued down the hall to retreat to the comfort of her own chamber.

CHAPTER 2

*P*eter of Normandy was dead. He just wondered why it was taking his brain so long to catch on. No blood. No visible wounds. No rushing need to get up and try to do something—like survive. But life *was* over for him. The blow from Jeanette's unexpected death left him as broken as if he'd had an axe to the head. Truth be told, he couldn't possibly live without her. He rubbed the dirt from his hands and turned away from Jeanette's grave.

Jeanette. The frigid air made it hard to breathe. His gray warhorse, Roman, wandered a few feet away nibbling at the grass, its withers covered with mud from the trail. Although Jeanette was long dead, Peter had pushed the poor beast hard, almost believing if he could just get here fast enough, it wouldn't be true. She would still be alive.

He stretched the rough, black scarf up to cover his nose from the cold and dug his fingers back inside his coarse, fleece-lined cloak. Peter glanced up at the late autumn sky. Snow was in the air. The babe would have been three months old now. That's what her brother had told him. Rotten bastard. He probably hadn't given a thought to her well-being.

Remorse tightened his chest and grief welled up, threatening to suffocate him. He finally let loose and bellowed his pain at the cloud-thickened sky. And again. His throat raw from the deep sound he expelled, like cries from hell. If only he'd known she was with child. It would have changed everything. They'd have been wed.

Peter would never have been like his own father. Leaving her to fend for herself. To die alone in childbirth. But unlike Peter, his father's babe had survived. Survived to remind him every day of what he'd lost. With each pummel of the man's fist, Peter knew the price of his meaningless life and the happiness he had taken from his father.

The overwhelming desire to lay himself down right there, close his eyes, and never open them again pushed him hard. To just hold her small body safely in his arms again.

"Peter."

A man's voice reached him, breaking through the morbid thoughts. John. He'd found him. Damn. The Queen must have told him about Jeanette. What did he want? To see how he fared?

"Peter?" The voice was closer.

John's horse nudged Peter's arm and snorted.

"Peter. My heart breaks for your loss." John's voice was low, barely audible. He'd loved her, too. Not in the same way but they had cared for each other. They cared because they had one thing in common—their love for him.

Damn! The air pierced his lungs with each laborious breath. He bit back the rage he felt but his voice was surprisingly loud. "We've arrived a bit late."

The horse shifted behind him as its rider dismounted.

"Please, Peter," John's voice was loaded with pity and Peter wanted to punch him in the face. "You couldn't have known."

"I. Should. Have. Known."

John's hand was firm where he gripped Peter's arm. "Do not—"

Peter turned toward him with such impetus that John stepped back as if in surprise.

"We didn't have our farewells. I didn't get to tell her how I felt." Peter stepped toward John, forcing him farther back. "I wanted her to know I loved her."

Peter turned away. He walked quickly to the lone horse now at the edge of the forest. He hesitated when he saw Rowena, John's wife, a short distance away. His angry facade splintered, and pain threatened to erupt again, but he would not give in. He did not seek their comfort. He did not want their comfort. It was Peter's fault the love of his life was dead.

His face hurt as he fought for composure, his muscles twitching. He could not be here, not with these people who had tomorrow and the next day and the next day. Even now Rowena bore the evidence of John's child beneath her heavy cloak. They had their whole lives in front of them. They waited expectantly for something that had been ripped from Peter's grasp before he had sense enough to grab onto it.

"Peter."

Peter tensed at the commanding tone of voice.

"The King requires your presence," John said.

Peter closed his eyes and took a deep breath. The King was not to be disobeyed.

He tipped his head in acknowledgement without turning toward John. Peter was a soldier again. Any life he may have wanted to build for himself was set aside for the pleasure of his King. That was the life he knew. For now, he must say his last goodbye.

John moved toward Rowena with his destrier in tow. She gripped his arm, her forehead creased in concern. He understood his wife's anguish. He'd never seen Peter like this either. Well, maybe once when they were very young but never since William had put a stop to the boy's self-deprecating ways.

"Is he going to disobey the King?"

John shook his head. "We should give him more time."

Her eyes rounded and her lips parted. "How can you think you should leave him be? He is beyond devastated. Who was this woman?"

John sighed. How best to put it. "She was his...his mistress, I suppose would be the best word to describe her. But make no mistake. He loved her."

"That is quite apparent. He would not feel so lost if it were not true love. But...did she not love him back?"

Jeanette's bright red hair and smiling green eyes filled his mind. Always smiling that one. "She did. She did love him in her own way."

Rowena frowned. "But not truly?"

John did not mean to be obtuse. He'd always thought theirs was a strange relationship. Peter would stay celibate for months and then spend days locked up with her. She was always nearby when he returned from battle. Being one of the many ladies attending the Duchess Matilda, now Queen Matilda, Jeanette never lacked for male attention. John had wondered more than once if she indeed had abstained herself.

"I would say she loved him in her way but it was hard to know, truly know, what she was thinking."

"I suppose it matters not what she thought but what *he* felt is more to the point. What do we do to comfort him?"

John was moved by the concern his wife had for his closest friend. "I do not believe there is anything that can be done. He must heal from this pain on his own."

She did not seem convinced. Standing beside her, a short distance from where Peter stood stiffly beside the newly dug grave, John was unconvinced as well. Perhaps his friend never would get over this loss. The loss not only for one he loved most dearly but for the one he'd never know, his child. John felt the sting of tears at the memory of his sweet, little girl born early as a result of the abuse his wife had suffered. He pulled Rowena closer against him as if to ward off any more hurt. She had been through enough. He wished for nothing more than to be able to protect her from any more sadness. Even if the sadness came in the form of concern for a dear friend.

"I believe it will take time. But perhaps we will see him smile yet again at some far off time."

Peter returned to kneel on the cold ground beside his dead lover's grave.

"We need to leave him like this then?"

"I'm afraid we must. The King has called for him. William will know best how to assuage his pain."

Rowena made a face of disbelief. The King had shown a definite lack of consideration when it suited him, as was the case with her people, the Saxons. He could also have great compassion for his own.

"He will keep Peter busy which may help him bear up under the burden of this loss."

"I pray you are right."

John gently guided her to where her horse stood waiting.

"Should we not say anything to him?"

John shook his head. It seemed cruel to Rowena but Peter was a proud man. He would not want to be seen in this weakened state, not even by them. He was a warrior. Warriors did not break. Warriors did not falter. Warriors fought on. John sent a prayer to heaven that it would be so.

CHAPTER 3

*B*right took in the surrounding green hills and cloudless sky, the moist smell of earth from the morning dew, and fought back tears. It was a beautiful day. Instead of being allowed to enjoy it, she stood stiffly beside her escort, Uncle Ronan. He and her brother worked out the details of her departure. She mattered very little.

She'd met her uncle when she was young but he had never left much of a shadow on her life. His barrel chest and muscled legs were those of a warrior. His speech and manner were gruff. He was an islander. Danish from her grandfather's side, her uncle had blond hair. Her mother had the darker hair of Brighit's grandmother, who had been a Celtic Princess. Brighit took after her mother.

The small man at Uncle Ronan's side leered at Brighit. Covered from head to toe with a dark cloak, he seemed to grow up out of the earth. She was properly covered as one becoming a nun. Ner a strand of her dark brown hair was visible, no indication that beneath this rough sack of a kirtle there was a woman's body and yet Ivan, her uncle's man, seemed to see right through her disguise. His crooked smile showed black teeth and a fat tongue that darted out between plump lips. Through narrowed slits, he perused her up and down as if imagining having his way with her.

Panic seized her. She moved closer to her imposing brother who would rip Ivan's face off if he ever dare touch her.

"Tadhg." The sudden need to be shielded from this man erupted in her mind. Certainly her brother would not allow her to be placed in such close proximity to this lecher. She needed him to notice, so she yanked his arm. "Is Sean coming for farewells?"

She tipped her head as much as she dared to indicate the little man but Tadhg merely appeared perplexed.

"He sends his regrets at being unable to see you off. He wishes you well, Brighit. You are like a sister…" She nodded her head the slightest bit to indicate where she wanted him to see, "…but he has…" She tried again to no avail, "…much to do at this time of year."

Tadhg stopped talking and frowned in irritation. "What is amiss?"

Smiling tightly, Brighit turned back to her uncle, but was surprised to see his lackey merely standing at attention at her uncle's side. Her shock must have shown on her face.

"Niece?" Uncle Ronan prompted her.

Her eyes flashed at the little man before she smiled at her uncle. "Forgive me, Uncle, I am under much stress in my preparation for this sudden journey. I fear I am not myself."

Uncle Ronan laughed at this, a loud, boisterous laugh which caused his body to shake. "Well, my dear niece, you've nothing to fear. We will see you safely to the Priory, just as we did your mother before you."

"Ah, yes, you were the one who brought her to Tanshelf," Tadhg said.

"It was none other. Your sweet mother looked to Elizabeth—beg your pardon—the Prioress now, as her protector as you should as well, Brighit. She'll let nothing evil befall you. I can grant you that."

Tadhg frowned and glanced toward Brighit before voicing his concern. "Then how did she come to be wed to our father? I mean after taking vows?"

The sudden silence was deafening. Uncle Ronan puckered his lips in a contemplative gesture that caused his chin to wrinkle. After a long moment, he nodded slowly.

"Well. I don't recall, except to say your mother was protected within that Priory until she was wed to your father in their chapel."

Tadhg turned a bright smile toward Brighit. "Ah, the last thing she would have imagined happening within the walls of such a place."

"That's true enough." Ronan said.

Tadhg glanced around, suddenly concerned. "Will there just be the two of you then, Uncle? Do you believe that will be enough?"

"No, we are meeting up with other men who will ferry us across and guide us to the Priory. There will be enough protection for Christ's future bride, to be sure. We will see her safely off, won't we, Ivan?"

The little man puffed up with the importance of the job. "We will, my lord. We know how to care for lovely women in our charge."

Brighit shivered at the double meaning.

"See?" Tadhg took both her hands. "You will be well cared for. Uncle Ronan has his men waiting for you at the coast. I wish I could come with you."

"How is father?"

"He is holding on. It will not be long now."

"Mayhap this trip should wait until later? When you can join us?"

"Father is afraid of what the O'Brien will do. If he compromises you—"

Brighit gasped. "He would never dare!"

"Your virtue is his only concern. I am sorry." He kissed each cheek, a sad smile on his face. "I will miss you, sweetling."

As if suddenly overwhelmed, he crushed her to him.

She swallowed hard against her tears. "I can stay at your word, my lord." She whispered in his ear. She longed to beg him to not make her go, to tell him her deepest fear, to convince him to let her stay.

Instead she stepped away. Her lips frozen into a tight smile. "But father's wishes will be seen to."

She tugged her wrap closer around her. The stable boy placed the step-up box beside the carriage. He gave her his arm to help her into the wood-sided conveyance. If she even breathed, she knew she would cry. She was a MacNaughton. She needed to be strong. She would get through this as she had gotten through everything else. She held her head high as she sat, unyielding, on the cushioned bench.

"Fare thee well."

Brighit found Ivan sitting in the far corner. His face averted. A study in propriety.

She turned toward her brother, now standing beside the carriage. "You will be foremost in my prayers." *Besides my own safety.*

The stable boy hopped onto the high seat. Immediately the carriage shifted and they were under way.

"God be with you," Tadhg called out.

Uncle Ronan raised his hand in acknowledgement from his seat beside Ivan, his knees occasionally touching hers. The curtains that would cover the square openings in each door were secured to allow air flow. Brighit wanted to yank them down, cutting off the outside, and enshroud herself in this moving casket that led to her grave. Instead, she remained seated and politely faced forward.

Her uncle's glances became less frequent by mid-morning, indicating he was lost in his own thoughts and paying her no heed. Ivan, on the other hand, kept a steady eye on her, or should she say her breasts, especially when the horse was led along the bumpy road which ran alongside the ocean. She tried crossing her arms about her until she realized his face brightened at that, pulling her gown tight against her as it did.

Brighit shook her head and looked out the window. She reassured herself yet again that she was fully clothed. Ivan could not see anything he should not be able to see. The man was just depraved. She prayed there would be no opportunity for this man to be alone with her. By dusk, her uncle had taken to his horse to escape the tight confines of the carriage. He rode ahead, leading it rather than protecting her.

"How fare ye, niece?" His loud voice boomed, startling her from her thoughts.

"Well enough."

"Perhaps some food and company? There is an inn down the road where we will stop to rest. Ivan?"

"Yes, my lord." His leering smile stayed on Brighit.

"Can you see to my niece's comforts while I search out our boatmen?"

Brighit shifted forward so her voice would carry. "No, ah—"

"Of course, my lord." Ivan spoke more loudly than her. That or her uncle chose to ignore her.

"Ah, Uncle—" she tried again.

"Do not trouble him." Ivan's quiet voice purred like a contented cat. "He has done so much for you already. He's disrupted his own duties to see to you. Allow him a few minutes to himself." He threw his cloak over his shoulder and rested his hand on the sword hilt at his hip, small as it was. Was he threatening her? With disgust, she noticed a little bulge fairly bursting through his breeches. "I will take very good care of you."

The thatched building, aptly named the Crossroads Inn, was set just off the much traveled crossroads that led down to the sea. The smell of salty water permeated the air but Brighit hadn't yet spotted the turbulent tides she'd soon be crossing. Not having spent much time on the ocean, she feared it. She was convinced the dark, churning depths that separated her from her new home were totally impassable. When her uncle returned, he assured her it was doable.

"The crossing to England is not a long one. I travel it myself quite often."

"You do?" This surprised her. "For what purpose?"

He stared blankly back at her before answering. "Now, now you needn't concern yourself."

His irritation with her was apparent by his tone.

"My apologies, Uncle. I meant no harm in asking."

He blew out his annoyance. "Enough! Just don't be daft now. You'll land with no harm coming to you. Come along, Brighit." Uncle Ronan grabbed her arm and directed her inside the small building to the center trestle before the fire.

The walls of the great room they entered were black with soot and ash and it reeked of urine and stale ale. The few patrons, dark and foreboding, blended into the shadows.

"That's a good girl now." He helped her to the bench but didn't sit down himself.

A small, elderly woman brought one plate with various hard cheeses and dried fish along with one tankard of cider.

Brighit's throat tightened. "Are you not joining me, Uncle?"

He looked about the empty room as if searching for someone. Having just sent Ivan off with the stable boy to care for the horses, Brighit had no idea who that could be.

"Do you know this place?" she asked. "Do you stop here often on your travels?"

Uncle Ronan seemed distracted. "You ask too many questions. I've some things to see to."

"Things?" Fear clawed at her insides.

His frown deepened. He glanced at her with a questioning look.

"Didn't you already see the boatmen?" Brighit said.

"Oh, yes. I have some other things... When Ivan returns—"

"Uncle, I wish to speak to you about Ivan. I do not feel safe in his company and—"

The older man beamed at Ivan who came up beside them, dropping onto the bench next to Brighit. He was far too close. She moved away, raising her voice.

"Uncle! I am not—"

"At your behest, my lord," Ivan spoke over her. "He has agreed to meet with you."

Brighit's jaw dropped. "What? Who? Who has agreed to meet you? Another boatman?"

Her uncle ignored her questions and headed to the door without a second glance. A tall, dark man waited by the door, his face concealed by the hood of his cloak.

"Uncle, I must object." Brighit began to stand but Ivan grabbed her hand, jerking her back down beside him.

She gasped. "How dare you lay hands on me?"

Ivan smiled toward the man at the table in front of the window who had leaned forward with her outburst and now watched them. "She's a bit slow."

Brighit pulled against Ivan's clenched hand, realizing she probably did appear mad. She struggled to keep her fear in check. The door closed with a thud behind her uncle.

"Unhand me. At once." She spoke with a tightened jaw.

"Lower your voice or I will claim you are my wife and no one will care what you say."

"You would not!"

"Do not provoke my wrath." His eyes narrowed. "It would not bode well for you."

He dropped his gaze to wander along her body. She stiffened, holding her breath against the violation.

"For me, it would be quite pleasurable. I could take you to the loft and teach you how to behave correctly. Not as the bride of Christ, but as a woman intended for a man's pleasure." He held her gaze. "I would be pleased to teach you how to lose your noble attitude."

Her nostrils flared. "How dare you speak to me thus. My uncle would never allow—"

"Your uncle is not here. Haven't you noticed how preoccupied he is? You are the least of his worries. And that attitude, sweet, innocent Brighit, is exactly to what I am referring. Here you are nothing. To me, you are nothing. Do you comprehend what I am telling you?"

Brighit searched the small room, hoping to find a sympathetic face. The others pressed back against the wall, into the dark recesses, as if to hide their identity.

"You are not the treasured, virginal sacrifice of the great MacNaughton Clan here. You are little more than a warm body to these people. And me? I am your only protection."

Many traveled these waters as men for hire and to gain political favor with no loyalty. The stories from this port carried tales of murder and kidnapping. No help would be forthcoming. Her fingers ached where Ivan held her fast.

"Where has my uncle gone?" Her voice trembled despite her best effort to show courage.

Ivan shot her a smile. "He has important matters of his own. Fear not. I will be seeing to your needs."

A shiver of fear slid down her spine. She lowered her voice to match his. "Please release my hand."

He raised a questioning brow. "Will you behave?"

Brighit nodded.

Ivan tipped his head, disappointment washed over his ugly face. "Are you certain? You did not wish me to announce that you are under my care? Even tell them you are my wife?"

She gasped, which made him smile. He loosened his grip and she jerked her hand away.

"I am not under your care." She spat the words at him.

"If you are under anyone's care, it is mine." His face darkened. "Do you see your uncle here to offer his protection?"

Her heart throbbed in her ears. "He will return." She spoke with more conviction than she felt.

Ivan's smile blossomed. "All things will be made plain in time."

Brighit began to shake uncontrollably. He leaned in closer as if sensing the overwhelming terror rushing through her. Placing his hands on either side of her face, he ran his thumb along her jaw before urging it tightly shut. He smiled pleasantly, his foul breath hot on her face.

"No one knows you here." His voice was low and threatening. "No one will gainsay me... but please do become overwrought." His closed his eyes and inhaled deeply. He smiled and opened his eyes again. "I welcome the opportunity to put my hands on you. Give me one reason to put aside my promise to your uncle to keep you safe. *Please.*"

Her breath quickened and she fought to subdue her panic. His dark eyes appeared bottomless—like the pits of hell. Hell. She feared she would not be making it to the Priory.

"Please," she begged through her clenched jaw.

He tipped his head, releasing his hold of her.

"As you wish." He sat away from her slightly and spoke more loudly. "Eat now. We have a room for only a short while and then we will be on our way again."

"We?"

"Forgive me. I misspoke. *You* have a room."

Ivan turned his little body toward the serving woman and snapped his fingers. She jumped at his command.

Tears threatened Brighit but she blinked them away. They would do her no good. She picked up the cider and took a deep swallow for fortitude. She was left totally at this man's mercy. She glanced toward the door. Her uncle could not be far. Surely if he would listen to her, he would see her better protected.

"I need to relieve myself." Brighit stood slowly, fearful he would grab at her to keep her from rising.

Ivan kept his hands to himself. "Attempting to escape would not be wise."

The room was filling now, but any one of them could be more of a threat to her than Ivan. He'd said he would hold to his promise unless she gave him reason.

"I will not try to escape."

She darted to the door. Opening it, she assessed which way her uncle may have gone. The gloaming was quickly being replaced by darkness. To her right, two tall figures, heads together in close conversation, were barely distinguishable. Their voices carried.

"She's not a burden. It will be as we'd planned." Her uncle's voice.

"As if you can speak openly with her nearby? I need assistance not—"

She hesitated a hair's breadth before interrupting their impassioned conversation.

"But Leofrid, I promised—"

"Uncle?" The sudden silence fell like a sheet enshrouding them.

Uncle Ronan turned toward her and grabbed her arm. The other man gave them his back and receded deeper into the darkness.

"What is amiss? Why have you followed me?" He hissed and led her back toward the inn, away from the other man.

"I am afeared—"

"I care not how you feel!" He all but shoved her through the door.

She struggled not to lose her footing.

"Stay with Ivan. I will see you at the shore on the morrow. Now go."

Brighit stood stock still facing the now closed door. Her breathing was shallow. What should she do?

"Come, lady. You need sustenance." Ivan's voice resounded in the room. All turned toward her but Ivan.

Slowly, she confronted the only slim chance she had for protection. The slobbering sound of him shoveling food into his mouth grew louder at her approach. She moved as if in a dream. Sitting in the spot she'd just left, she picked up the leg of lamb and began to gnaw at the meat. She would need her strength if she were going to survive whatever they had planned for her. Something was happening that she didn't understand. She would follow Ivan's advice and give him no cause to put his hands on her. She only hoped he would be true to his word.

CHAPTER 4

Between avoiding Ivan's lecherous "protection" and trying to make out the land across the sea, it wasn't until Brighit was deposited on the curragh that she realized her uncle was not joining her

"Why are you not coming?" Her words were quick. Irritated.

Uncle Ronan stared at her before he answered. "Do you hear anything besides your own prattling in that head of yours? These men know the area much better than I. They will get you safely to the Priory."

He puffed out a sigh then took both of her hands. Was he finally aware of her dilemma? His lecherous friend stood close enough behind her that she could feel his breath on her neck. No, her uncle didn't seem to notice and was not aware of her distress.

"My dear niece," he said and kissed her primly on both cheeks. "You will arrive safely and your new life will be all that you could have imagined."

He had no idea what she was imagining. She leaned away from him. Ivan's hands grasped her bottom. She squeaked, twisted away, and shot a glare at the little man. He smiled innocently.

Her uncle frowned with a why-are-you-interrupting-me look. He cleared his throat. "Don't worry, my dear, Ivan will stay by your side." He misunderstood the exchange. "No harm will come to you under my watch."

She yanked her hands away. "But it's not your watch. You're handing me off. Does my brother know of this?"

His eyes narrowed, tightening at the corners. "Do you question me, girl? I was afraid that tongue of yours might be the very reason you are still not wed. They do not allow for such disrespect where you're going."

He turned away and mounted his horse without a backward glance. The curragh left the shore, jerking Brighit forward. The choppy water immediately made her nauseous and she leaned to the side rope, emptying the contents of her stomach until there was nothing but dry retching.

Exhausted, she dropped to the bottom of the small craft, one hand still on the side rail, and prayed for death to come quickly.

By the time they made land, her head was swimming and nothing seemed as it should. She was pushed and pulled up the grassy hill by strangers to a carriage even smaller than her family's. Rough hands grabbed at her to lift her none too gently and placed her beside a small cart. Bile flooded her mouth.

"There you go, lady." Ivan stood beside the bald-headed brute who dared to handle her like a worthless corse. More than a head taller, he made Ivan appear even smaller. "You've arrived unscathed."

She pressed back against the wooden side of the conveyance and away from the three men now surrounding her. Her skin crawled under their close scrutiny. But she looked right back. None offered the protection of which she was so desperately in need. She pushed her shoulders back and addressed the bearded man to her left. He had in no way participated in her mishandling.

"My thanks." She brushed down her skirts and tried not to appear as molested as she felt. "I'm truly sorry I was so ill."

"That is the way of it for some." He shrugged, then crossed the short distance to a disorganized pile of items, presumably their belongings. The bald-headed man followed close behind.

"I've seen you safely across." Ivan pronounced and crossed his arms. An arrogant smile puckered his lips. When he spoke, the scent of herring and turnips drifted toward her. She swallowed hard against the nausea that threatened to overtake her again.

"That should lessen after you get a good night's sleep." The heavily bearded man stopped behind her, bowing stiffly, a sack in each arm. "My name is Cole."

"Thank you, Cole, for your assistance." She moved away from Ivan. "Are you our guide?"

"Aye, I'll be taking you to Father Tinsley—"

"Father Tinsley?" Brighit had never heard of a Father Tinsley just Sister Elizabeth. "What about Sister Elizabeth?"

"The Prioress? She died, must be five years ago now. Father Tinsley. He keeps the place."

What of the agreement with the Prioress? Did this Father Tinsley know anything about her or her family? A rock settled in Brighit's stomach. She assessed the strange faces of the men before her. None could be trusted. Ivan had made that quite plain. She needed to convince them to do the right thing.

"Then the Priory may not be the best place for me to go." Her voice was quiet. She avoided direct eye contact.

This could indeed be the perfect opportunity for her to return home. She had no need to go to a Priory that was not expecting her. She steadied her breathing and prayed for that response from one of them.

Ivan snorted and continued as if she'd spoken not one single word. "Cole knows the land here very well. He will get us safely to our destination. Fear not."

"And then what?" Brighit snapped. "They're probably not even expecting me."

Ivan's eyes narrowed in warning. "Rest assured. Father Tinsley *is* expecting *you*."

Cole refused to even acknowledge her, glancing over her shoulder. Brighit turned to look, too. She saw nothing untoward.

"Will someone else be joining us?" Her tone was laced with irritation.

Cole jerked back and searched her face. "No." He cleared his throat. "We need to get a few miles between us and the sea before we stop for the night."

He took the high seat of the carriage. Ivan was there beside her, gripping her arm and forcing her inside the conveyance before she could protest. His hand grasped her backside once again before giving her a shove. She turned on him, the cart dipping with the movement.

"If you touch me like that one more time, I will carve out your heart."

His nostrils flared and his smile grew. "I like a good fight."

"Augh!"

The fact that she had no weapon to defend herself with was something she decided to take care of at the first opportunity. Unfortunately, they didn't stop at an inn that night where she might have been able to obtain a dagger, but rather in the woods with the sounds of unfamiliar animals howling in the distance.

She lay flat on her back, fully clothed, in the bottom of the cramped carriage. Heavy curtains covered the windows. Earlier, the men said they would be sleeping on the ground outside and assured her she would be well protected.

However, sleep was not on their minds. They were deep in their cups, talking loudly. The strains of Andrew's poorly played whistle permeated her little space. A lone howl pierced the night and the abrupt silence told her they listened as well. That was the last thought she had before falling into a deep sleep.

The tempting smell of the fire and the promise of food awoke her with a start. She found the curtains were pulled back all around her. A strange feeling that someone had been watching her slithered up her spine. Glancing down at herself, she was relieved to find nothing out of place except for the tight cap that had slipped off her head. The wimple lay in a crumpled ball at her side. Her long, thick hair fell in disarray around her. She sat up and shoved her hair back into the little hat. The carriage rocked beneath her with each movement.

"'Bout time you woke up, lady." It was the bald man—Andrew.

She swallowed a sarcastic retort and said, "I'm sorry if I overslept. You could have awakened me."

The looks they all exchanged with little knowing smiles startled her. They had been watching her! They were all but admitting it. Accusations flew to her lips but she bit them back. Instead of giving vent to her anger, she took a deep breath, finished tucking her hair up, and squared her shoulders before facing them again. Ivan caught her eye and winked. The other men laughed, sheepishly glancing her way. She refused to succumb.

It was not safe for her to be the only woman with these men, none of which were a relative of hers. Her brother would never have allowed it. Her father would never have allowed it. Her uncle could apparently care less. He'd even taken offense at her questioning if she was being protected. These three did not appear to value her as one that should be well-cared for.

Ivan had insisted she was not "the treasured, virginal sacrifice." That did not make it so. Tadhg had assured her it would take less than a fortnight to get to the Priory and learn her fate. That seemed a very long time.

The days dragged by with Brighit confined inside the carriage. They traveled by way of the Great North Road along the River Wharfe. She was kept inside the carriage with the windows covered. She didn't mind the added warmth, or not seeing where they traveled, or protection from prying eyes but she didn't dare ask any question. Instead she listened.

The men talked to each other in low tones. They took turns driving the carriage and, on occasion, one of the men would ride with her. Never as a companionable guest but more like a stiff-mouthed guard. By the fourth day, Brighit discerned that the timing of these visits coincided with her guides being joined by other travelers. It was almost as if the men were ensuring she did not call attention to herself. Then their voices would be loud, friendly.

This realization stoked her rebellious spirit. Were the other travelers a threat to her? Or was it more likely that part of her "protection" was making sure no one saw her? She doubted other travelers cared about her one way or another. Irritation rose, making her itch to show some type of defiance to this predicament.

Andrew sat across from her, using his dagger to clean his teeth after their midday repast. She glanced out the window. Three unknown men now rode abreast of Ivan. As different as three men could be, one had a long, dark hair and a big smile. Another was fair-haired and shorter than his companions. The last man had the red hair of the northerners—a Scot. They were having a lively conversation with Ivan and Cole, who was driving the carriage. She cleared her throat.

"Ivan." She stuck her head out the small opening before Andrew could react. "I need to see to nature's call."

Andrew leaned forward, his hands flexing at his side, but stopped short of pulling her out of the opening. She leaned back against the wooden seat and smiled sweetly. He growled and tapped the side of the carriage to signal Cole to stop.

Ivan and the other men did the same a short distance away. She jumped from the carriage and the jaws of the three visitors dropped at the sight. Apparently other travelers may indeed have some interest in her.

"Gentlemen," Brighit said, tipping her chin in acknowledgement before heading toward the side of the road. She paused. They were in an open field without so much as a bush to hide behind. Brighit squared her shoulders and headed to the right of the road.

"Hold!" One of the three men dropped from his horse and ran to her. "Might I assist you? There is a small area to this side of the road just a ways."

It was the man with black hair and a beguiling smile. He had bright, green eyes. He took her elbow, directing her the opposite way from which she had been heading.

Brighit exhaled her relief. "My thanks, uh—."

"Lachlann," he offered and bowed most gallantly. "My pleasure to assist such a bonny lass."

Ivan stomped toward them. "Unhand her." He took her arm out of his hold, jerking her against him. He pierced her with his gaze. "What game are you playing at?"

Lachlann stepped away, a bewildered look on his face. Brighit's insides recoiled.

"I nee—need to relieve myself." Her voice quivered, unsure whether Ivan would take her up on his threat now that she'd apparently overstepped her bounds.

"What is amiss?" Lachlann's eyes rounded in concern.

Ivan smiled at the man. "My apologies."

"Ivan!" Cole's voice bellowed. "We stop here for the night."

Ivan turned back toward her, his lips curled into a tight snicker. "You will obey me." The words were whispered, so Brighit doubted even Lachlann, who stood beside her, could hear him. "Do you comprehend me well enough now?"

Fear flashed through her. His grip tightened on her arm. "I do not know what I have done to anger you so."

"Ivan!"

Ivan turned to Lachlann, dismissing him with a smile on his ugly face. "I will see she is taken care of."

The other man's frown deepened, confusion marring his handsome features. "As you wish."

Lachlann went back to his friends, his shoulders rounded in disappointment. Ivan pulled her none too gently, trying not to be too obvious, of that Brighit was certain. The anger coursing through him was overwhelming. She'd played with fire and gotten burned. What was she thinking? Perhaps they'd just leave her on the side of the road now. Then what would become of her?

Her "protectors" all treated her with little regard, as if she were a loose woman. They spoke of inappropriate sexual conquests and large-breasted females. Over the past few days, Ivan had often dropped his voice mid-story, speaking low to the other men. They each turned toward her, their eyes roving hungrily over her body. She was in desperate straits and had no one to help her. She didn't even know where she was.

She trudged back, following behind Ivan.

Cole's disarming smile brought the attention of the three travelers back to him. "You know the area then?"

"Well enough." The red-haired man stepped toward Cole, extending his arm. "My name is Niall. Perhaps we can be of some assistance to you."

Cole grasped his wrist. "I am called Cole. Thank you for the kind offer. I'm sure you can, Niall. And your friends?"

"This is Lachlann," Niall answered, then indicated the blond. "And this is Aldred."

"I'm thinking the lady still needs to piss," Lachlann blurted out.

Brighit blanched. All heads turned toward her. She wanted to crawl into a hole.

"You're an arse, Lachlann." Aldred screwed his face up in disgust. "You don't talk about pissing and shitting with the ladies present."

"You just did," Lachlann defended himself, his feet wide apart, ready for a fight.

"I beg your forgiveness," Niall said as he searched her face. His expression changed to one of appreciation before he continued. "My friends are simple men without courtly graces."

Brighit noticed their bare legs which were clearly visible beneath their long shirts, the dark smudges on the blond's face, and food stuck to the side of his mouth. "You are forgiven."

Ivan's firm touch on her back, in warning, wasn't missed by Brighit, before he stepped toward the men, offering them his arm. "She doesn't need any airs. She's a plain woman herself."

"If someone could direct me?" she asked.

The three young men began to speak at once, fawning over her to see who would indeed be her guide to a private area. Brighit's cheeks heated until she noticed Ivan behind them, a scowl on his face and his fisted hands on his hips. She swallowed hard before answering.

"Please, if you could point me in the direction I can go?"

"There is a small loch just over that rise, a short distance."

Brighit nodded before heading where Lachlann had directed her. Even if for only a few minutes, a break from these men would be greatly appreciated.

CHAPTER 5

At the King's orders, Peter headed to York. The road through the north of England vacillated between being overcrowded with travelers and not seeing another soul for days. He wished to be alone but his flamboyant traveling companion did not choose to be ignored. Not only was he dressed in fine silk, silver bells and feather adornments, he refused to be quiet.

"So when William came to York, it was really just to visit FitzOsbern whom he had the greatest of respect for, you understand, but he does like to keep even his closest friends under his thumb—though I mean no disrespect, but the man truly is a tyrant at times…so sorry, do not mean to offend—"

"Mort! Will you please just shut up?" Peter tried yet again to get the man to give his mouth a rest. The subject of his irritation turned his head quickly, the feather tucked securely in his cap flapping up and down.

"My lord, you know I have nothing but the greatest of respect for you and for our mission here but you need not be so obviously disgruntled with the fact I am a talker and, as the King knows I am a talker, I believe it is the reason he put us together. Do not think for a moment I did not have better things to be doing…" Peter rolled his eyes and prayed to be struck down by lightning though the skies were finally clear. Listening to this man blather on and on was going to be the death of him. "...and it was true I was never far from the King's side during most of his conquests but—"

"Desist!" Peter maneuvered his gray warhorse in front of the palfrey the plump, little man rode, causing it to stop. With the sudden movement, the bells at his waist jingled slightly. "I mean now."

The man was clearly surprised by Peter's direct orders and dropped his jaw to make his defense but Peter held up his hand. Holding his gaze, the other man turned away abruptly as if being insulted by a man of lesser value than himself.

"I know not why you feel the need to speak without end but I can bear it no longer."

The plump man turned his evil eye on Peter who tried not to laugh at the absurdity of the situation.

"Hear me! Either you stop talking or..." Peter drew his sword from his saddle with slow deliberation until it was held up before him "...I will cut your tongue out."

The little man really knew nothing about him. Peter could very well be the sort to do just that. Mort definitely tried his patience. Admittedly, Peter had been sorely tempted over the last week's travels to do just that— and more—to keep from listening to the man anymore.

Mort pursed his lips and crossed his arms. When he opened his mouth, Peter lifted the blade slightly higher.

"Do we understand each other then?"

The feather that drooped from his floppy hat quivered with his angry grunt.

"Good. Then I will be allowed to travel unmolested by your tongue and perhaps plan my strategy for possible assault?" Peter paused, quirked a brow, his lips pressed tightly together. "York does not hold kindly to the King sending yet another envoy to her gates. They prefer to rule themselves."

"That is what I was telling you about," the man huffed his response.

"No. You were just talking. You said nothing of the sort."

His nostrils flared and Peter swore he could hear the man's teeth grinding. "You, my lord, have no sensitivity to the finer art of conversation."

"So I have been told."

"Hah!" The man's eyes widened on him. "I knew that was the very problem at the last inn. You did not show that woman the proper amount of attention before trying to get her beneath you."

Damn. Peter had hoped the man was too drunk to have remembered that embarrassing scene. Truly, Peter had been too long without a woman. How else could he have bungled such a simple job as bedding a very willing wench. He replaced his broadsword and gave the man a withering look.

"You talk again, yet I have not asked you to do so."

"You're surly because you've been without a woman." Mort spit the words at him. "Do not take that out on me!"

"I most certainly will not." Peter pulled the reins to head the horse back along the little path. "I have no need for a woman."

Mort's *humph* could be heard even across the distance he put between the two of them. Perhaps he was right. If Peter could be left alone to think, he might be able to figure that out as well. The hill sloped down below them at last and a castle in the far off distance came into view.

The wooden structure sat formidably raised on a hill and surrounded by a palisade of timber but seemed no worse for wear. FitzOsbern's fort building days had long passed, however, and having this one controlled by an Earl of questionable loyalty was just one more thing for King William to be unhappy about. Peter had been sent by the King to make known a strong and loyal presence to those who might wish to question his leadership again. No doubt the harrying that had taken place could never be forgotten. Peter accepted the duty as an opportunity for space and time to overcome the loss of his lady love.

His love. Thoughts of their last night together came slamming back and he fought against the desire that burned his loins. It had been too long and this craving was becoming unbearable. That ridiculous attempt at carnal satisfaction the night before had given him hope and dashed it just as quickly. Enough. They crossed the gentle slope at the edge of the glen. The lake came into view.

Peter reined in his horse and dropped to the ground. "We'll stop here.'

He ripped his tunic off in one motion. His companion *tsked* behind him, mumbling of this and that. Peter removed his braies and hose. He dove deep into the crystal blue lake before his unappeased appendage could be commented on. At the muddy bottom, he pushed himself back up, his lungs near bursting. The water was ice cold and it felt good. He flipped his hair back and dove again, savoring the numbing chill.

The barrenness of the countryside would take Brighit some time to get used to. Perhaps it was only this area, but it seemed nothing like her home which was so lush and green. She missed her family. A tightness began to build in her throat but Brighit refused to acknowledge it. A splashing sound came to her from just beyond the tree stand.

She glanced back the way she'd come. The need to return immediately or confront Ivan's wrath had her clenching her teeth. That splash sounded very much like the lake Lachlann had mentioned. A chance to clean her face and hands in a refreshing body of water rather than with a soaked cloth? The heat in that confined carriage was making her wilt. She sniffed and confirmed her stench was overwhelming. Before even thinking it through, she headed in the direction of the sound.

Brighit paused on the barely discernible path. Sure she heard rustling, she glanced behind at the open field she'd come from. It was empty. Nothing behind her that could make such a sound. Was it a deer perhaps? Taking a few steps farther, the small rise gave way to the breathtaking sight of a small lake. The top glistened like glass without a ripple to disturb its surface.

The slight breeze carried the pungent aroma of honeysuckle and lavender. The plants would be a wonderful thing to find and put in with her few belongings. Each night she would be surrounded by the smell of flowers. Without another thought she headed through the bushes to her right, careful to not make a sound in case the deer were still nearby. Movement along the banks drew her attention and she froze.

A man stood there dripping wet and naked. He pushed his hair away from his face. A handsome face with a strong jaw and a thick brow. She followed the movement of his hands, sloshing the water off his chiseled body. Blond hair spanned his broad chest and across his rippled torso, leading down his muscular legs, glistening in the fading light. His tarse was visible even from this distance. She looked long and hard. Her breathing became labored. Magnificent.

He turned in her direction. She ducked. She held her breath and shivered in the bush, willing her heart to stop pounding so loudly. When she ventured another peek, he was gone. Disappointment welled up inside her gut. She'd wanted nothing more than to sit and watch him, imagine how it would feel to run her hands down his expansive chest and firm body as he had done, to appreciate the rippled strength there. She blew out the breath she'd been holding and licked her dry lips. That certainly wasn't going to happen, not in this lifetime—as a nun. A small bush of purple flowers brushed her hand and she snatched it. Lavender. The sun was dropping below the hills in the west and she needed to get back. Enough of these wasted desires.

Desire made things happen. It was her grandfather's favorite saying. As the seventh son, he had been a man of some notoriety among Irish nobility. He was given the Celtic Princess, Faighrah, to wed. When he sired his own seventh son, the other leaders turned to him for guidance, for wisdom, in return for unfailing loyalty. The belief always that the seventh son of the seventh son of the seventh son had a special anointing from God. No evil could befall him.

Brighit was no son and evil seemed a little too close. Ivan had told her he would not hesitate to make up a lie about who she was. Even saying she was his wife. Others would believe him because he was a man. Perhaps a little more protection from the same God who made her a female was not asking too much.

CHAPTER 6

*P*eter returned from the lake to find his traveling companion sitting and nibbling a biscuit.

"Feel better?" Mort asked. He carefully licked the crumbs from every one of his fingertips.

Peter wondered at the man's own appetite and he didn't mean food. At none of the inns they'd stopped at had the man shown any interest in the local women for hire. He seemed only attuned to Peter and his comfort. To call that loyal was an understatement. Peter had even encouraged the man to take his leave earlier in their travels. But that was back when Peter was determined to remain celibate. The man just shrugged and said his place was at Peter's side.

"I feel refreshed," Peter said.

The man quirked a smile. "I can see you do."

Peter bent to retrieve his clothes. "You might want to take a dip as well. Help put a lock on those lips of yours."

"My lips are at your disposal alone, my lord. If you no longer wish to hear my stories, I will indeed cease and desist."

"I never wanted to hear your stories." Peter popped his head through the neck of his shirt. "Why ever would you think that I did?"

"You must be prepared for what you may face here. The King wishes you to stay on to settle the matters disrupted by FitzOsbern's departure."

"That departure was quite a while ago. Why the sudden interest in the area now?"

"Ah, so you do have need of my knowledge?"

"You're prattling thus far has not demonstrated knowledge." Peter shook his head like a dog to help the drying process. Too late he realized his words had finally struck a nerve. The man was tight jawed, his gaze locked on the dark forest behind them. "I am sorry, Mort. I do find my tongue is not well kept when I am so clearly frustrated."

The man did not respond. Instead, he straightened and extracted his sword from his palfrey's saddle.

Three or four riders quickly approached. Peter stepped beside Mort, wondering how the man could have spotted the group before he did. "Can you tell if they are Normans?"

The Normans were not well liked in the area. This had been one of the last areas of England to be subdued under King William and their loyalty was still highly suspect. By the looks of the surrounding area, the tactic the King had used against them had been savage with the harrying still quite visible everywhere they went. Peter had his orders. He also had compassion.

Mort shook his head, his voice low. "They are not, my lord."

As one, they mounted their horses. Peter drew his blade. "I do not believe they know we are here."

They exchanged looks and retreated into the darkened, western woods to watch their approach.

Three, young riders burst onto the field laughing, their horses winded beneath them.

"And you cheated as always, Lachlann!" A tall, red-haired man atop a courser had spoken. He reined his mount in to face the other two riders. His accent difficult to understand.

The one called Lachlann had long, black hair and a smile from ear to ear. "I know a shorter way is all."

The stumpy blond puckered his mouth. "And you're being chased by the devil."

Lachlann rubbed at his groin. "Aye, the devil in the form of a brown-haired fox. She's riding me hard."

He leapt from the horse then led it to the edge of the lake. He dropped to take a drink as well.

"Methinks you *wish* she was riding you hard," the first man replied then followed suit.

They laughed, relaxing alongside the water. They had bare legs and knee-length coverings of course material. But they appeared young and strong.

The blond stood beside the water, about a head shorter than the other two but stockier in build. He crossed his arms, taking a wide stance beside his horse.

"She would have been well-bedded if I'd laid hands on her."

Peter settled himself but remained wary. Like a spark to dry grass, relaxed teasing could quickly turn to death blows.

"Don't believe that'd be true, Aldred," Lachlann said. He closed the distance between them. "If I couldn't succeed, why do you suppose you'd have gotten any?"

Peter sensed the growing tension between these two and, as if on cue, their voices were suddenly tight. The smiles a little less jovial.

Lachlann shoved the other against the horse. The beast skittered.

"Enough!" The last one still squatted beside the water spoke. His voice held the ring of authority. "You're wasting your strength fighting with each other."

The two dropped their battle stances and turned toward their apparent leader. "What are you thinking, Niall?"

"It was a strange setup is all. Those three men with the one lass." He dragged his hand across his wet mouth and stood.

"Perhaps she was their hostage?" Aldred said.

"And they passed her around when they wanted some." Lachlann guffawed at his own joke. Aldred shoved him gently, their past disagreement forgotten.

Niall nodded, his expression tight with suspicion. "No, he could be correct, Lachlann."

The long hair on this one made him appear younger than the other two but Peter would have guessed at perhaps sixteen summers. Surely too old to be traipsing around the countryside in search of a good swiving.

"It could be something like that." Niall went to his horse and adjusted the saddle with quick gestures before straddling it again. "We can catch them if we cut them off through the glen."

Shouts of excitement surrounded him.

"We shouldn't have any trouble rounding them up." The blond directed his horse around in preparation of mounting as well. "Are you game, Lachlann?"

Lachlann, suddenly serious, stood frowning, unmoving. "But who will get the lass?"

So pathetically desperate. Peter knew it'd be the leader who got the girl and he felt somewhat sorry for the female. These three were pups.

Without the slightest hesitation, Peter urged his mount forward, emerging from the darkness. Sword in hand, he approached the suddenly silent group. Their hands empty, they glanced at each other as if to ask where this man had come from. Mort followed behind.

"So what is this talk of a brown-haired fox I hear? Are they common in these parts?" Peter was surprised how much he sounded like his father. Also a powerful soldier. He flinched in remembrance. "Perhaps you need leave it to men who can handle such a hunt?"

Niall tipped his head, a definite tenseness. Perhaps he only feigned nonchalance. He surveyed Peter before answering. "Norman?"

Peter nodded and waited for the inevitable ranting that usually followed but ready in case they wanted to fight it out. The King was the usurper and he needed to go back to Caen. This young man did not seem so inclined.

"I am Niall of the MacDonell Clan." He came abreast of Peter. His confidence was surprising for one so young. Peter felt an instant liking to him.

"A Scot?" Peter asked. He'd not met many of the northern tribes.

Niall smiled, causing a crease at the corner of his eyes. "We try to come upon our prey unidentified. It gives us the advantage."

In a flash like lightning, the three lads shifted from being individuals to a unified fighting force. They were armed with swords and their war cry but they were also armed with something less tangible. Their shoulders shifted back. Their heads tipped, as if attuning to each other's movements. As one they moved, circling Peter. They forced him from his horse. Mort put his hands up in surrender. Peter dropped his weapon carefully to the ground.

The point of Niall's long blade stopped short of Peter's chest even when the lad dismounted. Peter allowed himself to break into a broad smile and clapped his hands in a slow rhythm.

"Well played, lad. I thought you to be three untrained villagers and yet here you have me at a disadvantage."

They did not break from the unified front. Their faces remained stoic.

"You'd have done better to stay hidden and let us pass than to confront us, my friend," Niall said.

"I see you are right." Peter bowed slightly in acquiescence, both arms outstretched.

He turned his arm slightly, curling his hand in a fist. He knocked the loosely held sword hilt, the edge of the blade hitting against the silver band at his wrist. Peter stepped in tight to grab Niall around the chest, moving him in front. The sword fell harmlessly at his feet.

"Weapons down. On the ground." Peter took the dagger from his belt and held the tip to Niall's throat. "Don't make me ask again."

Niall struggled to loosen the man's grip circling his neck, his horse shifting beside him. The other two quickly placed their swords on the ground in front of them.

"So you are quicker than you appear, old man." Niall managed to squeeze out the compliment.

Peter snorted. "And you are far more aggressive than *you* appear." He pushed him at his two friends. "Do you provoke a fight with anyone you come across?"

The three exchanged glances, seemingly confused by the question. Finally Niall turned back and shrugged. "Yes."

Peter laughed out loud at the audacious answer.

"So the Scots have earned their battle-loving reputation."

Mort just shook his head.

What should he do with these enthusiastic would-be warriors?

"Should I speak to you about chivalry and the proper way to woo a lady rather than to just take and jump on anything that has breasts?"

Aldred's jaw dropped, aghast. Peter bit his lip to keep from laughing.

"No wooing!" Aldred sounded as if he'd just been ordered to cut off his arm. "We would have no interest in that."

Niall shook his head and rolled his eyes in apparent embarrassment at his friend's outburst.

"What about you?" Peter asked. "Is that your true name? Niall?"

Niall sized Peter up once again with a very somber look on his face. "I had no need of jumping on anything I came across. The travelers were from across the sea and they were on our land."

Aldred jerked his head toward Niall. "What? You said you'd like to get a piece of that!"

Niall reddened slightly. Peter knew how it was. Boys needed to impress each other with their constant virility. Well mayhap it was just to impress each other.

"They got away from you then?" Peter asked, his brows rising.

Judging by the blush creeping down Niall's neck, Peter believed he had the right of it.

He couldn't resist adding. "And they don't even know the area? *Tsk. Tsk.*"

The intended jab struck home. Niall started breathing heavier and his friends gathered closer, their chins dipping lower. Any divisions were closed up tight.

"Rest easy now, lads. I'm just trying to anticipate what I should do if I come across this…much sought after…wench."

"Give her to me!" The blond burst out, easing the tension, a smile on his young face. "I'll know what to do with her."

Peter shook his head. "Well, if you'll leave us in peace, we have no quarrel with you." It was to his benefit if he could get through this encounter leaving them unscathed. Their unity as a fighting force was inspiring. He'd like to be able to tap into that for his own use. Allies were more beneficial than combatants. "Would that be to your liking, Niall?"

The relief appeared heartfelt. Peter was glad he'd read the boy correctly. "We've no quarrel with you either. We can be on our way—"

"To hunt our prey," the black haired one added, his big grin splitting his face.

Niall gave him an irritated look. "—on our way and leave you unmolested."

A humorous statement since Peter was the one holding the blade. "That would be much appreciated."

CHAPTER 7

*P*eter and Mort heard the commotion long before they came upon the scene. Hurrying through the woods, they needn't worry about being heard above the din they were seeking the source of.

"What the hell?" Peter grumbled, irritated to be yet again interrupted from his mission.

After their encounter with the team of Scots the day before, they'd decided to set up camp and begin their travels bright and early the next day. Bright, however, was not to be found and by the time the clouds gave way to filtered sunlight, the morning was swiftly passing.

Mort laughed quietly. "This is a hell of a busy place for being in the middle of nowhere."

The two dismounted and dropped down at the edge of the clearing. They edged along on their bellies through the tall, wet grass.

"Do you see anything?" Mort came up behind Peter.

The scene was strange in the mist, the voices hung in the air around them but their source was hard to locate. "I think I see three men...no maybe four. Wait! Is that one of our Scottish friends' horses?"

Mort turned in the direction Peter indicated. The black mount Niall had been riding the day before wandered off to their right. "I would say it is. We are not the only ones who did not get very far this day."

He turned back to the mist. "Well, is this the prey they were stalking?" He laughed at his own joke.

"God's Bones!" A loud voice carried, followed by a laugh. Perhaps it was the man whose back was closest to him. "You whoremongers sure don't give up."

The piercing sound of steel on steel had Peter up on his elbows, edging closer.

"So do we just step in?" Mort's expression conveyed urgency as well.

The sound of grunts and fists carried better than the voices.

"I wouldn't know which side to take," Peter said.

A shoulder here, a body falling there, and the wide carriage that blocked his view seemed to shake every now and then with the swirling mist.

The sound intensified. Peter had to step in. He was the authority in the area, direct from the King. It seemed his first duty as such was presenting itself.

He edged back to where they'd left their horses and mounted in one motion. Mort was lagging behind but that no longer fooled Peter. It was just Mort's persona. A better, quicker fighter Peter had never met. Dragging his sword from the scabbard along his saddle, Peter urged his horse forward. He had no doubt Mort would be there to back him up.

Peter made a run at them across the meadow. The men were surrounded by the lifting fog. They appeared as if fighting within a cloud. Aldred dropped to the ground with blood seeping from a head wound. A bald man grabbed at his shoulder. Checking his condition no doubt. The other Scots seemed to have their adversaries, one per man, held in check. For the moment, at least. They were being distracted by concern over Aldred's condition.

Quick glances toward his friend gave Lachlann's opponent an unfair advantage which rewarded him a blow to the side of the head. Despite the other man's shorter stature, Lachlann fell hard. He lay unmoving on the ground. The man raised his weapon to finish the job.

Rounding his horse just short of Lachlann, Peter's shout received the expected look of surprise. Eyes wide with fear, the little man dropped his weapon and threw his arms up. Peter didn't hesitate to push his advantage, jamming the man against the carriage before dismounting. He aimed the point of the blade at the man's throat.

"Desist!" Peter shifted to take in the scene and be sure his blade at the man's throat would not be missed.

The unknown fighters responded at once, quickly backing away at the threat against their companion. Lachlann stood, apparently unharmed. The bald man moved from Aldred. It was Niall who kept it going. The bearded man he was fighting was much older, Peter could see that now. Taller and more seasoned. Niall's anger, perhaps at the felling of one of his own, was pushing him beyond reason.

"Niall!" Peter's voice rang through the surrounding trees. The small man before Peter shook so much the carriage rocked beside him. He peered behind to see he was finally being listened to. Niall was breathing heavy but when the other man laid down his sword, he did the same.

"Stupid shit!" The older man's voice was low, more like a growl than coherent speech.

Niall reached for his weapon again. "Me? Who the hell do you think you are?"

They both started yelling at the same time.

Mort came alongside Peter and put his own weapon on the first man. Peter pushed his way between the two before Niall had lifted his sword all the way. His vision burned on the bearded man. His nostrils flaring. He did not spare a glance for Peter.

Peter shoved his arm away. "Enough."

"I'm thinking this isn't a simple act of abduction," Mort stated the obvious and pushed the short man against the carriage with so hard a shove the vehicle rocked again. The man dropped where Mort pointed.

Glancing about, Peter shook his head. "What goes on here?"

"The bastard thinks he can take anything he wants," the bearded man answered.

Even taller than Niall, he was an imposing creature.

"And who are you?" Peter asked.

He sized Peter up before answering. "I'm Cole."

Niall grunted but held his temper in check.

The bald man finally spoke. "You're far from your home to be making accusations against us."

Niall spat on the ground. "No, *you're* the one far from home—"

Peter had to shove Niall back again. "Sit—Sit ! Now! All of you."

With the swords out of harm's way, Peter rubbed his chin and thought about how best to handle this. "Do you all know each other?"

Niall glared at Cole. "I know a whoreson when I see one."

Peter shoved Cole back down with the toe of his foot before he could get all the way up.

"Enough. Or should I just be on my way? And let you all kill each other?"

Aldred moaned where he lay unmoving. Niall quickly crawled over to his friend.

"Aldred? You got a hell of a lump on your head." Concern for his friend came through in his tone. The other men looked concerned as well.

"Do you all know each other?" Peter repeated.

The bald man covered his concern with a snicker. "Know is such a strange word."

"A poet!" Mort said. He hooted. "Here in the wilds of England. Imagine that."

Lachlann wiped at the blood dripping from his mouth. "We'd shared a meal together last night. Like friends. Even enjoyed our time together."

"Friends? Not likely," Cole said.

"Clearly not you!" Niall tossed back just as vehemently from where he was helping Aldred sit up.

"You got that right," Lachlann agreed.

The conversation made little sense to Peter but he wasn't sure he wanted to understand. It seemed nothing more than a family spat and yet there was a man bleeding profusely not three feet away.

"Mort, can you help our Scottish friend?"

It was going to be a long day.

~

Brighit shifted on the hard floor of the carriage, afraid to move. She did not want to call attention to herself. She'd stayed squatted in the small space through all the fighting and arguing. Surely they'd all settle down and go back to drinking as they'd done the previous night. Wouldn't they?

She shook her soaked chemise out again and tried to work her way down to the opening. It had seemed a simple enough task. Get the water. Bring it to the carriage. Wash as quickly as possible. Get dressed.

Spilling the heated water onto her chemise had not been part of the plan. Then the loud men from the night before came traipsing back into camp. She had questioned her own hearing. And this just as she'd pulled the sopping wet material off, over her head.

Urgency slapped her in the face. It set her fingers to quivering. It also made it even more difficult to move quickly.

"If they gave you friendship last night, why are you fighting so early this morn?"

She stilled. The voice was that of a man she didn't know. Brighit shivered. She tried to calm her nerves and focus on her task.

"We find their ways offensive and told them so." That was definitely Niall's voice. She'd had to listen to him enough the night before, trying to woo her after he'd had too much to drink. Why hadn't Ivan just allowed her to leave them?

"Are you jesting? Those aren't our ways. Those are *your* ways."

Cole sounded extremely angry. In the short time she'd known him, he got irritated easily enough, but never angry.

"What?" Niall again.

Brighit rolled her eyes. They'd all gotten along well enough last night. What could have set them off this time?

Settling for a quick wash had seemed harmless enough. Especially since what she actually wanted was to submerge herself in the lake as the handsome man had done. She took a moment to close her eyes. And took a slow deep breath. She could again see the man... in full detail. The hard lines of his muscled body. The warm blond of his sopping wet hair.

She had dreamed of him! All at once it came to her. He had taken her into his strong arms and held her tight against that hard body. Every muscle pressing into her. Then the touch of his warm lips sliding along her cheek to meet her mouth with a hungry kiss. Brighit had actually felt his lips on hers and that same heat swirled through her now.

She sighed. Yes. It was a very nice dream.

The shock of cold air accompanied with the sound of the curtain being dragged back had her eyes flying open. There in front of her was the man from the lake... the one in her very real dream. In the flash of a second, his eyes changed from wide with shock to a look she'd swear spoke of pleasure.

"And what is this?" He tipped his chin toward her, a knowing smile gracing his pleasing face.

Brighit covered herself. One arm across her breasts and one hand over her private parts. She felt like Eve posing in the Garden of Eden.

The sudden silence stole her breath away. She refused to confirm it but knew all eyes were on her.

"Do you mind?" Ivan's voice cut through the awkward moment as he stood next to the carriage. He yanked the curtain from the fine-looking man's hand, dropping it back in place. Brighit was again cocooned in darkness.

"Yours?" The man's voice was low, resonating through her core. It was as appealing as his body.

She took a steadying breath, trying to calm her nerves enough to cover herself. She couldn't have done a better job of calling attention to herself if she'd tried.

Just how many men were out there? How many men had seen her without so much as a stitch of clothing? She yanked the chemise down but it refused to cooperate. The sopping material bunched at her hips. She grabbed at her gown, her hands shaking with the rage coursing inside her.

That now familiar sound of fist-against-flesh cut through the silence.

An unfamiliar laugh. *His* laugh. A slight tremor responded through her insides.

"Mort," the handsome man called to someone.

The indistinct image of a shorter man with a gaping mouth came to mind. "Yes, my lord?"

"I believe this man was about to take a terrible misstep with his fist.

Does it seem to you these men have a certain…lack of knowledge?" he asked.

What arrogance!

Ivan's angry face came to mind. She shivered. The handsome man did not know who he was dealing with.

"I would say that it does." The shorter man was closer now.

"Mayhap some learning is required?"

"Do you believe it's possible, my lord? Are they trainable?"

"They have a naked woman in a carriage while they fight out here over who will get her."

She gasped, a soundless intake of air. Like a standard being dropped, the men talked at once. Tears threatened and a few leaked down her cheek. She wiped them away. She was only trying to clean herself not be fought over. Who was he to say such cruel things about her?

The morning had started out so promising. They'd had a nice time breaking their fast with very little interaction at all. Cole's offer of extra water had come as a surprise but not one she wanted to miss.

Sudden silence. Brighit held her breath.

"And what would your name be?"

"I am called Ivan."

"And this…young lady?"

This was just getting worse and worse. His words fairly dripped derision.

"Brighit." She answered for herself albeit through a clenched jaw from within the carriage.

"Ireland? You've taken her from Ireland?"

Brighit was surprised at his ability to name where she'd come from. She wished she were still there… any place but here. This was infuriating. She could not go out there now. They may have imagined her naked and their occasional lustful glances assured her that they did. But to have them actually see her was beyond embarrassment. Embarrassment only increased by the fact that at least two of them weren't even known to her.

"That I have." Ivan's smug voice drifted to her.

Whoreson!

"Please clothe yourself forthwith."

He must be facing her now for he sounded very close. A warmth tingled up her spine. No! His voice may be low and quiet but there was nothing intimate about this situation. She struggled with the ties up the front of her dress.

"It's what I've been trying to do." Her irritation came through in her tone of voice. Good!

"And I wonder why you have not been successful thus far." *He* had the nerve to sound irritated? "Just do it... and be quick about it."

Arrogance oozed from the man!

"Yes, my lord." She clipped her words, struggling with her wimple, and hoped her sarcasm carried through the curtain.

"Hurry up."

"I am hurrying!" Her thick hair refused to cooperate but she was not about to go out there with so much as a single strand visible.

The man cleared his throat. Brighit would like to take a knife to it. He may be pleasant to look at but his manners lacked even the slightest courtesy.

"Can you please enlighten me as to what is going on here?" He was turned away again.

"My ward and—"

"Ward?" His disgust at the word was apparent.

"Yes." Ivan's voice was quieter. "Is that a problem?"

"Ward? As in 'one you are sworn to protect'? So you were merely protecting your 'ward'?"

"Yes—"

"Not likely!" Niall spoke up. "You tried to sell her to me."

Brighit stopped her movements. Fear lurched in her stomach and halfway up her throat. Sell her? Is that what Ivan had been planning?

"I did not!" Ivan blurted. "You misunderstood me."

"I heard you myself." Brighit recognized Aldred's voice. In the short time she'd spent with him, she'd use one word to describe him. Sincere.

"You lie," Ivan accused. "You are ignorant northerners."

Ivan was the one lying. She knew it in her heart. He had tried to sell her!

"Dare *not* say that to me, coward!" Niall was closer now. Any charm he'd shown her last night was well hidden. Rage alone encompassed his well-chosen words. "You *know* the truth."

"But I didn't mean you could try her out first."

Brighit's gasp sliced through the conversation. Too late, she covered her mouth with her hand. Tears burned. She would not cry!

"Why would I pay so much for soiled goods?" Niall again.

Soiled goods? If Niall "tried her" she would be soiled. How dare they speak of her thus.

Brighit whipped open the door and jumped from the carriage. She glared at each man in turn before finally speaking.

"I am not for sale! And..." she took a step up to Niall, who towered over her. The top of her head barely reached his chest. "I am not to be tried."

She moved in closer. Niall's face softened. How dare he even think about using his charm on her now? The tears were there again. This slightest show of compassion for her and she would wallow? Hell no! She swallowed her emotions.

"Enough!" The arrogant man stood far too close to her and shouted his orders about as if all should obey him. She turned to him, put her hands on her hips, and stared.

"Yes?" He finally asked. His honeyed voice vibrated through her. One heavy brow tipped up expectantly. "Did *you* have something to add to this discussion?" His words dripped with sarcasm.

Brighit snapped. She slapped him roundly on the side of the face. The sound resounded in her ears. "How dare you reveal me in such a state of undress!"

"Had I known why the carriage rocked of its own accord, I would not have needed to pull back the curtain and...reveal you." His full lips dipped in at the corners as if suppressing a grin. "Perhaps it was not your best idea to be hiding naked."

Peter's face throbbed and he wanted to rub his cheek. This time he saw the hand coming and stopped it short of its mark. He gripped her small wrist. Her vein pulsed beneath his fingers. Her eyes black with anger. She was a feisty one.

"Once, I may forgive, but twice will have you over my knee. And I will not mind your embarrassment." He spoke in a low tone for her ears only.

For a moment, he saw the fear and indecision cross her face. His heart lurched. She relaxed her arm and allowed him to lower it to her side.

"I was merely trying to dress in a very small area. I was not 'hiding naked'." She spat the words at him. Her expression spoke of her betrayal at his hands. The unspoken accusation hit him hard.

But she continued her tirade and stomped right over to Ivan and kicked him in the shins. "How dare you try to sell me!"

A fearsome look of rage swept across Ivan's face. He raised his hand to her so quickly that Peter hesitated, but was able to block the man's fist, pressing his body between them.

"Desist," Peter said.

This man had shown little fighting ability among the other men, yet he vented his anger and frustration on an unarmed woman? Not while Peter was nearby. He shoved at him.

A glance behind him revealed a changed woman, like night and day, one who now backed toward the carriage, cowering. He turned to face her.

"What is amiss here?"

Now her wide eyes spoke only of her mistrust. She shook her head and took a shaky breath. "There is naught amiss."

The memory of her in the carriage, surprised but defiant, flashed through his mind.

Ivan moved closer, swaggering, and pulled himself up to his full height which was only as high as Peter's shoulder.

"Do you often lay hands on women in anger?" Peter asked.

"She is in my care," he answered, sounding more like a growling animal than a man, then sneered at his "ward".

The implication of that statement came out of nowhere. The sight of her standing naked in the carriage assailed him again. One arm across her lovely breasts which swelled over it, leaving one fetching, pink nipple exposed. Her other hand placed over the silken triangle of hair, merely calling attention to the promised treasure that lay within.

"Are you truly in this man's care?"

"I am." Her voice quivered. There was something unspoken. Desperation!

"We appreciate your assistance, my lord," Ivan's tone dismissed Peter. "I'm sure we can work this out amongst ourselves from here."

Ivan extended his hand toward him as if nothing untoward had transpired. Peter seethed. He refused the hand.

Ivan dropped his arm. "I have been given the charge to see her safely to a convent not far from here."

Peter glanced again at the woman. "Your name is Brighit? Of what clan?"

"The MacNau—"

Ivan stepped in front of her. "She is called Brighit. We are taking her—"

Peter turned sharply toward the short man. "Ivan? Methinks I would like to hear her answer."

Ivan shrugged as if it were of little importance what she would say. "She's not in her right mind."

"What?"

"She's a bit of a loon."

Brighit turned her face away.

She didn't appear unhitched.

"And you're bringing her where?"

"The Priory."

"At Tanshelf." Her voice startled them both and they glanced toward her. She kept her face averted.

The Priory? A ripe body like hers was intended for a man's pleasure. His sex-starved body immediately reacted, filling in the scene for his imagination. Those dark eyes deepening with passion. Those succulent, sweet, red lips parted into a sensual smile. Those firm, full breasts filling his hands.

He took a moment—and a slow, deep breath—to form a coherent response.

"Tanshelf?" The image of a monastery finally came to him. One of many King William had put under the control of his brother Odo. It solidified his rightful rule of the area. "Are you fleeing there for protection?"

Ivan watched him with a hardened expression. The other men were alert for the answer as well. The tension was thick.

"I am to become a bride of Christ."

Peter's chest tightened. The audible gasp from Lachlann mirrored his own disappointment. But Lachlann was young. Peter should know better.

"And where have you come from?" Peter focused on the task at hand. He needed to ascertain if this was really something he needed to become involved in.

"From across the sea," Brighit answered, then turned to face him. Her eyes rounded. "From Ireland."

The tenseness of the woman's body reached out to him. He didn't trust Ivan's intentions. He sensed the woman was in danger.

Peter confronted Ivan. "Do you have any thought on how to get there? Do you not know where you're headed?"

The little man's eyes narrowed. Peter's insult hit the mark. "I know where I'm going."

Brighit took a quick step away from Ivan.

Peter didn't acknowledge her this time.

"I fear you have been misled," Peter said.

Peter moved to the center of the group. "Mayhap I should introduce myself." He glanced around the little group of troublemakers. The Scots and the Protectors. The Normans could use more loyal soldiers in the area. Could these men follow orders? He needed to remain open to the possibility. "I am Peter of Normandy and come here at the behest of the King."

Their uneasy glances assured him they were now thinking better of the problems they were making for themselves by calling attention to themselves.

Niall spoke first. "Where is the King now?"

Peter translated the question to "How much time do we have to get away?"

"King William will follow anon. Upon his arrival, all men here will be swearing fealty. The cost of not doing so is immediate exile."

Peter stopped on each man as he spoke, measuring their understanding. Their averted gazes said it all. The Scots may not be intentional troublemakers except they had too much time on their hands. He could certainly take care of that little problem. "If any of you choose to follow King William into battle, I can help with your training once I am settled in the castle."

"We are proud Scotsmen. We could not fight for a Norman," Niall explained, speaking as the leader again.

"Well, I believe your leader, Malcolm—"

"*King* Malcolm," Niall corrected him.

Peter paused. "You are not in Scotland."

Niall stiffened at the reminder that he was indeed within Peter's realm of power.

"Being in England causes you a little problem, Niall."

Peter did not seek to have enemies right from the outset. If these men could be made to see reason, they might be good allies against any of the few remaining Godwinson and Dane strongholds in the area.

"Will we be given the chance to leave without incident?" Niall stood tall and proud. Peter could definitely visualize this man leading Norman soldiers. He certainly didn't want to break his spirit. He also could not leave him with any doubt of who controlled the area.

"I believe you have come farther south than you intended. You must be more careful from here on out. These areas are no longer in dispute. These are Norman lands along with all of *England*."

The lad's face became unreadable.

"If you come to see me, I will greet you as a friend," Peter said.

Niall exhaled and visibly relaxed. The two grasped arms above the wrists as men do in camaraderie and competition. When the lad moved to release his hold, however, Peter held fast. Their eyes met.

"If I have reason to think otherwise, I will not hesitate to kill you," Peter said.

Niall gave the slightest nod but it was enough. Peter let loose his arm. They had an understanding.

The leader of the Scots contingent glanced once more toward the lady, now modestly covered with a wimple and loose-fitting kirtle. There was no indication of what treasures lay hidden beneath. With downcast eyes, she appeared much younger than Peter knew her to be. The eyeful he'd seen was of a well-formed, womanly body.

Niall and Lachlann helped Aldred to mount and they headed north at a slow pace. One situation handled.

"And you two? What part are you playing in all of this?"

The two exchanged looks of disbelief. The bald man spoke first. "My lord, we are men for hire, paid to see this lady to her new home."

"And you are?"

"My name is Andrew. We don't hold any to be our personal responsibility. Understand?"

He did indeed. They had taken pay for a job they weren't actually seeing to. Peter wished he hadn't noticed the sadness that passed over the woman's face before being replaced by a look of nonchalance.

"And who hired you?"

They both pointed to Ivan. He didn't flinch but glared back at Peter.

If this is the total of the lady's protection, she didn't have any. And a sincere attempt to sell this woman? He did not doubt the Scots' story. What benefits Ivan received from her as his "ward" Peter had yet to ascertain.

The real question was whether she was she headed for the Priory as a soiled dove or a virginal sacrifice. If she left her home as a virgin, her protectors would need to see her arrive at the Priory in the same condition. And if she was a soiled dove? That didn't mean she was to be used by those protecting her. She could even be with child. A picture of Jeanette holding an indistinct bundle in her arms flashed through his mind. His chest hurt. Perhaps at the Priory, there were ways to see a child and mother safely through delivery. He exhaled to ease the tightness.

Either way, they were passing through King William's land and that alone gave Peter the right to step in. Fear for her safety, however, hardened Peter's resolve. He would see her to the Priory. And he would see her safely ensconced, whatever her condition. His arrival at the castle in York would be postponed.

He was surprised to see Mort staring intently at the woman in question. He cleared his throat and turned away with feigned disinterest only to find Peter's eyes on him. The man's color deepened. Peter glanced toward Brighit, trying to discern the reason. Her downcast eyes. Her hair primly out of sight. Her hands demurely clasped—Peter checked himself. Two nipples, perfectly outlined against the dampening material of her gown, were now quite visible. The chemise beneath appeared to be the source of the wetness.

"So, gentlemen," Mort's suddenly lilting voice caught the group off guard, giving him a chance to grasp each of their shoulders and turn them back toward the fire and away from Brighit. That left Peter with Ivan and Brighit.

Peter blocked her from the little man's view. "Ivan, I've decided I will be of assistance to you—"

"Oh no need, my lord."

Ivan's sudden stiff-lipped deference turned Peter's already soured stomach.

He shifted to move around Peter.

"I insist." Peter shifted with him, adjusting his shoulders to block her as well. "I cannot possibly allow the lady... and her entourage... to travel these lands without proper protection."

No doubt Ivan saw through the veiled threat.

"Then I accept your offer. Come, Brighit." Ivan reached around Peter and grabbed her elbow.

Her entire body tightened like a bird captured in the claws of a starving cat. Fear and loathing wiped away any feigned nonchalance from her face. Something snapped inside him. She was not a loon and if Peter did not quickly put that lie to rest, the little swine would be using every opportunity he could to lay hands on her.

"Ivan, I must insist however," Peter gently took Brighit's arm out of his grasp, turning her away from the other man's perusal, "that we treat this future bride of Christ's with greater esteem than I have seen demonstrated thus far."

Peter released her arm. "I believe it is unacceptable to have a woman of the cloth, so to speak, to be exposed to handling or ribald treatment of any kind which would include fighting. Am I correct?"

"Uh, I can't say that I know—" Ivan said.

"Yes!" Brighit's face lit up at his suggestion and she turned toward him, unaware of her dampened, and now nearly exposed, state. Peter tapped down the sense of pleasure her relieved expression gave him. He had to force himself to not look lower than her smile.

"Then let us allow you the privacy you have lacked thus far."

Her face relaxed.

"Please return to your carriage and join us when it suits you."

Ivan opened his mouth to protest but Peter roughly took his elbow as the man had just done to Brighit.

"Come now, Ivan. Surely her being in your care does not allow for an invasion of her privacy."

The little man harrumphed. Peter all but dragged him to join the group at the fire. A backward glance caught him a glimpse of Brighit retreating into her carriage. If she had a few moments to herself, perhaps she would change the chemise soaking her gown and giving him another eyeful of her bounty before anyone else noticed.

CHAPTER 8

*O*nce she was safely within the carriage, Brighit grabbed at her bodice. She was sopping wet. Glancing down, she gasped at how transparent the material had become. Heat crept up her cheeks. Was that the reason Peter had sent her away? She whipped the gown over her head, pulling her hair loose at the same time, and stretched the offending garment across the bench. It wasn't enough the man had an eyeful of her totally naked but now he saw again what no man had a right to see—no man but her husband.

But she would have no husband.

The realization pierced her chest, splitting her heart right down the middle.

No husband to look on her with pleasure. No husband to hold her close at night. No husband to meet her in that secret place where two become as one.

Her breath hitched.

But she had seen him naked as well. She closed her eyes and saw him again as he had appeared. As she should only see her husband. A well-honed warrior. Powerful. Strong.

His hand at her elbow, however, had been gentle, and the look on his face had been... appreciative.

The memory of him surveying her nakedness caused more heat to her face. He'd seemed surprised, yes, that was to be expected. But there was something else. For just the smallest of seconds, there had been... longing? The tightness in her stomach was there again.

"My lady?" The voice of the man traveling with Peter startled her. He was right outside the carriage.

"If I might offer some assistance? Perhaps the gown may dry faster beside the fire?"

"What?" Brighit had herself covered even though there was no way for him to see inside the carriage. He had noticed it, too? She felt sick.

"They'll know I am near naked in here."

"Ah, but I also have some things to stretch out for drying and will be sure yours are not visible."

Brighit hesitated. His help was welcomed but she was uncertain about this man.

"The hot fire I built will have your gown dry in a very short time. I will return it to you as soon as it is." His voice sounded reassuring. Perhaps he anticipated her reluctance.

She grabbed the gown, shoving it through the curtain to the man's waiting hands. Then she whipped off the chemise as well.

"I will have it back to you before you even have need of it."

"I have need of it now," Brighit's lowered voice dripped with sarcasm.

"My apologies, fair lady, I do see your point. I will do my best to return it to you anon."

Brighit was embarrassed that he'd heard her. "My thanks, ah,..."

"Mort," he filled in her sentence. "A great pleasure to meet you even under such conditions as these."

Peter stood beside his horse, its foreleg bent with its hoof in his hand. He tensed at the sight of Mort returning from the carriage, Brighit's gown in hand. The others were too busy grumbling amongst themselves to notice anything else. Peter continued the scraping out of mud and stones.

"I don't know that I will be needing to stay on," the bearded man announced in a loud voice, to no one in particular. "If you have sir knight at your disposal, what use have you for me?"

Peter clamped his jaw tight to stop from responding to the jab. This was a matter they needed to work out amongst themselves. He stood by his decision to see the young lady to the Priory himself.

"Cole, you know I've still need for your services." Peter caught Ivan's head tipping toward him but didn't let on. "You will not receive your payment until that time."

The big man's dissatisfaction with the answer was apparent in the way he stomped about the area, collecting wood so large, it would be impossible for a smaller man to even move. Ivan rocked on his heels beside the flames, quite pleased with himself. Mort moved about the fire, staking the sturdy limbs into the ground.

"What are you about?" Ivan finally asked Mort.

Mort ceased his movements before the first freshly laundered piece of material was draped. "Excuse me?"

Ivan frowned. "I said what are you doing?"

"Seeing to my things. Is there aught amiss?"

Ivan made a face of disdain. "No. But there's no need for you to do your own washing when we have the girl here."

"She is not a girl. She is a woman, full grown," Mort added, his tone clipped.

Ivan exchanged knowing glances with his men. Their smiles indicated they knew more than they were saying.

"Aye, that's true enough," Cole said.

Mort tipped his head, his full attention on the men before him. "You seem to be saying you have first-hand experience with the woman. Would that be from the unfortunate incident earlier?"

Peter dropped his horse's hoof and moved to pat him down, alert for the answer.

"No. We knew long before that," Andrew chimed in. He rubbed his hand across the smooth globe of his head. "Her skin is soft, too."

Peter stilled. He gripped the small, iron pick still in his hand and waited.

"Soft? I'm surprised you have such detailed knowledge of your ward. Is there more to your duty here than bringing her to the Priory?"

Ivan stepped forward. "No, there's naught. Just saying she *looks* soft is all." The passing punch fell short of being as surreptitious as Ivan probably would have liked and the other man was slow in realizing why he'd received it.

They turned away from Mort, sitting beside the far side of the fire. He continued to stretch his few articles, which included some carefully obscured woman's garments, across the limbs of the sturdy branches along one side of the fire.

Peter wanted Mort to ask more questions, force them to tell him how well they knew her. They insinuated much, as if theirs was a more carnal relationship. Especially Ivan. If he had a more intimate knowledge, was it by force or her choice? After having witnessed Ivan's treatment of her thus far, Peter doubted it was her choice. If Ivan, or any of the men, were forcing themselves on her, Peter would put an end to that. If she took them willingly into her bed, protecting her would be more difficult. It would mean she was allowing improper behavior and she may not want his protection. There was only one way to know for sure. Peter needed to find out from Brighit. He needed to get her alone.

CHAPTER 9

The evening meal was uneventful. Peter expected to witness some sort of tension but Brighit kept her face averted and spoke little. It was Ivan who kept the conversation going without actually saying anything. Peter assumed this was intentional. The occasional grunts from Mort gave Peter a certain amount of satisfaction that the man found the useless prattling annoying.

"So, Brighit," Peter said. It was time he drew her out. Her body tensed so that he'd wished he had let her be. "Are you from the east coast of Ireland?"

She glanced at Ivan before answering. Peter did the same, catching the slight nod.

"Yes," she said.

"And you have been promised to the church? Or are the provisions to be decided upon your arrival?"

"It has been decided," Ivan answered.

Cole wiped his greasy fingers on his shirt and stood. "I'm in need of a walk."

"I'll join you." Andrew stood as well.

They walked off toward the lake Peter had swum in earlier. The idea was appealing to him but he set it aside. His duty called.

"I wonder, Ivan, if I might converse with Brighit without your interruptions?"

"No!" Ivan said, his chin jutted out in a belligerent manner.

"I was being courteous to pose the question in that manner. I would have you leave us now."

Brighit's eyes widened, the glow of the fire reflected in her deep, brown eyes. Her fear of the man ran deep.

Ivan stomped away, following after the other two.

Brighit dipped her head, avoiding Peter's gaze. He moved in closer, careful not to touch her, and spoke in quiet tones for fear of upsetting her.

"Brighit? I would have you face me when I speak to you."

She acquiesced but continued to glance the way Ivan had gone.

"He cannot hurt you. I am here now."

"Methinks you don't know him as I have come to know him."

Peter tensed at that cryptic statement. Were they intimate then? He rubbed his lip with his thumb. Deciphering soldiers and predicting their movements was something Peter was quite good at but this was beyond him. If Brighit were with child and bound for the Priory then perhaps Ivan's touch was not as reprehensible as Peter believed it to be.

"How long have you been with Ivan?"

She frowned. Was it at the choice of words? He hoped so.

"My uncle gave him charge of me before we made the crossing."

Ah, an uncle. Now they were getting somewhere. She glanced into the darkness.

"And where is your uncle now?"

She shrugged, still searching the darkness. Unexpectedly she moved in close to him, her eyes imploring him. "My family cannot know what has happened to me. They would never allow such treatment—"

"Brighit!" Ivan burst out of the woods as he'd been listening. "Are you ready to retire?"

She stood abruptly refusing to make eye contact with Peter again. "Yes."

Soundlessly she moved across the camp and into the carriage, closing the curtains around her.

Peter assessed Ivan, sitting across from him, his stubby legs stretched out in front of him, his arms across his protruding belly.

"I wonder... What part of 'leave us' you had trouble with?"

Ivan tucked his feet in, leaning toward Peter. "Sir, I beg your pardon. I believed she was disturbing you. I thought only of your welfare... and hers of course."

Did the man just insinuate Peter was being inappropriate?

"Why is she being brought to the Priory?"

The other two men joined them, sitting on either side of Ivan. Mort returned at the same time and stood just beyond the firelight, behind Peter. He was prepared for something but Peter was not sure why.

"It is where her father wants her to be brought. I follow the orders I receive. Much as you, no doubt."

"I do follow orders, that's true. I have a moral code by which I live as well so that when a situation presents itself, I know what I am called to do even without direct orders. Can you say the same?"

"Yes, I can. I see to my own comfort during these times and make the most of any situation I find myself in. Do you not?"

"I might look to my comfort but not if that comfort imperils one within my protection."

Ivan guffawed. "You, sir, are a knight of the first order! I cannot say I would be quite so discerning."

"And have you taken liberties with your ward?"

Ivan's smile froze on his lips. "You disparage me, sir!"

"Do I?"

Ivan thought for a moment, almost as if measuring the best course of action. Peter wondered for the first time if this man had been a soldier. Cole and Andrew shifted, perhaps to signal readiness. Ivan narrowed his eyes slightly then stood, breaking into a huge grin.

"Ah, Sir Peter, dear Brighit is at your disposal. I ask only that she is returned when you are done with her."

Peter threw the punch without forethought, hitting Ivan squarely in the jaw. The sting shooting up his arm assured him it was a solid hit. He did not shake his hand out but stood ready for the return blow.

The men on either side of Ivan merely shifted away, as the little man fell back on his arse. Getting as far as his knees, he rubbed at his jaw, moving it side to side, then stood. The huge grin returned. The three men turned and walked away, disappearing into the darkness.

Mort grunted and stood beside him. "Well played. Round one to Ivan."

Peter's eyes widened. "You think so? I thought my fist would have quashed his comment."

"But his was still the last word. He is a wily player."

Peter rubbed his knuckles. "I didn't even know we were playing. I had the man pegged as a lecher of the worst kind, one who defaces sacred shrines and deflowers innocent virgins without much thought. Could I have been so wrong?"

"Perhaps you saw only what you chose to see. I am not sure he does not do just that. Lady Brighit is the only one who can answer those questions."

"Lady? You believe she is a lady?"

"With a certainty. Her bearing is noble and she is well educated. I just cannot fathom why she is with this group."

"I believe she was about to divulge that information when Ivan interrupted."

"Oh?" Mort shifted closer as if to ensure he didn't miss a single word. "What did she say?"

"She said, 'My family cannot know what has happened to me.'" Peter scratched at the stubble on his chin. "I cannot say exactly what it means, however. Is she saying she does not want them to know or they have no way of knowing."

"I'd say you have much to discuss with the lady."

"And you have a true knack for stating the obvious."

Mort snickered. "This would be a good time to sit and wait to see what happens next."

With the moon casting strange shadows about their little camp, Peter rested against a tree in the darkness along the forest's edge. Sleep eluded him. That was just as well. Ever since he learned of Jeanette's death, his dreams were dark and macabre. Sometimes the dream would be of his own birth and his mother screaming for help with her last breath. Sometimes it was Jeanette delivering their babe, alone and abandoned. Always he awoke in a sweat, emotionally sucked dry, unable to return to sleep.

The men had been passed out in a drunken stupor for just a short while. The banked fire glowed a distance from Peter, but the occasional snore still carried. Mort, too, slept but twenty feet from him. His feathered cap within an arm's reach. His head against his forearm. It promised to be a long night.

A dark form moved between him and the fire. He squinted, trying to identify the shape. It could be a wild animal. The shadow was small but appeared to be upright. It paused beside each of the sleeping men, an arm's length away. When it drifted to the right, the dim light revealed it was indeed a person. Peter couldn't be certain it was Brighit but he had definite suspicions. Who else could it be?

She stopped beside Andrew. He rolled onto his back. She jumped back soundlessly, out of the reach of his arms. Perfectly still. Then he turned back over, tucking his hand back beneath his head. He imagined she counted to ten before she moved again, reaching to the pile of his belongings, rummaging through, looking for something in particular. Slowly she withdrew a long stick and held it in the air.

Peter tensed. The muscles of his legs coming to full alert, ready to stop any bloodshed she might be planning. Instead she dropped her arm and backed away, disappearing into the darkness just to his right. She hadn't seemed to notice him.

Peter stood without a sound and followed her into the woods. The muffled crunch of branches breaking beneath her feet was like a beacon guiding him. He glanced back to assure no one else was aware of their movements. It didn't take long to come upon her. She sat beside the small loch, still within the shadows of the forest.

With her back to him, he moved in closer. A tentative high pitched noise, then slightly fuller but just as high, whispered through the air. She turned toward the camp. Peter ducked soundlessly against a tree just short of her sighting him. She returned to the pilfered whistle. The instrument sounding much better than the noise Andrew had gotten out of it. A quiet tune soon drifted across the water, its haunting melody sad but sweet. Peter settled on the ground.

After playing two more tunes, Brighit leaned her head forward and placed a hand over her face. No catch in her breathing. No unintelligible words. But her shoulders shook in the moonlight. She was crying. It tugged at his heart. The beautiful music she had played spoke of her talent. Mort was correct. She was indeed a lady bred.

He filled his lungs then exhaled before standing. He walked toward her.

"That was a lovely tune."

She jerked herself to standing, feet spread in a defensive posture, the whistle hidden behind her back.

"Do you follow me?" Her sharp tone surprised Peter.

He paused in front of her. The moon made a sudden appearance, casting her in full light. Her cheeks were damp from tears, her lips appeared soft to the touch, and her long, brown tresses promised the same. With a start he realized she was not wearing her wimple. His manhood stirred. She was quite provocative. Was she aware of the picture she presented? He licked his lips.

"I thought my new ward was making an escape."

"Your ward, now?"

"Perhaps I will take my duty more seriously that Ivan."

She turned slightly. In this light, she appeared quite the seductress. The gown she wore was tighter than her kirtle, outlining her breasts and dipping in at her narrow waist. He was shocked to see her ankles were exposed as well. Perhaps he had misjudged her. She could easily be a lady-bred but fallen from grace.

"Please." He gestured to the ground she'd been sitting on.

Brighit sat as if alighting on a throne rather than the cold, hard ground. She moved the whistle to the folds of her skirt.

"So why do you skulk around in the darkness?" Peter asked.

The moon hid behind the clouds so he could no longer see her features. "I do not wish to awaken the others."

"I thought perhaps you didn't wish to be caught stealing the whistle you were just playing."

"He won't miss it. I will return it before he awakes."

"You were quite adept at obtaining it... and moving among the sleeping men with them none the wiser."

"So now you believe I am a thief?"

"I do not know what to believe."

"Hmph, you knew well enough when you made accusations about me sitting around naked in the carriage."

Peter turned away slightly to hide his grin. "My apologies if I was wrong."

"If?" Brighit stood again, her voice louder now. "I have given you no reason to think I was a wanton woman. Why would you behave as if I am?"

He remained sitting, leaning his head back to look up at her. "I am at a loss to explain this situation. You are the only woman with three men. None of which I believe are your relatives. Am I mistaken?"

The sob carried to him. He took his time standing.

"Are you Ivan's property? Do you warm his bed?"

An open-mouthed sob now. She covered her hand with her mouth.

"I do not wish to cast stones but to understand."

"I—I am no—not his whore!"

She gave him her back.

"I don't expect you to believe me," she said. "I don't expect the other men to believe me. I don't expect anyone to believe me. Ivan has said as much."

He placed his hand lightly on her shoulder. "Please tell me what is amiss. I will do my best to assist you in whatever you need."

She faced him. "I wish only to be taken to the Priory."

Brighit shoved past him, pushing the whistle at him. He followed. She returned to the carriage.

The men slept on, oblivious to the goings on around them. It was just as well. Peter had missed a chance to learn what he needed. He returned the whistle to Andrew's bag and returned to his earlier position. He settled back against the same tree.

"I take it things did not go well," Mort spoke without moving. Naturally he was awake to witness his failings.

"Go back to sleep."

The little man was quiet and Peter was shocked to think he was finally obeying his orders.

"Perhaps you will get a chance to question her alone again and you can be more... judicious in your questioning."

Peter stretched out on the ground, his back to Mort. "Perhaps *you* should take your sleep when you can. I believe you will have your hands quite full come daybreak."

CHAPTER 10

Brighit turned once again in the cramped confines of her carriage. She knew the moment she fell asleep the sun would rise and the rest of the camp would be stirring. She was right.

"Hey!" Ivan poked at the curtain. "You need to join us, not lay about all day in your private chambers."

The other men laughed at his jest. She couldn't be sure she heard Peter's laugh with the others. He probably did laugh, finding it quite funny even.

Are you Ivan's property? Do you warm his bed?

What audacity. If that were so, wouldn't Ivan have joined her in the carriage? She jerked herself up. That would be awful. Her stomach lurched. Surely if the little man wanted to lay a claim to her, that would be all he would need to do. She sent up a prayer of thanks he had not done so thus far, promising anew to give him no reason.

She tugged her cap tightly over her hair and slipped her kirtle over her bed clothes. Thank goodness she'd found something else to sleep in rather than to wear her dampened gown. The night had turned cold once the clouds broke. A few moments by the fire now would help the last bit of material dry more fully. Mort had showed her kindness and didn't seem to be cut from the same cloth as the knight he served.

Brighit jumped down from the carriage. All eyes were on her as usual. It seemed odd that they always watched her. She imagined their tongues nearly touching their chins like a dog eager to receive a bone. As usual they all grinned at each other as if she had done something quite alluring rather than just stepping out of the carriage.

She caught Peter's eye before he turned around. He had a scowl of disbelief on his face. Mort, however, smiled and stepped toward her.

"I will do my best to be closer to assist you the next time." His words were for her ears only. Gallantly, he took her fingertips in his hand and escorted her to the side of the fire, even brushing off a rock for her to sit on.

"My thanks." Such kindness.

Peter appeared as a man ready to strangle someone. Was he angry that Mort had shown her such thoughtfulness?

"You have missed the turn off to Tanshelf," Peter announced to the group.

Ivan's face screwed up as if trying to discern if Peter spoke English. "What are you talking about?"

Peter blew an exasperated breath. "You have missed the turn off to the Priory." His tone was precise and impatient.

Brighit took the offered biscuit from Mort who then sat beside her. Her stomach turned to mush. Could they have intentionally missed the turn? She kept her eyes downcast.

"I'm sure you are mistaken," Ivan responded.

Brighit could tell by his tone he was lying through his crooked, yellow teeth.

"I am not," Peter said. "You did say you knew where you were going?"

Ivan sat perched on the edge of the rock, his cup of mead halfway to his mouth. The innocent look she had become so accustomed to stuck on his face. "I know I can trust my lead man, Cole, and he mentioned no such turn."

Peter licked his lips before turning rounded eyes to Cole. "If you know the way to Tanshelf, then you know you've passed the turn off."

Cole tipped his head back, his lips puckering in thought. "I recall no such turn."

"Recall or not," Peter's tone demonstrated he was out of patience, "I am telling you," his tone was low and menacing now, "we will go back. You missed the turn."

Cole rubbed at his dark beard, mayhap considering the wisdom of the man. "Yes. Yes, you could be right. I may have forgotten the turn. My thanks."

Peter relaxed his stance, nodding his head as if in answer to some internal question and began to pick up his few belongings from around the fire. "We leave shortly. Finish breaking your fast and make provisions for our water. There is little available between here and the next village."

He came close beside Brighit, but she assumed he was leaning in to speak to Mort.

"Methinks you may call attention to yourself a purpose. Fear not, I aim to be certain."

She drew back and watched him walk away. Mort's finger under her chin, gently closing her mouth shut, brought her out of her shock. He smiled at her.

"Did I hear him a right?"

Mort shook his head. "Methinks you did indeed."

"Why does he speak to me so?"

"Brighit!" Ivan barked at her. "Gather our things."

She glanced toward Peter, knowing full well that Ivan's use of the words "our things" just gave Peter the proof he sought of her intimate relationship with the disgusting man. She pulled together the few items strewn about. Let the arrogant knight believe whatever he would of her. She didn't deserve it but that seemed to matter even less.

Mort handed her his bowl, a small smile on his lips. "You missed this, my lady."

My lady? That title was foreign to her ears of late. Although not usually used in Ireland, she accepted it as a title of deference. She was the daughter of the clan leader after all.

"My thanks, kind sir." She dipped her knee before walking toward the carriage.

Mort treated her kindly, even reverently. How could he easily see what his master could not? Surely, it was apparent to all who came upon her.

She was a lady, nobly bred. Why did it matter? Their time together was limited. What he did or didn't believe about her should not matter at all. But it did. That was the most frustrating. She wanted him to think better of her. She wanted him to see her goodness. She wanted him to see her for who she really was. Why that was, she couldn't explain.

CHAPTER 11

*P*eter was anxious to get to the inn. He and Mort had passed it
a few days earlier but certainly it could be reached by nightfall
if they hurried. He wasn't just anxious to have a roof over his head and a
warm bed to sleep in, but to find some female companionship. Most inns
had at least one woman for hire. He could forge steel with his unrelenting
erection.

To slake himself now would surely help him keep his mind focused for
the trip to the Priory. One day on the road with these four and Peter was
at his rope's frayed and tattered end. He'd had more ornery travel
companions in the past, so it had to be this unreleased sexual tension
driving him.

When they arrived, Peter strapped his sword to his side as he perused
the inn, such as it was. No surprise he had given the inn so little attention.
It had a more comfortable looking shelter for the animals than for paying
guests. There was not a person in sight. His heart pounded quickly with
barely controlled anger. He shoved his way through the door.

"Hail." Peter peeled his gloves off sweaty hands and allowed his
irritation free reign with his booming voice. "Is anyone here?"

The smell of food cooking was the only indication he was not alone.
The open room had two, small, wooden tables—marred, nicked, and

looking as if they had been pieced together from scraps. Various bottles, flasks, and wine skins sat on a shelf to the left of the open fire. He did not hesitate to help himself.

"Is no one about?" Mort asked from the open door, his hands rubbing along his belted waist.

Peter took a long sip of some sort of barley water that went down smooth. "I've seen no one."

Mort gave him a disgusted look. "You have ridden us hard, my lord. I believe I am not the only one who thinks so."

"You're complaining?" Peter tipped back for a second swallow.

Mort locked his jaw then walked through the door at the far corner.

One small window faced the road with enough grime on it to convince Peter that although the place was quiet now, it was not always so. A sure sign they would be able to meet all his required services.

Ivan walked in like the captain of a ship and towing Brighit close behind. He stopped, made a sweeping glance around the room and laughed. "Well? Does this place seem familiar to you, Brighit?"

Brighit paled.

Peter stopped mid-drink. He moved toward her. "Have you been here before?"

She shook her head. A slow, emphatic "no".

"Speak up, dear Brighit," Ivan said. "Tell Sir Peter what this place reminds you of."

Peter wanted to smack that do-as-I-say-or-else look right off Ivan's arrogant face.

"If it is a troublesome memory, you need not share it with me." Peter spoke quietly, sorry for having walked right into Ivan's latest attempt at belittling his ward.

"It was our first place... together." Ivan spoke the words as if speaking of some memorable, deeply treasured place.

Together.

Brighit stared straight ahead.

"Tell him, Brighit. I'm sure he is curious. Aren't you, Sir Peter?"

"I said she does not need to tell me." Peter clipped each word. This man was surely the vilest creature he'd ever met.

"No. No! You should be told." Ivan suddenly became serious, his eyes widening as if not telling him might stop the sun from rising on the morrow. "A room very much like this one was where I offered her my complete protection."

Ivan moved in closer to Brighit, sliding one hand down her forearm to rest on her clasped hands, the other hand unseen behind her. Brighit gave a stiffened jump. The bastard had grabbed her arse.

Her color deepened three shades but she said nothing. Peter took a deep, slow, deliberate breath. It was gain control or gut the man right here.

"Ivan." He moved in close to the little man, a breath away from spitting in his ugly face. "If you *ever* touch Lady Brighit in my presence again, make no mistake, I will see every last bit of your blood spilled beneath your feet."

Ivan released Brighit's hand, took two steps away from her and appeared to be actually shrinking in size.

Peter stared him down, unflinching. He *wanted* to reach down Ivan's throat and rip his lungs up through his mouth. He *wanted* to rip his entrails out as well. He *wanted* to stab him right through his black heart.

Instead, he took Brighit's trembling hand, placed it lightly on his forearm, and escorted her into the room. He brushed off a bench for Brighit to sit upon. "Please, rest here."

Peter straightened. Perhaps Mort could locate the owner of the inn and get some food for her. He dare not leave her alone. "Mort?"

An older man entered from the corner door. He had a thick cloth wrapped around his middle and a large pitcher in each hand. The innkeeper. Mort followed behind.

"Here, my lord," Mort said.

"Andrew, grab the mugs from yonder wall." Peter sat beside Brighit.

The bald man did as ordered, placing them upon the tables. He sat beside Cole who had already chosen the other table for himself. Ivan stood by the door, shuffling his feet and skulking like a child who'd lost the cat he'd been torturing.

Peter wanted him out of his sight.

"Ivan, sit with your men or be gone from the room."

The innkeeper reappeared with a well-browned pheasant, speared with a knife, on a wooden platter. This time he was followed by a gray-haired woman, probably his wife. She carried a tray of dark bread and offered the upper crust to Peter. Her head bowed slightly.

"My thanks," Peter said.

Mort smiled, no doubt pleased by the deference being shown Peter. The man had probably informed the couple of the honor they were being paid by the presence of one of the King's own favored knights.

After properly serving the knight, the couple brought in the victuals for the other table.

Peter removed the knife and cut the meat. He pierced a small, juicy piece and offered it to Brighit.

Her warm eyes held his for a moment before accepting it, the pink tip of her tongue catching the liquid that dripped off it.

The tension in his body doubled.

"My thanks."

"I hope you find everything to your liking."

"It is very good," Brighit said.

The innkeeper's wife topped off Brighit's mug.

"Is there no one else here? Are there no wenches about?" Peter asked.

The gray-haired woman paused beside him and searched his face before responding. "A young woman helps sometimes."

He waved his hand to decline the mead, opting to continue with his own filched libations. He took a long sip. The sudden, delicious warmth in the room may have been from the fire, but he suspected it was not. Release would be sweet. "Will she be here tonight?"

Brighit frowned at Peter. He speared another piece of meat.

"She only comes when needed," the older woman said.

Her gaze was unwavering. He need only admit his need for the wench and it would be done.

Peter missed Brighit's mouth.

"Ow!" Brighit gingerly touched her lip.

"My apologies," Peter said.

No blood. Peter put the knife down.

Brighit drank from her cup, watching him over the rim. She placed her mug on the table beside the knife then glanced over at Ivan. Peter did the same before turning back to her.

The little man dropped his head to slurp his soup as if he'd not eaten for a week.

"Do not vex yourself," Peter said.

"I am under his *protection*." Although she kept her face down now, her eyes widened at the word protection.

He couldn't resist asking. "And is that all?"

Her eyes widened then narrowed into little slits of unspoken indignation. Her entire expression closed down. When he offered her more meat, she held up her palm, then turned away.

She sat perfectly still—stiff as the wooden plank she sat on. Her shoulders pressed back. Her chin in that ever-so-defiant tilt. Her full breasts pressing against the coarse material of her sack-like kirtle. Her nipples puckering beneath his gaze. Large, rosy nipples if he remembered correctly.

"How soon could she arrive?" Peter asked the innkeeper's wife.

Mort's annoyed intake of air was quite loud.

"We will get her immediately, my lord," the innkeeper said then rushed his wife into the other room.

"What is amiss?" Peter finally asked Mort. "I thought it would be appropriate to have Lady Bright receive assistance while she was here. Do you not agree?"

Suspicion flashed across Mort's face before his shoulders rounded suddenly. "Oh, no, my lord. You are very thoughtful."

The innkeeper returned alone.

"Do you have rooms for us?" Peter's irritation intertwined with his unquenched desire.

"Yes, my lord." The man bowed slightly then smiled. "We have enough room in our outbuildings to accommodate a small army."

He didn't have or need an army at the moment. When he needed was a willing woman.

Peter took another swallow of the warming liquid. He stood. The smoothness of his drink made a pleasant sweep through his body, down into his loins, and up into his head.

Brighit remained unmoving. Her head beside him, blurred slightly. He had the sudden urge to feel the softness of the brown hair that lay hidden beneath the stark, white wimple. Run his hands through it. Slide his finger along her unyielding profile and tip her chin up ever so gently so he could meet her mouth for a warm, wet kiss—

Mort coughed loudly from across the table. "You were saying, my lord?"

Mort's face appeared quite expectant but Peter wasn't sure what he had been sa—oh yes.

"Well, a warm bed or two would certainly suffice."

The arousing picture of being in a warm bed with the even warmer body of Brighit beneath him flashed through his mind. Her lovely brown hair splayed across the pillows. His manhood making its presence felt between her—she shifted beside him.

"Yes. Do you have a room?" Mort came up to Peter, blocking Brighit from his view. But Peter wanted to see her, watch her, think about making love to her. He stepped to the side so that he could continue to observe her. Some movement at the other table caught his attention. Ivan watched him, his face dark and unreadable.

"We only have the one bed in the loft." The innkeeper's wife spoke. "But plenty of room in the stables. It's warm and dry."

Peter crossed his arms and smiled at Ivan. "I'm sure our traveling companions would be happy with those accommodations."

"As will I," Mort stated. "Come, gentlemen, let us see this enticing area."

The four men followed the innkeeper out the front door. Peter glanced at the unyielding future bride of Christ. His arousal painfully tight in his close-fitting hose. He closed his eyes and breathed in her scent. A feminine scent that required just that gentlest of touches to bring her to full arousal.

Reality hit him. He opened his eyes. This was no willing wench. She was not to be seduced. There was no chance Peter could spend tonight in the company of this fetching woman. It must be his long abstinence turning her into a highly desirable morsel. He should know better. If Brighit wanted the only bed, that was fine. She deserved it. He wanted a willing wench beneath him, quenching his raging need—perhaps more than once. Hopefully they would both get what they wanted.

Peter's eyes bore into her. She knew it as well as if she could see his face. The bench beneath her was unyielding and uncomfortable. Her numbed bottom begged her to shift but after his last insult, she refused. She couldn't understand why he would treat her respectfully one minute then ask about this imagined, intimate relationship with Ivan the next.

That whoreson smacking her bottom was the last straw. The innkeeper's wife would be back any second to clear away the remaining items on the trestle. The small knife sat among the wooden plates, mugs, and bones on the table. It had taken long enough but she was not about to pass what may well be her only opportunity to obtain a means to protect herself. With the others gone, it would be hers if Peter would just turn away.

"Well?" Peter asked.

She started at his voice. Indecision held her immobile. If he could be distracted before the woman returned, she could grab that little knife.

She would engage him and get him to leave. "I'm sorry?"

"As well you should be, but what will it be?"

What will it be? What was he going on about? He did not seem inclined to leave. She glanced toward the back door. She had only a fleeting moment to act.

She leaned closer to the table, her fingertips curling around the wooden edge. She pushed herself up, swung to face him, and scooped the blade into her hand.

Brighit stood, squared her shoulders, and held her head high. Behind her back, she clenched the hilt of the pilfered knife. Elation coursed through her body like a river overrunning its banks. She now had a means to defend herself against anyone who would harm her. She bit her cheek to keep from smiling.

His brown eyes were unusually bright. The hint of a playful smile on his full lips.

"Is this stubbornness now?" Peter moved in close, his steps a little unsure.

"Not intentionally stubborn." He misread her yet again.

He licked his lower lip. When his gaze dropped to her breasts, the air was knocked out of her. A full smile now. He was appraising her with total appreciation. The way a man looks at a woman he desires. Her breath returned with a solid *whoosh*.

"What. Will. It. Be?" He leaned in closer, whispering each word.

"Whatever you think best?" She spoke as calmly as she could but the room was getting very hot.

He glanced up as if trying to read an unclear sign but then that assured smile returned.

A tiny quiver rippled through her. Before she could speak again, he was closing in on her, his body up against hers.

"Whatever I think best?"

She wavered for a moment, unsure why he answered her with that tone. She wanted nothing more than to melt against him, envelope herself in his heat. This was just like in her dream. Hot and heady.

Then his firm lips were on hers. His hard length pressing her into the table, as if trying to meld them together. Her body would gladly have done just that if only it could have turned to pure liquid instead of just a growing warmth where his hips grinded into her.

He pulled his head back enough to search her face. He was breathing hard. He looked bewildered. "Is this what you want then?"

Her body arched towards his where the pressure had eased. "I...I'm not sure." She should not be feeling this way. "Please."

The answering sound from deep in his throat surprised her but then she got what she craved. His lips on hers again, then trailing across her cheek and down her jaw. An intense ripple of pleasure shot straight to her core. His hips undulated against hers, the heat, the dampness. She moaned.

He suddenly stopped, his head still dipped into the crook of her neck. She didn't dare breathe.

"I do not believe your *protector* will be happy with the outcome if we continue." His voice was husky, his breath warm against her skin. He shifted away.

Her body immediately missed his. Her eyes closed, she took a slow, steadying breath.

"I believe you need to think more carefully before you answer a man who asks you where you prefer to sleep."

She put her hand to her throat.

His eyes narrowed, clearer now, pierced hers. Her disappointment tripled.

The innkeeper's wife chose that moment to make her presence known.

"Lady Brighit will make use of your bed." Moving in close to Brighit's ear, he added. "And if you need a bigger knife, you have only to ask me."

The forgotten knife was nearly dropped onto the floor before she grabbed it tight in her hand.

"Yes, my lord." The older woman bent a knee.

Peter took a step away. A respectable distance.

"And what of our young woman, my lord? Where shall I send her?"

"To Lady Brighit." Peter grabbed the last remaining jug from the shelf and left the same way the others had.

Brighit blew a long breath. She noticed the older woman was still there, a knowing smile on her face.

"This way," the innkeeper's wife said.

Brighit followed the woman up a ladder at the far end of room. The small area was cozy, cut off from the few stairs by a heavy tapestry that was short enough to let in the heat from the fire below.

"Ursula will bring some fresh water for your ablutions."

"My thanks."

Alone in the room, Brighit tucked her little weapon beneath the pallet that sat on the floor, hilt side out. Peter knew she had it and didn't take it from her. Mayhap he understood her need for protection. He told her she needed to be more careful in what she said. Had he kissed her because she gave the wrong answer? It did not feel like a lesson on protecting herself

She placed her cold palms against her flushed face. The longing deep inside was still there. She wanted him closer. Even now. She had never felt like this about a man... about anything.

Brighit stretched across the stiff straw mattress. It crunched beneath her. She placed her palms over her breasts, imagining they were Peter's strong hands. Remembering the look of appreciation in his eyes. She would dream of him tonight. In her dream, she could be brazen. She would take him into her bed, as naked and splendid as he'd looked by the loch. He would hold her against his hard body and have his way with her. And she'd have her way with him. She'd know what it was to be a woman. Then she would wake up and continue her journey to the Priory where woman did not think of such things.

Peter rested his elbow on his bent leg, rubbing his lip with his thumb. His thoughts remained with the woman who slept soundlessly in the bed that should have been his. She had certainly ignited a fire in him.

Whatever you think best.

He'd only hoped to put a little fear in her. Her tight-lipped kiss and rigid body spoke of her lack of experience. He should have behaved better, released her, and explained why her answer was asking for trouble. Instead he became acutely aware of the way her breasts flattened against him. He could still feel her nipples hardening into nubs, pressing into his chest. His mouth watered with the need to take that generous peak into his mouth. Her scent drifted to him as it seemed to shift from fear to desire. It intoxicated him. He needed to have her. So he coaxed, encouraged, seduced with his mouth, tongue, hands. She didn't slap him or shove him away but inch by inch she responded. Leaning into him. Opening up to him. When he rubbed against her, revealing his hardened need, her hips pressed closer. He ached to rip off that unbecoming sack— her disguise—and stroke her silky skin, grasp her buttocks with both hand to yank her even closer, and touch her core to see if she was as wet and ready as she seemed. It took every ounce of his control to draw back. Her disappointed moan nearly called his bluff.

Damn.

He was not being a protector of the woman but a defiler! As bad as Ivan with his vicious mouth. What she needed was his protection. Protect her from himself, more correctly. Or perhaps protect her from herself. He needed to keep his guard up. That was plain to see. The only way to do that would be to keep his passion in check and see her safely within the Priory walls. The latter would be hoped for continuously but the former would require a huge amount of restraint. Planning to practice just that restraint, Peter didn't get a bit of sleep.

CHAPTER 12

Bleary eyed, Peter staggered toward the rain barrel at the far side of the small inn's yard. The anvils in his head rang out with every step. Animals bleating and pecking all around him made sleep impossible. The other men were dead to the world.

"God bless you." He spat the words.

He stilled. He stretched, scratching at the stiffness in his crotch. Wasn't he going to see someone about that?

Unbidden, the dreams came back to him. His own warm bed and his love splayed out before him. Him taking his time, his hands overflowing with her generous assets, sucking at her tightened nipples. Stroking her warm, wet treasures, delving inside, his hand wet with her moisture. Her moans of pleasure. Whispered promises of love and faithfulness. Suddenly it was Brighit's face, her smile of pleasure, shifting into Jeanette's face—smiling with dark, sunken hollows for eyes. The ghastly scream still sounded in his ears.

Peter doused his head in the ice cold water, then whipped his hair out of his face. He sloshed his hand down his face. Why would he be dreaming of Brighit? Jeanette was the usual bed partner of his dreams. His own personal hell. Now the future nun was haunting him? It was going to be a long day. The light burst over the hills and he had to shade his eyes from the onslaught. Stumbling, he made his way into the still darkened hall of the inn.

He plopped on the bench, his head in his hands. Whatever happened to the wench he'd asked for? Ah, yes. Lady Brighit got a servant and he got aching balls.

A bench creaked nearby and he lifted his head. The vision before him had long, red hair and a very revealing red gown that seemed to be lacking its under dress. Red. The color for whores.

"My lord?" she spoke in a seductive whisper.

"Ah, the missing wench." His cock jerked to attention.

Her smile was sheer enticement.

"Come here." Peter adjusted his legs and patted his now accessible lap.

She closed the distance and sat sideways on his lap to face him, pressing her breast against him. The opening at her neck ran down to her belly. He slipped his hand inside. Her breasts were small, without much life to them. She met his lips. Her tongue seemed too rough and he pulled back.

"Easy." He rubbed his palm along her nipple, tugging it, purling it into a hard little nub. Brushing aside the material, he took it into his mouth with a hard tug. She squirmed on his lap.

He withdrew again. "Have you never done this before?"

"I heard you liked virgins."

"Where did you hear that?"

"The innkeeper's wife."

The sole witness to his advances on Brighit. The memory of Brighit's body shifting from tentativeness into passionate eagerness shot straight to his groin. The innkeeper's wife had come to the same conclusion as Peter. She was indeed a virgin. Ivan had absolutely no basis for insinuating anything else. That would come to an end this day.

The redhead, willing or not, didn't have a chance of satisfying Peter now. He moved her off his lap. Wood scraped against the floor overhead. The object currently inflaming his desire was awakening.

"See if you can locate the rest of your under clothes and present yourself to Lady Brighit. She requires your assistance."

"Aye, my lord." The wench dipped into a curtsy and left to do his bidding.

Peter crossed into the kitchen and stopped in the doorway. The open hearth blazed. Both husband and wife moved about the small area. A kettle sizzled over the fire.

"How fare thee, my lord?" the innkeeper asked, scraping the ashes off the bottom of a dark loaf of bread before dropping it onto a wooden platter.

"Fair enough. I will see the other men roused and will return anon to break our fast."

"As you wish, my lord."

Peter went out the way he'd come. The tension grew in the pit of his stomach the closer he got to the stable, anticipating his encounter with Brighit's guardians. They were scoundrels of the worst kind. Not to be trusted. And the only ones with any information about Brighit. That was about to change.

"Ivan!" Peter shoved the little man with his foot. Ivan rolled onto his back and wiped the spittle from his mouth. He blinked several times before answering as if trying to get his wits about him.

"Aye. I'm up."

Ivan's obvious annoyance was a boon to Peter's irritation.

"We need to talk. Now."

Peter walked a short distance past the stable, away from any possibility of being overheard. Ivan joined him, his face scrunched up into a nasty grimace.

"Tell me about Brighit."

Ivan stood a little taller and his face just about split with his arrogant smile. "I thought you would take a liking to her."

Peter grabbed him by the front of the tunic and jerked his face in closer. "Enough with your arrogance! *Never* speak so of the lady again or you will find your entrails spilling onto the floor."

Ivan lifted his hands in surrender. His eyes two wide orbs. "I yield, my lord. Beg pardon."

Peter gripped the material tighter. "I know you have threatened her bodily to make her afraid."

Ivan shrugged against his grip, his feet half off the floor. "I don't know what you speak of. I've said nothing."

Peter's nostrils flared, his teeth clenched. "You lie."

He paused, fighting to cool the rage coursing through him.

"If you lay a hand on her, I will cut that hand off. If you look at her askance, I will pluck out your eye. If you offend her with any part of your body, I will remove it."

Every pore on the man's face bulged with fear. Peter unclenched his fist. It took Ivan a moment to move again. Peter stood before him, crossed his arms and waited.

"Her uncle was to see her safely to the Priory from Ireland."

Peter glanced around, raising his hands palms up. "Uncle?"

Ivan shifted and averted his gaze. "My master, her uncle, ordered me to see the job done."

Peter tightened his chin. This missing uncle was the root of the problem. "Where can I find this uncle?"

Ivan blanched. "He is not with us."

"My question was not a difficult one."

"He is in Ireland."

"While his ward and niece is here? Unattended by family? At your mercy?"

"It's not the way you're presenting it."

"It is exactly this way."

"I'd never touch her."

"You were going to sell her!"

"That's not true. Scots are all liars. Their tales are spun bigger than their pricks."

"I will not discuss this with you. You are no longer in command here."

"These are my men. They're in my hire." Ivan's face was suffused with color now.

"What happens to you or your lackeys matters little to me. I will see the lady safely to the Priory. That is my only objective." Peter rubbed at the growth on his cheek. "I may allow you to continue with us unless you become a problem for Lady Brighit."

"Lady Brighit," Ivan muttered the name under his breath.

Peter placed his hands at his hips and tipped his head. "This is not the way to go about ingratiating yourself with me so that you may remain in good standing with your hired help."

"Beg pardon, my lord."

Peter doubted very much this man would be with him until he reached the Priory. He didn't seem intelligent enough to keep his mouth shut. If he followed orders, Peter would allow Ivan to go with them so he could report to his master that Brighit had arrived safely.

"Rouse your men and break your fast. We leave on my orders."

When Mort escorted Brighit to the carriage, the sun was still low in the sky. He placed the step-up box that lay beside the wheel in front of the door and offered his hand.

Brighit smiled and took his hand. It was much easier to get into the carriage.

"My thanks, Mort," Brighit offered and sat down on the hard bench.

Mort picked up the box and placed it at her feet within the conveyance.

"Is there anything you need before we begin our travels for the day?"

Brighit was taken aback at such courtesy. "I am sure I have everything. Unless..."

"Name it, Lady Brighit."

"Perhaps some company?"

"My pleasure." Mort jumped into the carriage and sat across from her. He adjusted his legs so they were not even close enough to accidentally bump her knees. His palfrey was already tied to the back of the carriage. She smiled. He had once again anticipated her requirements.

Peter, ready and mounted, guided his horse abreast of the carriage. He glanced in her direction then addressed Mort. "Shall we depart?"

Mort turned toward her, his brows raised in anticipation of her response.

"Yes. I am ready."

Mort turned back to Peter. "Yes, my lord. All are ready."

Peter tipped his head slightly and urged his mount to the front of the carriage, out of her view. "Move out."

The carriage lurched into a steady pace and Brighit relaxed into her seat. It would be a pleasant ride. Cole and Andrew paid little attention to their speed or how much the faster speeds jarred the carriage. Her comfort being of little importance.

"So Lady Brighit, tell me about yourself."

It had been a long while since she'd had an opportunity to speak of her home or family. She swallowed. "What would you like to know?"

"Where do you come from?"

"I am of the MacNaughton Clan."

"Ah, a name I am not familiar with."

She giggled. "Your accent tells me there are probably more names you could say that of than not."

He blushed slightly. "That is true enough but I have a wonderful memory and pride myself on remembering such things."

Brighit glanced out the window. Ivan caught her gaze where he rode his horse. Her stomach lurched but he averted his face. If she didn't know better, she'd say he seemed fearful. When she'd passed him earlier, he'd not a word to offer to her.

"Ivan seems to be keeping to himself." Brighit regretted the words as soon as they were spoken.

"I believe that is in response to advice he recently received."

She faced Mort. "From you?"

Mort's look of shock was almost comical. "Oh no. Certainly it is not my place."

Brighit hesitated before asking, "Does Peter lead us?"

"Yes. He sees to all the arrangements for your journey now."

A weight was lifted from her shoulders. She needed to understand where she stood though. "And Ivan is allowing this? Is he p-paying him as well?"

Mort's gasped. "My lord would never accept money for doing what is right."

Relief flooded her. "My apologies. I didn't mean to impl—"

"Ivan has no say in the matter, Lady Brighit." Mort searched her face before he spoke. "Sir Peter is from the King's personal guard and acts in his stead. There is no discussion. There is only his will."

Brighit shivered slightly at the idea of Peter's will being tantamount.

"Thank you for sharing that with me."

With nothing to add, Mort nodded then leaned back and closed his eyes.

She turned to watch the scenery. It wasn't the hills and glens she saw but the glistening body of her dream lover.

He came to her again last night. His hands hot on her skin and so much more real now that she'd actually experienced Peter's touch. He'd barely noticed her this morning. She had willed him to look on her again, to see the appreciation that had been there before. And have him touch her with hands that spoke of a desire to handle her even more intimately. To have his mouth on her lips, her neck, her bare skin. Skin that begged for more. Her pulse quickened. Her breath quickened. Her heart quickened.

Brighit closed her eyes. In her dreams, Peter wanted her desperately. She stroked her lips, remembering every sensation from his kiss. Her first kiss had not been disappointing. His lips had been coaxing, his tongue tracing her lips as her fingers did now. His arms were strong but didn't crush her. Instead he drew her into his own body, surrounding her with his heat. Again, her stomach did that little flip. Opening her eyes, she turned toward Mort who appeared fast asleep. Brighit blew out a slow, inaudible breath.

Last night, Peter had indeed seemed like the man in her dreams but today that man was gone. Not even sparing more than a glance her way. No interest at all. Perhaps what the red-headed servant girl had told her was true. Quite talkative, that one. When she should have just helped Brighit to lace her dress and brush out her hair, she'd prattled on and on about her other duties at the inn and her encounter with "the knight". Brighit would have wished her to keep her mouth closed as she had the night before but no. Ursula had even shown her the gold coin Peter had given her after he'd lain with her.

Brighit said nothing. She was shocked to hear someone speak so brazenly about something she knew little about. She was also curious. Did he kiss her? Did he stroke her? Was his touch hot? Of course she'd said nothing. She listened to her speak of Peter in that way. Her chest tightened.

And as if all that wasn't enough, the servant had stopped at the ladder and said in a very matter of fact tone, "And he doesn't even like virgins."

The afternoon dragged by. Several times, Peter stopped for a respite. The men would dismount and stretch and go out of their way to avoid him. He didn't seem to notice. He was always busy seeing to the carriage, the supplies, the horses, the road.

Mort, however, saw to her. He made sure she had everything she needed. A drink. A blanket. A helping hand out of the carriage. A comfortable rock to rest on. He even went so far as to stand guard when she saw to nature's call. Peter gave her only a cursory glance.

When Peter gave the order to stop for the evening, it was just past dusk. He delegated who would build the fire, unpack supplies, and see to the horses. There was no grumbling in response. Something had definitely changed since they left the inn. Despite her questions, Mort had refused to elaborate on what his master's course of action had been. He assisted her out and saw her settled in front of the fire before seeing to his own duty—the food preparations.

Brighit stretched, her arms reaching over her head. Her deep breath turned into a big yawn. It felt good to relax a little. There was a calm around her that hadn't been there before. It had to be due to Peter's presence. Her stomach rumbled and for the first time since she'd left her home, she found she looked forward to the evening meal.

Alone for the first time that day, she observed the interchange of the men around her. When going to the carriage, Ivan made a wide arc around her. Cole and Andrew kept their heads down, their eyes averted. They didn't seem to want to have anything to do with her.

When she twisted to work out a kink, however, their heads snapped up to leer at her. That lustful gaze she knew so well. Andrew winked. Fear struck at her like a snake. Brighit hunched forward, crossing her arms about her. She sought out Mort but couldn't find him. Peter was missing as well. The bald man quickly approached and searched the area around her.

"Our little Brighit is being well taken care of now, isn't she?" He reached for the wood behind her as if that was his objective but his words were for her ears only. Low and menacing. "Fear not. We'll be nearby as well."

There was a movement behind her. Andrew took a wide step away, going back to drop the wood on the blazing fire without a backward glance.

"Is there something amiss?"

Brighit jumped at Peter's voice. Her hand went to her throat.

"No. Nothing."

Peter frowned and searched her face just as her brother, Tadhg, did when he was trying to decide if she was lying. He pressed his lips together.

"Mort!" he called without taking his eyes off her. He sounded angry.

"Here, my lord." Mort came at a quick pace, wiping his hands on a towel wrapped around his waist, a questioning look on his face.

Peter's look of accusation thickened the guilt seeping through her veins. Mort hadn't done anything wrong. If she spoke in his defense then Peter would know something had indeed transpired. Andrew had approached her as if he'd been waiting to catch her alone.

Brighit glanced from Mort to Peter. Unheard words seem to be flying between them and Mort nodded before turning his full attention to her.

"My lady, if you could assist me with the preparations, I would be forever in your debt."

Peter placed a fisted hand on his hip but said nothing.

Brighit dipped her head. "Of course."

She followed Mort to the far side of the carriage. An iron pot sat on the ground. It was already overflowing with various root vegetables. A hunk of meat lay on a wooden slab, the huge knife protruding from it. He kneeled beside the makeshift carving table.

"I was having some trouble with the quality of the tools here." He gave her a sideways glance. "The knives are not as sharp as I am used to."

Her hand instinctively went to her belted waist where her small knife lay hidden beneath her outer gown. She dropped it just as quickly. Mort tipped his head up to her and smiled.

"I'll be but a moment." He tossed the meat into the pot, grabbed it by the leather handle, and stood beside her. "We'll get this to the fire."

Brighit followed him back. Mort snatched the wooden box beside the wheel with his other hand and placed it next to the fire.

"Please." He gestured to the box then went to get his would-be stew close to the glowing embers.

Brighit glanced around. There was little talk but much was being accomplished. Always before, Ivan and his men took out the mead and beer before anything else was seen to. They would drink as they worked, throwing ribald comments her way. Comments that would make her face heat. There was none of that now.

Mort looked around as if assessing the situation. He half turned toward her.

"If you will excuse me, I will be but a moment. Not out of sight or out of ear shot." He gave her his most charming smile and walked past her.

The others still kept their distance. Andrew's threat had been delivered. Her peace was shattered. Peter may believe he was in charge but it was only as long as these men allowed him to think so. It wasn't possible for Mort to be with her at every moment and they wanted to make sure she knew that. She wasn't safe from them even with Peter and Mort nearby. She no longer had any desire to eat.

CHAPTER 13

The darkened woods were very near but the clearing they'd found for their camp would suffice for one night. It gave the others a place to retreat without knowing exactly how far they'd gone. Ivan's lackeys would surely make as good a use of the cover as Peter did now. Unlike them, he chose to still be seen. Mort needed to remain vigilant. Peter crossed his arms and gave the man his sternest look.

"What were you thinking?" He kept his voice low.

"My apologies, my lord. The men were busy jumping to the tasks you'd given them. I saw it as an opportunity to give her a few minutes to herself. She has much on her mind."

"How do you know that?" Peter snapped his mouth closed. The urgency was there in his question but he would have preferred not to be quite so transparent. The entire situation with this woman was becoming more and more intense. His tension was rising as if preparing for battle.

"I can see it in her movements, my lord. She is in a fragile state."

Peter had sensed that as well.

"And yet you left her alone."

"I was wrong to do so. These men are more observant than they appear."

"Hmphh."

Mort shook his head. "I cannot possibly be at her side every second."

"Then she is not well protected."

"Who was it that approached her?"

Peter knew Mort was more astute than most so he didn't mind telling him what he should have already known. "It was Andrew I saw collecting wood near her. I found her trembling while she stood there. Her face blanched. I did not hear what was said and she refused to tell me."

"I fear she does not trust any of us."

"Were you not at least *trying* to alleviate her fear? Alone with her in the carriage all day?" Peter snorted. He sounded far too accusing and by the surprise visible on Mort's face, it hadn't gone unnoticed. "My apologies. I fear I did not sleep well last night."

"Guilt, no doubt."

Peter frowned. "You overstep yourself when you make such accusations."

"I am torn between protecting the fair lady, as you have ordered me to do, and being respectful. The two duties are warring within me!"

"How so?" Peter demanded an explanation.

"Your behavior last night was less than chivalrous."

Peter shifted his feet. "I lost sight of our objective."

"Since when? You are a great fighter. It would not be true if you could so easily 'lose sight of your objective.'"

Peter knew he was correct. Without a single word, Brighit demanded his total attention whenever she was nearby. He seemed unable to tear himself away from her. How many times had he stopped today to check on her? Feigning a need to relieve himself. When Mort finally asked him if he had eaten some bad beef, he knew it had been too many times.

He needed to look at her, check to see that all was well, see if perhaps she would ask to ride outside the carriage for a while. She never said a word to him.

"The knife?" Peter asked.

"She has it on her, hidden beneath her kirtle."

"Do you think she plans on using it?"

Mort thought for a moment. "She will use it if she needs to."

"If she is attacked? She will use it in her own defense?"

Mort strummed his fingers against his lips. "No. I think she may feel she needs to use it even now."

"As in commit murder?"

Peter turned back toward the fire. Brighit gently rocked, her hands wrapped tightly around her waist. His heart sank. Without waiting for the reply, he walked to the fire with enough noise to assure he did not startle her.

"May I sit?" Peter asked.

She looked up at him, her eyes wide with her fear. "You may."

Peter settled himself beside her. He still had hope he could offer some bit of peace.

"Were you comfortable enough in the carriage?"

Her smile brightened her entire face. "I was. As Mort reassured you all afternoon, it was quite comfortable."

He shifted on the cold ground, his legs stretched out before him. "Are any of these men known to you?"

Her face shifted to a guarded anger before his eyes. He regretted his choice of words immediately. That was something he needed to move beyond with her if she was to ever feel safe with him.

"Known? As in the way you know Ursula?"

He did not anticipate the question. He paused before he asked, "Who is Ursula?"

"You don't even know the woman you paid to lay with you?"

"I paid no one."

"She showed me the gold coin." Brighit's head tipped to one side, her jaw tight.

"I've lain with no one."

Brighit's mouth closed tight.

Peter searched his memory. The woman in the red dress came to mind. "Ah, the wench at the inn?"

She turned toward him with eyes wide with outrage. "Now you remember?"

"I do not know what she told you but I gave her no gold coin and I did not lay with her."

"So she lied to me? Why would she do that?"

Peter thought for a moment. "Perhaps she tried to make you believe I had lain with her?"

"Why would I care?"

"You do appear irritated."

In a better light he was certain her coloring was turning a deep red.

"I do not know. I barely spoke to the woman." He didn't want to tell Brighit that she may have been insulted at his lack of interest in her. "I believe I was asking you about these men you are with. Have you met them before?"

Her lips tightened. "No." She turned away.

"And your uncle hired them?"

She gave an exaggerated sigh. Peter resisted the urge to smile, instead waiting patiently for her answer.

"Ivan is my uncle's man. Ivan hired the other two."

"And your uncle?"

"I never met him before—at least that I remember, before the day we left my home to come here."

She turned away. Her nostrils gently flared. Her throat constricted with her swallow. She struggled to keep her composure.

"It must have been very difficult to leave your home."

Her tear left one single clean streak down her travel-weary face. "It was."

"I take it that it was not your choice?"

Her look spoke of the absurdity at such a question. "I am a woman. I do as I am told. May I return to the carriage?"

Peter wanted to take her hand... no he wanted to take her in his arms and let her cry on his shoulder. He wanted to comfort her with reassurances of her safety. To tell her he would not let any harm come to her. He didn't move.

"Yes. If that is what you choose."

Brighit rose slowly and walked back toward the carriage. He followed her, waving Mort aside, but not before seeing the angry frown on his face. Peter assisted her into the carriage. She closed the door in his face with a quiet thud.

~

Peter sat on the cold ground and leaned against the tree in the darkness. A cloudy sky offered no clear view but silhouettes of black, hulking objects where the men sat before the fire. Ivan, Andrew, and Cole huddled around the dying embers still drinking their fill. Loud and unruly, the occasional quiet drew Peter's attention back to them. Their heads close together, they talked of things among themselves. He would not be surprised to have them inform him that they were departing on the morrow. The evening had gone that badly.

Ivan pushed to have Brighit ordered out of the carriage to eat with them. All but falling short of ordering her to be dragged to the fire. Peter was not so inclined and said as much. If she wanted to be alone, they should allow her that. He and Ivan had nearly come to blows over it. The man was single-minded and loose-mouthed from the drink. Peter's insistence jeopardized Ivan's leadership in the eyes of his lackeys, no doubt. Neither was willing to back down. But when Mort quietly pointed out to Peter that it may be her pride that was keeping her inside, he had second thoughts.

He approached the carriage to ask her to join them. The door opened and she jumped down again. He couldn't miss the mumbles of appreciation erupting with the movement or the back slapping from the three at the bawdy entertainment. Brighit seemed unaware of the amount of leg she displayed with every unaided ascent and descent from the carriage. All the way up to her knees. Peter refused to acknowledge that her ivory-skinned ankles and calves were indeed the most comely he'd ever seen. The sudden silence assured Peter that Mort had silenced them with his god-awful glare.

Brighit returned to her earlier seat. Mort quickly handed her a trencher.

"My thanks. This smells delicious."

The courtesy she displayed indeed spoke of noble breeding but her inability to keep herself completely covered—no, that wasn't fair—her inability to get in and out of the conveyance without showing far too much leg belied it.

The men proceeded to pass around the mead throughout the meal, filling in the quiet with their own boisterous laughter and vulgar comments. Peter did not object. Men needed to relax. Even if he found their company far from desirable. So now he lay again in the quiet of the night, thinking. He needed sleep and he fought against it. His sleep was not restful. His dreams were tortured. He didn't awaken refreshed, he awakened with a raging need for release. Guilt. Misery.

Peter stood abruptly. The men were settling down now, the fire nearly out. They didn't notice him. Mort was nearby. He followed the path that led deeper into the woods and isolation. He needed to be alone.

CHAPTER 14

*B*righit shifted again. The hard wood of the carriage floor pressing against her shoulder blades made it impossible to sleep. The men had quieted and she knew from experience they were passed out. Peter and Mort had not been a part of their nightly gathering. She wondered where they were. The night before, they had slept apart from the others as well.

She sat up, hugging her knees into her chest. This was the time of night when she could safely venture out. The men would not hear her. They slept like the dead. As carefully as she could manage, she stood to open the door. No movement. She hopped down.

The fire was nearly out. She didn't sense anyone closer. Perhaps Mort and Peter slept in the woods. That would be foolhardy with the wild animals around. She stilled. Maybe it was not a good night for this. An owl sounded in the distance. Fear tripped up her spine. The cold night air left goose bumps where it caressed her exposed skin. The carriage at least was warm.

Brighit turned to go back inside, the shadow of Mort beneath it. She froze. He shifted suddenly, turning his back to her and pulled the rough, woolen blanket over his shoulder. She smiled. If she called him, he would surely come, but for now she did desire time outside of her tight quarters. Peter was nowhere she could see so she moved closer to the fire.

Ivan lay on his back, his arms flayed out on either side. He mumbled something but she couldn't tell what he said. Moving in closer, Cole and Ivan had their possession in close proximity as always. She searched the area beside Andrew but found nothing. She bent in closer then heard a movement behind her. She jumped, glancing back toward the sound at the forest's edge. A tall silhouette of a man emerged, a sack hanging from his hand. It was Peter. Fully clothed. His sword at his side. He held Andrew's bag up higher as if to say "Come and get it".

Indecision rippled out from her stomach. Peter knew what she was after. She moved in closer.

"Is this what you search for?" His face was in shadows but he sounded as if he had a smile on his face.

"Are you stealing from them?"

He reached inside and pulled out the small whistle, dropping the sack to the ground. "I believe you were looking for this?"

She snatched it from his hand. Infuriating man. "You'd best not awaken them."

Peter stretched his arm the way he'd come, directing her into the woods. She hesitated but a moment before heading down the little deer path she'd noticed earlier. He followed close behind. It gave her a strong feeling of safety to have him with her.

"Here." Peter veered to the left and she followed. "There is a small clearing just ahead," he whispered over his shoulder. "I do not think they'll hear your music from there."

"I don't know what you're talking about."

He stopped abruptly and turned toward her. She stumbled into him, the heat shooting up her arms where they slammed into the solid wall of his chest. She pulled back and righted herself.

"What do you think you know? One night I played a whistle so you think I do that every night?" she asked.

He stood up straighter. "I don't think I know anything. I saw you searching Andrew for the whistle. Was I wrong?"

"You'll never know." Brighit shoved past him into the clearing then stopped.

Several large trees had fallen, creating a little shelter. A rotting log lay in the center. She settled herself next to it, leaning back, and brought the whistle to her mouth. She blew one long note, then a shorter one, and began her tune.

In her mind she heard the words of her mother's favorite song.

The handsome knight of one score and ten
  He gave his hand to me
  His touch so light I could ner believe
  He came here just for me
  Throughout the night he held me close
  And I cleaved unto him
  For in the morn twould be farewell
  And never more to see

A sudden sob choked her breath. She dropped her face into her hands, the whistle forgotten beside her. The tears poured out for all she had given up. The security of her family. The loss of her mother and probably even her father now.

A gentle hand lay against her shoulder and she jumped. She swiped at her tears and stood away from him. "I'm sorry," she said.

Peter did not touch her again. "Why are you sorry? What wrong have you done that you seek forgiveness?"

She shook her head, still swiping at the tears. "M-my weak-kness."

"Tears are a woman's right. They come from deep in her soul. You need not apologize for the depth of your feelings."

Brighit swallowed hard and struggled for control. "No. It is not right for you to see me thus."

Peter shifted slightly closer, his arms at his side. "Do you wish to be alone with your sorrow? Or will you allow me to offer comfort."

Her breath hitched.

He raised his open arms slightly.

She stepped into his embrace, burying her face in his shirt. He smelled of smoke. The flood of emotions raged within the firm safety of him surrounding her.

He murmured words of comfort, one hand stroking her back, the other holding her tight. She let loose her fears. The loss of her dreams. She would allow herself this respite, a chance to experience peace. However fleeting or untrue. Shifting against him, she turned her cheek and the strong, steady beat of his heart comforted her. Her tears subsided.

"I will see no harm comes to you. You can trust in that."

His whispered words soothed her and she snuggled closer still.

"You can trust in that."

His lips by her ear.

"I promise you."

Feather light, he kissed her hair.

"I will see you safe this time."

His lips moved against her head. His breath was warm and a shiver swept over her.

"I vow this to you."

She pulled her head back to look into his shadowed face.

"You speak from the heart," Brighit said. "I feel it in your embrace."

Peter stiffened slightly. "I will protect you."

There was something—something she could not name.

"I believe you," she said.

Heat radiated from him, swirling through her, the tears forgotten.

"What pains you so?" he asked in the same low voice.

"The loss of my family. I am alone here."

His arms relaxed as if giving her a chance to step away. She held fast.

"That is a heavy loss." His sigh expanded his chest. "You will have a new home."

He would bring her home if she asked him to. Her heart quickened. Dare she ask for this from him? Her heart sank at the truth. It was a matter of honor to her family. She could not return now.

"Yes."

He dropped his arms from her. She moved back, the cold surrounding her where his heat had been.

Peter retrieved the whistle, then gave her a coy smile. "If you would like to play, I can stay nearby."

"Stay with me." Her words came out before she could stop them.

He searched her face, nodded, then settled down beside where she had been sitting.

She took the whistle and resumed her spot on the cold ground. As she took a deep, slow breath she closed her eyes and focused on happier times. A memory came to her from when she was young. She brought the whistle to her mouth. It was a celebration between the MacNaughtons and the O'Briens. She played the jig as she remembered it.

In her mind, she saw Tadhg holding hands with Tisa. That look of love. Her father smiling as he danced the lively step with her mother. Her mother's warm smile and flushed face. The moon overhead. The laughter surrounding them. She shifted into another tune, then another until her memories receded. She put the whistle down and turned toward Peter. She could make out his smile in the darkness. He put his arm around her shoulders and pulled her close to him.

"You will have a new home." He repeated the words.

She closed her eyes and fell asleep in the warmth of his strong arms.

Peter jerked awake, a warning sounding in his head. The sun was just coming up over the horizon.

"My lord." Mort burst through the trees, a look of surprise covered his face.

Brighit shifted, awakening beside him.

Peter's arm was asleep where he'd been holding her. He came to stand in front of Mort. When the man glanced between the two of them, Peter didn't miss the I-know-what's-happening-here expression that flashed across his face.

"They've taken the carriage and our horses," he said.

"They've taken—"

Peter shook his arm to stop the pins and needles attacking it and strode the short distance back. He stopped at the edge of the clearing. The blackened earth where the fire had been was the only thing that remained. The carriage was gone. The horses were gone. The men were gone, along with all of their belongings.

A laugh threatened to erupt. "Buggar me! They have balls, those three."

Peter stepped closer to the fire and turned in a circle, assessing the empty view. He couldn't believe what he saw. Or did not see.

Irritation slithered into his chest. He turned on Mort. "And where were you?"

Mort gasped. "My lord, I got up to relieve myself. I realized you were not here and went in search of you. I returned to—to this." He made a sweeping gesture with his arm.

Brighit staggered into the field, wiping the sleep from her face. "Where is everything? Where is Ivan?"

Peter's fighting instinct took over. Had she been a ploy to lure him into the woods? "And you? Did you know this was their plan?"

Brighit gave a quick shake to her head and stepped back as if scorched by his accusation. "Surely you jest."

She looked as shocked as he did. And she had nothing, too. Peter fought to cool his ire.

"My apologies. Of course they would not inform you of their plan."

"You think they planned this?" Her sharp words cut through his annoyance. "They were not so cunning. They were near imbeciles."

Mort's jaw dropped before he started to laugh. "Methinks she does not think highly of her guardians."

"So it would appear."

Brighit's face turned bright pink. She averted their gaze. "Beg pardon, my lord."

Peter stepped near her. "Oh, no, fair Brighit. I would not have you apologize for words spoken in truth."

She faced him. He sensed the lovely lady he'd witnessed ascending from the carriage, mad as hell, was hovering just behind her stoic features.

He needed to encourage here so he repeated his earlier words. "You are safe with me."

A smile as bright as the sun burst across her face. "They were imbeciles." She made the pronouncement as if she were a judge declaring her decision.

He smiled back at her and tipped his head. "And I agree."

Mort cleared his throat. "As do I but what are we to do? We have nothing."

Peter tapped down the delight he found in her brash statement. He sighed. "You have a point, my friend."

A perplexing dilemma because of all he'd lost, but there was only one answer.

"We walk to the next town."

Mort stepped closer and pointed at Brighit with a shift of his head. "What are we to do about our predicament?"

Peter assessed her. In the bright light of morning the problem became transparent. She stood in her nightdress. A flimsy material. Too short. Too revealing. Although he enjoyed the view.

Mort and Peter turned to each other at the same time.

Mort shook his head as if reading his mind. "There is nothing remaining."

Peter removed his tunic and moved closer to Brighit. "Please cover yourself."

She glanced down at herself and back at him, her eyes wide. "I have nothing else."

Peter shoved his shirt at her. "So cover yourself with this."

She quickly donned his tunic. It fell well past her hips. She glanced between the two with such a look of expectation. Her ankles remained exposed. Her bare feet as well. And her uncovered hair fell about her shoulders. She looked like a peasant woman for hire.

"It will have to do," Peter said.

Bare-chested now, he paced around the camp. The grass still flattened from where the men had lain sleeping.

"Although I agree without reservation with your assessment of your guardians, my lady," Mort started, "I'd venture to say this was their plan all along."

"To take off and leave us here? Then why take the carriage? That would only slow them down," Peter said.

Mort's frown turned into sudden realization. "They believe Brighit is still inside!"

That made sense. They had thought to only be leaving Peter and Mort with nothing. There was no reason for them to believe Brighit was not asleep in her carriage as she was every night. He glanced toward her. Her already fair complexion blanched before his eyes.

"What will they do when they learn she is not?" Mort put to words what they were no doubt all thinking.

They tortured her with their vulgar behavior, instilling her with fear, even offering to sell her. Would they just walk away from her?

"I cannot even venture a guess," Peter said.

Brighit dropped to the ground, tucking her bare feet beneath her, but said nothing.

"If they hadn't offered to sell her to our Scottish friends, I would say she was of no value, but clearly they were willing to be rid of her," Mort said.

Her head snapped up and she glared at Mort but he paid her no heed.

Peter smiled. Her spiritedness was definitely returning.

"If she is not found in the carriage, they may indeed return for her." Peter said. "No doubt that wouldn't be until they stopped a safe distance from here. I believe there was a house not far down this road."

At the road, Mort dropped low to the ground. "Perhaps I can tell which way they've taken the carriage."

"The tracks should be simple enough to find."

Mort paused then said, "They're returning the way we just came."

Peter nodded and placed his hands on his hips. "That's as I had suspected but *we* will not."

Mort stood and brushed off the knees of his hose.

"It was a ruse that they had missed the turn to the Priory." Peter said.

Brighit stood and blew a breath. "They were taking me somewhere else?"

The three were quickly moving as one down the dirt road.

"They may have planned on getting you to the Priory eventually," Mort said.

"Just not before they saw to whatever was the other way first. Can you think of anything else they might be doing beside what they claimed?"

Brighit paused. "They talked constantly to all the people we passed on the road. Some were responsive. Some were hostile. I could never tell what was being said. They seemed to take great care that I would not have an opportunity to be seen or speak to anyone."

Peter pondered this for a moment. "Did your uncle have any encounters while you were with him?"

"Yes!" Brighit stopped in her tracks. "There was a tall man at the inn by the mouth of the river. My uncle left me with Ivan to meet him. I assumed it was because he didn't want me to hear them."

"Do you remember anything else about the man?"

They began to walk again.

Brighit continued, "He and my uncle were arguing. I had been hoping my uncle wouldn't leave me with Ivan. I thought surely my uncle would want to know what inappropriate remarks the man was making. My uncle cared very little."

She stopped talking, hesitated mid-step, then continued on.

Peter waited for her to continue until his patience was up. "Is there nothing else?"

Mort touched his arm and shook his head. Brighit's head was down so she missed the gesture.

"My lady, did he threaten you?" Mort asked.

She glanced sideways at him for just a moment. "I'm sure I've said too much already."

Peter stopped.

Mort said, "Lady Brighit, it is clear to me that you have been ill-treated by these men. Mayhap we can work together to find out why."

"Will you not accept my protection?" The words stung Peter's heart even as he spoke them.

He had not been there for Jeanette but he would be for Brighit. Resolve settled in the depths of his heart. "My protection will not be withdrawn, my lady. I will see that no harm comes to you."

"Indeed. We will reach the Priory with you none the worse for wear—" Mort broke out into a smile "Maybe a little worse for wear since we are now forced to walk."

Brighit sighed. "Beg pardon, Sir Peter. I take your protection as my own but wonder if Ivan and his men were to return, would I be handed back over to them?"

"We will not gainsay your decision to stay or return." Peter had an almost overwhelming desire to punch something.

She smiled. "Yes. Then I will take your protection with the understanding that Ivan no longer has any hold over me."

"And that is at it should be," Peter said.

"We should keep walking," Mort reminded them both and they all started out again.

"The tall man was hooded and it was just getting dark," Brighit said. "He and my uncle were arguing when I came upon them. My uncle had just yelled something about someone not being a problem. I was afraid he meant me and that he was changing his mind about seeing me to the Priory."

"They ceased their talking as soon as my uncle spotted me. Then he dragged me back into the inn. I was told Ivan would protect me until he returned. When it was time to board the curragh, I was immediately sick at the movement and my uncle never got on with us."

Her pace quickened with the ending of her remembrance.

Mort gave her a reassuring smile and nodded.

"Not a lot of information," Peter said.

"I'm sorry. I was upset to be leaving my home."

He knew he was being harsh but the frustration at not being able to complete one simple task—like seeing her safely to the Priory—was grating on his nerves. The King would be sending soldiers to support Peter taking the castle in less than a week unless he sent word that all was well.

The morning stretched on and they kept a clipped pace. Their silence was broken only by occasional greetings from the few travelers they passed, all going in the opposite direction. Finally a young boy went by with an older woman Peter assumed was his mother. He had an excited look about him and a big grin.

"Mornin'," he said. "Fine day."

The child passed Brighit and handed her a tiny, blue flower.

Her face brightened.

"Look out for the cooper," his mother said over her shoulder. "He seems fair and honest but he had no problem taking from my son."

Peter turned back to face the departing pair. "It must be market day."

Brighit smelled the flower. "It smells wonderful."

"That flower looks quite fresh. It is probably just ahead."

"Thank you!" Brighit yelled to the two who were already twenty paces beyond them. The little boy waved back. She placed it carefully behind her ear. "Wait." She turned back at the departing pair. "We may have passed them."

The three exchanged glances. Peter trotted after the pair. "Please. Can we have a word with you?"

The mother and son stopped and waited.

"How can I be of assistance?" the mother asked.

Brighit moved in closer and smiled at the little boy. She touched the flower at her ear. "My thanks, again. Do you remember passing a wooden carriage a few days ago?"

"Of course," the mother answered. "It near blocked the path and the men were rude. Did they bother you as well?"

Peter gave Brighit an expression of encouragement, so she continued. "Did the men say anything to you."

"Aw," the little boy's mouth dropped open. He screwed his face up. "You mean the dirty men? They asked if we knew where we could find Tostig's soldiers."

His mother nodded. "They were crazy. Tostig's been cold and dead for a long time now. We just rushed by them. Loons."

Peter nodded. He patted the little boy on the head. "My thanks."

They returned to walking toward the market.

"My thanks, Brighit." Peter smiled at her. "I'm glad you recognized them."

"There wasn't much else to do but look out at the people we passed. The boy was very cute. He carried a sack for his mother."

"They must live in the area somewhere," Peter said. "Just who are these men and what are they doing here?"

"Now we know they're asking about a Godwinson," Mort said.

"Yes. The one who held the territory in this area. But he was killed just as Harold and the rest of the family."

Lowering his head, Peter caught a glimpse of Brighit's near naked state. His eyes again perused her shapely calves. He blew a noiseless whistle. Mort noticed his focus shift.

"Perhaps we can find something for Brighit to wear at the market ahead?" he asked.

"Chances are better there than a single home," Peter said.

At the crest of the hill, a wide, green valley spread out before them. Perhaps ten different vendors lined the road with colored flags waving from their carts. The din of caged animals and voices hawking items for sale drifted to them.

"We cannot dally here. Just renew our supplies," Peter said.

The view of the castle was obscured from this direction and the reminder that he had other duties he should be seeing to made Peter ill-tempered. That and other distractions.

A glance at Brighit showed her excitement at the prospect of a market day. Peter smiled to himself. Ivan had made things quite difficult for her and being without a proper gown just made it that much worse. She wasn't part of the Priory yet. These worldly things would be a part of her past very soon. He couldn't begrudge her a few minutes to take in their wares. Her features turned dark suddenly.

"What is wrong?" he asked.

She turned toward him, an incessant shaking of her head adding to his trepidation. "I cannot be seen like this."

He didn't need to be reminded of her shapely calf and near transparent clothing but his eyes wandered of their own accord, stopping at the precariously placed flower in her hair.

"We know that," he said and immediately regretted the harshness of his tone.

She pushed her shoulders back in a determined stance. "All will be well. Whatever you may find for me to wear, I will be grateful."

Her voice was clipped as if reassuring herself as well as him.

"We will do our best," Peter replied.

Her bravery was admirable but he noticed her step slowing as they approached the carts tightly gathered at the crossroads ahead. Why wouldn't she be embarrassed to be seen in her night dress? Even one covered by a man's long tunic. She could easily be mistaken as a kept woman and the tunic, along with his bare chest, certainly marked her as his. Ivan had been treating her as such throughout the trip. He snorted and stopped.

"Mort will you look ahead to see what can be found for Brighit to wear? We will wait here."

The little man frowned. "I will do my best."

Peter sat at the ground beside Brighit, just off the road. "We will see you respectable again, Lady Brighit."

"My lord, we do not have such titles in Ireland."

"Are you not of noble birth?"

"My father is clan leader—although it may be my brother by now."

Peter ripped a piece of grass from the ground in front of him. "How do you mean?"

"My father was on his death bed when I was spirited away." There was a little slant to her tight lips. "At his death, my brother will be clan leader."

She swallowed hard before blowing out a loud sigh. "Apologies, my lord, I have much weighing me down."

"No need. As the daughter of a clan leader, I believe lady is the correct title for you."

Her eyes sparkled. "My thanks."

She stretched out on her side, bending her knees slightly so that her legs were covered, and rested her head on her arm.

"Not even a blanket to cover you with," Peter said. He crossed his legs before him and leaned back on his arms.

She gave a small laugh. "It is certainly not for lack of planning on your part. Being robbed can definitely leave one short of many necessities."

Idle conversation was not Peter's way but he decided he would try. "Do you enjoy the markets in Ireland?"

"We have a few tradesmen who would travel through but we are mostly on our own."

"In Normandy, the market days were quite frequent... at least whenever the fighting stopped."

She bent her head back to face him more fully. "Fighting sounds like it was on going."

"It is a part of our everyday life. William has unending plans for the acquisition of lands."

"I have memories of a lot of fighting when I was younger, as well."

"I suppose we should be glad when celebrations begin and we can have a peaceful market day."

She smiled. The dark image of a man coming toward them was indeed Mort and Peter stood to greet him. He carried a large sack and a basket full of hard bread, colorful cheeses, and a skin near to be bursting.

"You've done well, my friend." Peter relieved him of the wine skin. "My thanks."

The liquid was cool on his parched throat and it gave him a distraction from Mort handing Brighit the newly acquired gown. He drank and glanced around but saw no place for her to have even the slightest privacy to dress. There was also no one else nearby. He handed the skin to Brighit.

"I'm afraid you'll have to change with our backs to you."

She drank a sip and wiped her mouth with the back of her hand. "I will trust you not to look."

Mort accepted the skin and they walked a few feet away, turning their backs to Brighit.

Peter's senses tuned into the sounds behind him. First the tunic dropped to the ground making a sound as loud as a tree falling to his ears. He held his breath and saw again in his mind the way her dampened gown had clung to her curves.

Mort all but slammed the skin into his chest. Peter's hands scrambled to grab it and saw Mort's dark visage. "Keep your mind where it should be."

Peter grunted and took another drink. He tried to concentrate on the refreshing liquid but the rustling behind him reminded him of the way she'd felt against him. Soft and yielding. He thought again of her mouth against his. Her lips parting to allow his tongue access. Her breasts crushed against him.

"All done. You may turn around."

When Mort shoved at him to obey, reality felt like cold water splashed on him. However, Peter was in no condition to face her. His hardened cock bulged quite visibly against his hose and he had no tunic to hide it with. Ever observant, Mort noticed and quickly retrieved Peter's tunic. Peter pulled the clothing over his head and tugged it down over his demanding appendage. Unfortunately her scent surrounded him, fighting against any inward resolve to cool his ardor. He breathed in deeply, giving in to the memory of her shifting against him in submission. Clearing his throat, he steeled himself before turning to face her. His jaw dropped at the vision before him.

The tightly-fitted gown was made of a simple material but the way it hugged her womanly assets, it might as well have been silk. The generous swell of her bosom strained against the material so much so that her pearled nipples were clearly visible. Peter's mouth went dry.

"You look lovely," Mort offered, no doubt to cover Peter's foolish response, and stepped in front of him.

Brighit accepted his compliment with a smile. She glanced shyly at Peter, the flower gone from behind her ear. Like a parched man, he drank in the fluidity of her graceful curves. His gaze gliding along her narrow waist to the swell of her hips. Mort cleared his throat. Peter glanced toward him again.

"The color becomes you, Brighit." Peter frowned slightly and turned away.

In his mind's eye, he saw her again as she had looked standing in the carriage. Her spirited response more desirable than the willing red-haired wench he could have easily slated his sexual desires with. The vision he had of Brighit was of a passionate woman whether in anger or... and Peter knew he was taking liberties even thinking about it... in his bed. Briskly, he began walking the rest of the way toward the market.

"Are you coming?" he asked without actually turning back.

He breathed deeply, trying to clear his mind. Celibacy required a certain deadening of the senses that he had yet to master. Her scent drifted to him again from his tunic. He pulled the offending material over his head and tossed it to the ground.

"Can you see to this, Mort? I believe I require some new garments, as well."

Brighit's voice could be heard behind him. She questioned Mort about his response but Peter ignored her, walking even faster. The sooner he got to the little group gathered at the market, the quicker he would be able to... Peter didn't know what he planned to do but he needed distance from this woman.

As he'd hoped, the first cart he came upon had several tunics. He grabbed the first dark tunic he found.

"How much?" He pulled it over his head. It was tight in the shoulders but it smelled of wool which was better than to have Brighit's scent teasing him. Mort stepped forward to pay the required amount. Brighit moved closer to Peter.

"Have I done something to anger you?"

The man beside the cart heard her question and looked toward Peter, waiting for his answer.

"Of course not."

She turned away and moved along the table, admiring the items for sale.

"Are you looking for something else?" The man spoke in a low voice and looked sideways at him. "I can find almost anything you need."

It was the way the man said it that Peter recognized his offer to find him a willing wench. Either Peter was going to commit to celibacy or find some release. "Yes."

Mort turned toward him. "My lord!"

"Monk's pepper," Peter said. "Where can I find it?"

The tradesmen looked Brighit up and down and smiled. "Third cart on the right side of the road. That's where all the herbs can be found."

CHAPTER 15

*B*righit soaked in the scene before her. A dozen tables laden with every imaginable necessity from pots to swords to spices to fowl to clothing to breads. Brightly colored banners fluttered in the breeze every few feet as if heralding in the festivities. Strange smelling herbs and bleating sheep all vied for her attention. She hadn't been to market day since before her mother had passed. The MacNaughtons of late had little to offer to sell and even less to buy something with.

Peter provided her with clothing and she was grateful. She wanted to thank him but he seemed irritated. He wanted to buy something... Monk's pepper? She didn't even know what that was. Mayhap later on she could thank him... with a kiss. Her lips curled into a secret smile. A pleasant thought but never would she be so bold.

Mort offered his arm, escorting her down the little swell in the road toward the other carts. She went from vendor to vendor, each one offering more exotic items than the one before. It wasn't possible for her to keep the grin from her face. It was easy to forget her circumstances and become entranced by her surroundings.

"And you, my lady," an ebony-skinned man called to her. His eyes as dark as his skin, drew her toward him. "This flower would look exceptional on you."

The table behind him held fresh flowers, several small jars of various hues, and a brightly colored bird in a cage hanging from the corner. She gawked at it.

"Ah, you like my pet?" he asked.

"What is it?"

"It is called a parrot. I won him in a game of chance from an interesting traveler I met. The man has gone both north and south, east and west in his travels on the sea. This—this fine feathered friend is from one of those trips."

Mort laughed quietly beside her.

"Why dye him so many colors?" she asked.

"Ha ha, no. I did not dye him. He came that way."

"Monk's pepper! Have you never heard of it?" Peter's irritated voice interrupted what she was about to say. She turned to the cart behind her.

Mort went to Peter's side. "My lord, are you having no luck in securing the item you seek?"

Peter turned toward them and his gaze fell on her, roaming once again up and down her body. It might have been the dress he saw but the way he focused on her bosom... her breath hitched. His expression spoke of longing. Heat radiated off him. When he brought his gaze to her mouth, she wetted her lips.

"What vexes you so?" Somewhere inside she noticed the breathiness of her question and tried to stop from reaching toward him.

Mort coughed. Peter caught her hand, stilling the movement, then released it. His expression closed off, his inner desires no longer visible. "I find markets annoying—the people, the noise, the smells." He turned toward Mort. "Do you think anyone here is going toward the Priory?"

"I found only one man headed in that direction but he doesn't leave until the morrow. He is the entertainment for tonight."

Peter's jaw tensed. "So we will have to stay the night as well."

Her heart sank in disappointment. There had been something in Peter's look that had promised so much. She'd swear he'd wanted to touch her. Caress her.

When she had awoken in his arms, it took her a moment to make sense of his nearness. She remained still, feigning sleep. His scent drifted to her but she dared not turn into his chest as she longed to. Instead she listened to the steady beat of his heart and his quiet breathing and pretended she belonged there. The man's arms were as comforting as a boat in a harbor.

The longing she'd just seen on his face brought that all back to her and sparked an ache in her soul. A desire to experience his strength again. And more. To feel his hands gliding over her. His light kisses along her cheek, her jaw, her neck. His warm breath against her skin.

"Come, my lady, let us find a place to settle down and partake of the food we have." Mort's hopeful expression included Peter. "My lord? Will you join us?'

"No. I have more pressing matters requiring my attention."

He brusquely walked away. Her sigh bubbled up from the depth of her disappointment.

Mort led her back to their earlier spot but he seemed preoccupied. Once under the tree, he seemed to force a smile. "The weather is certainly mild."

She nodded.

"The sky is very blue."

She glanced up and nodded again.

"Do you enjoy music?"

"Music?" Brighit brightened. "For certain."

Brighit thought of her mother's love of music and dancing, knowing she took after her. They ate in silence but her thoughts remained on her mother. Had they stopped in this area so many years ago when *she* was brought to the Priory? Is that where she met her father? There was so little she knew about the two of them save for their happiness. They were a couple deeply in love.

"Are you married, Mort?"

Mort took a sip of mead before answering. "Yes. I am happily wed." A far off look came to his eyes, one she'd never seen on his face before. The look made Brighit certain he was seeing his wife in his mind.

"You must miss her."

"Every day." Mort smiled sheepishly. "And what of you? Had you always known you were destined for the Priory?"

Brighit turned away. The question was not expected and she found it hard to swallow. "No. I was to be happily wed and expecting to be near my family always." Her voice sounded unusually low. "My father changed my destiny when he told me I would become a nun."

Mort's intense gaze searched her face, perhaps seeing more than she intended. She cleared her throat and reached for another piece of cheese although she was no longer hungry. "I will accept my father's decree."

"Yes. I can see you would never give him any reason to be ashamed. You are a good daughter."

Mort brushed the crumbs from his hands and stretched out. The afternoon dragged by. She regretted her harsh decision to leave Andrew's whistle behind because of the memory it would stir. Being at those men's mercy was not something she wanted to remember.

Mort's loud snoring grated against her patience and his words echoed in her heart. She was a good daughter and would never shame her father or her clan. He wanted her to take her vows. Vows that would make her spend her life alone with no one to love.

Tonight, though, she was not secluded. Tonight she was here. Tonight she was surrounded by new and exciting things and would take full advantage of her situation. She wished Mort would take her back to the market.

The sun finally began to set in the distance. The sound of carts being closed up drifted to her. They were led into a wide circle in preparation for the impending festivities. One by one, lights appeared out of the dusk, hung from the cart posts, all adding to the magical feel of the evening. The fireflies came out in force to twinkle among the heather and tall grass that grew across the meadow beyond.

"It sounds as if the evening's entertainment has begun."

"It does." She twisted her hands in her lap, struggling to tap down her excitement.

"Do you wish to join them?" The sounds of music drifted to them.

Brighit took a deep breath, not wishing to betray her enthusiasm. "Yes. I believe I do."

Mort's knowing expression, however, assured her she had not been successful. He stood, extending his hand. "Then let us be off."

The scene was indeed surreal. After her days stuffed inside a carriage, afraid to speak, afraid to look askance, afraid to listen to the conversations around her, she was being escorted with great care into a gathering that promised her frivolous entertainment and her heart soared.

Vendors were transformed from unbending purveyors to easygoing participants, even changing into more festive outfits for the occasion. Musical instruments appeared from carts and wagons and several vessels of libations were generously being passed from person to person.

The mead went down smoothly and Brighit enjoyed the sweet warmth spreading through her limbs. For this night, she would relax and enjoy her surroundings. Her time with Ivan was over. She was safe with Mort. He would never let any evil befall her. Nor would Peter.

The stringed instrument was a surprise. It was played by the ebony man. His parrot squawked in its cage. She stood off to the side. The man's deep voice resonated through her. He sang in a language she didn't know, but with enough passion that she knew it was a song about love. When he finished his song, the silence hung there. Then the listeners in the small area broke into spontaneous applause. He bowed.

"Wonderful." Brighit joined the clapping with enthusiasm. "That was beautiful."

The man tipped his head in her direction.

"He has a mighty voice," Mort said, taking Brighit's attention away from the entertainer.

"Oh, he does! My brother has the voice of an angel as well."

The memory squeezed at her heart but she set it aside. Music meant celebration. Tonight was a celebration of her freedom.

"My fair lady." The tall, dark man stepped up beside her, bowing at the waist. With a suddenly coy expression, he handed her a large, blue flower. "A beautiful flower for a beautiful lady."

"Oh." Brighit took the flower to her face to fully appreciate its heavenly scent. "It is lovely."

"You put the flower to shame with your beauty. It blushes to be in your presence."

Brighit couldn't hold back her pleasure at the compliment, her smile widening even more.

Dancing started behind him, both whistle and drum beginning a lively tune.

He raised his eyebrows, offering her his arm. "May I have the pleasure of your company for this dance?"

Brighit gasped in pleasure. "Oh, ye—

"This lady is spoken for." Peter stepped up from behind and gave his back to the man. His eyes were overly bright and a smile played across his lips. Extending his own hand toward her, he asked, "Brighit?"

The string player dropped his head in acquiescence and backed away but brought his hand to his heart as if injured. "Of course."

Brighit's breath ceased at the touch of Peter's firm fingers on her hand. She gladly allowed him to lead her into the dance. The effect of the mead increased her awareness of his long length beside her, his handsome face smiling down at her. This was her celebration of freedom and this handsome man was her love.

One dance led into another. The sweat trickled down her back. She couldn't even try to curtail the smile on her face. To and fro she danced, her hands lightly held by Peter. They sashayed up the line and back, pressing toward each other, then retreating. The whistle and drum were quickly joined by the string player. When they passed him in the circle, he smiled at her. No bad feelings.

The full moon rose in the sky as the night progressed. A few men appeared among the dancers with masks covering their faces and hay tucked inside their shirts. They were the Mischief Makers. They darted along the dancers, stopping to steal kisses from the ladies and making mock challenges to the men. All laughed in good fun.

The late evening chill finally took its toll on the worn out crowd. One by one, and sometimes in pairs, the crowd dispersed. Peter led her to sit beneath a tree, the moonlight filtering around her. She leaned back, waiting to catch her breath and he returned with a bursting skin of some sort of liquid.

"Wonderful. I am parched." She accepted the offered skin. It was lighter than the mead and very refreshing.

"You dance well." He rested his elbow on his bent knee where he sat beside her, his face obscured in the darkness.

"We loved to dance, my brothers and me. My mother and father, as well."

"Brothers? How many do you have?"

Brighit handed back the skin and wiped at the juices that dripped down her chin. "I have six brothers. Well, I had six brothers."

A cloud passed in front of the moon and she felt the weight settling back onto her shoulders. "Three of my brothers have died in battle over the years and two moved farther south to protect their wives' clans, leaving just me and my brother. Now Tadhg is the only one who remains."

"And he will be clan leader now?"

"At my father's passing. He is the strongest of all the six boys. Our clan will be well guarded under his leadership."

Not that she would ever know for sure how well they fared. The night's happiness seemed to be slipping away. She would have liked to hold on to it a little longer.

Peter wiped his face and brushed the hair back from his forehead. The evening's festivities had taken their toll on him or perhaps it was the Monk's pepper. God knows his reaction watching Brighit's shapely figure, now displayed for all to see in her well-fitted gown, dancing about in total abandonment certainly hadn't indicated it was working. The growing urge to pull her against him and allow his hands free reign over those curves hadn't lessened in the least. Were the Monk's actually successful in using it to alleviate lustful thoughts? He certainly had his doubts.

"Did you find your Monk's pepper?"

He started slightly before he realized she hadn't read his mind but was remembering what he had been searching for earlier in the day. "Yes."

She nodded then turned away.

"And I see you've been very careful with the flower you received."

She brought the flower to her nose for the hundredth time and smiled. "Yes. I wonder how long it will last."

"Most flowers don't last very long once they've been cut off the plant."

"That's very true."

"They need to be fed from the plant to stay alive. Once they're separated, it's just a matter of time before they wilt and die."

She kept her eyes on the flower and nodded but the look on her face spoke volumes about her attachment to this flower.

"You can put it in water. Perhaps that will keep it alive longer."

She nodded again.

It suddenly occurred to him that perhaps they were no longer speaking of the flower, but of her. That realization quickened the blood in his veins.

"Are you going to the Priory against your will?"

Brighit snapped her head up and looked at him with wide eyes. "Of course not. You're not making me go."

"Is it not where you wish us to bring you?"

She swallowed loudly, as if fighting other words that wanted to come forth, before answering. "It is where I must go."

"I will take you wherever you want me to, Brighit. You need only ask."

Her bright eyes remained on him, searching his features, and his temperature rose. The moment dragged on. And the monks were lying about their guarded pepper.

"No. I will honor my father's agreement with the Priory and do as he bid me."

"You speak of honor as if you were a man."

"Why would a woman not have honor as well?"

"My experience is more with woman who display their wiles and prefer to have their whims seen to than rather than to behave with dignity and go without hesitation as they are bid. You surprise me."

"Perhaps if I were able to reveal my heart, you would not be so surprised."

She had enjoyed the dancing, accepted the gift of a flower, and now sat in resolute determination to see her family bestowed with the honor of a grateful daughter who reveres her father's wishes rather than stating her personal desires even when questioned. "I have much admiration for your stalwart attitude. I will see you arrive at the Priory unharmed and unmolested."

Mort's sudden arrival made Peter's suspicious that the man had been listening.

"Ah, shall we see our ward gets a good night's rest, my lord?" He stood off to one side, as if waiting to assure he had chosen his moment correctly.

Peter rose with a heavy sigh. "Of course."

"I have acquired a small blanket for your comfort, my lady. Let us return."

"Thank you, Mort. You are very good to me."

She rested her hand on the little man's arm and they headed up the hill.

"It is my pleasure to see you comfortably settled for the night."

They continued on the road but Peter remained where he was, watching them. Had she just professed that she would prefer to not be taking vows at the Priory? It did seem so. Did he have any other choice for her? No. She was indeed a determined, virginal sacrifice for her family and would wear the mantle until the very end of her days no doubt.

The idea somehow managed to enflame his desire rather than quench it. Pulling the small jar from his pocket, he swallowed down the rest of the tincture before following them to their camp. His need for sleep would go unmet again this night he'd wager.

A short time later, Mort snored where he was curled up beside Peter, his two hands tucked between his knees for warmth. It was going to be a long night. His own stomach growled loud enough for everyone within a mile to hear. He didn't realize the Monk's pepper would take his appetite for food and make him forget to see to his evening meal.

Covered with a blanket, Brighit lay a short distance beyond. She lay on her back, her hand tucked beneath her head. It made her appear not as one in sleep but one who lay patiently waiting for her lover. Peter turned away. His imagination was running amuck. Perhaps the pepper was not fresh. That must be it.

At some point, hopefully sooner rather than later, he would acquire the fresher weed and would no longer be racked with lustful longings he could not satisfy. As long as it didn't lessen his fighting ability or stamina on the battlefield, the herb could easily become a mainstay in his diet. It would keep his focus where it needed to be. He just needed to remember to eat.

His stomach growled again.

"Your stomach seems to have a mind of its own." Brighit's quiet comment surprised him.

"I believed you to be asleep."

"I am very sensitive to the noises around me. Between your stomach and Mort's snoring, I am unable to sleep."

Mort mumbled and shifted. Peter leaned in closer to see if he was awake as well.

"I'd say he sleeps like the dead," Brighit said.

Peter laughed quietly. "And so he did when we were traveling alone. I thought perhaps with you nearby to guard, it would be less so."

She sat up and the blanket fell to her waist. He quickly looked away since he didn't know whether she slept in her newly acquired gown or her sleep chemise. He didn't need to know.

"Would you like to take a walk?" Peter wanted to slap himself. Why would he ask her to come away from the only protection she actually had, when he had such a strong desire to seduce her?

"If you wouldn't mind."

No, Peter didn't mind getting her alone. He shoved his urges back into his gut and rose. "Of course I wouldn't mind."

She was again clothed in her night shift but sensibly kept her blanket pulled tight around her and joined him.

"I appreciate that you are a light sleeper as well."

"Yes." He agreed although he knew it was guilt and lust that kept him from sleeping. "Let us walk back toward the crest of the hill."

"That would be lovely. I can hear the river but don't remember seeing it."

They walked in silence. At the top, she went to the right and led the way through the heather until she found a small clearing where perhaps a deer had been resting during the day. She looked to the east. "I think I can spot the river. Do you see it?"

Peter tore his eyes away from the vision of her visible in the moonlight where her blanket had fallen off her shoulders. "Yes." The water glistened slightly. "That is the river that runs beside the Priory."

She glanced back, her face in shadows. "Oh. It's that close?"

He'd swear her expression was sad now. "It's further than it appears from here."

Suddenly remembering the whistle he'd acquired for her earlier and the anticipated pleasure it would give her, he indicated the grass beneath them. "Let us sit. I have something for you."

He retrieved it and handed it to her. Her delighted gasp pleased him. It satisfied him that the price he'd paid in giving up his smallest dagger that usually lay hidden in his left boot was well worth it.

"Thank you." She put the whistle to her mouth and played a quick run up then down. "It has a wonderful tone. Is it yours?"

"No. I bought it for you. I didn't want to hear you were arrested for pilfering from one of the merchants in order to have your nightly concert." The sound of her quiet laughter encouraged him. "I would have a difficult time explaining that you would have returned it if they'd only given you a few minutes to yourself."

The sentiment squeezed his heart. That was really all she wanted. A few minutes to herself.

"I don't know for certain that the nuns will allow you to keep the whistle but I knew it would give you great pleasure now."

"Yes. Great pleasure."

He stretched alongside her to enjoy the music. She played a quick little tune then smiled again. "I knew you were a great warrior but, with this, you have certainly shown yourself as my gallant knight."

Closing her eyes, she played a slower tune. The emotions flitted across her face, giving him a good idea of what the song was about. The blanket slipped from her shoulder and he looked again on her loveliness. Her breasts pressed against the flimsy night dress with each breath and his fingers itched to follow the swell, to let them fill his eager palms. Then following the curve of her waist, he would tuck her close against him. The feel of her firm bottom in his grasp, rocking her against him, urging her closer still.

The music stopped and he reluctantly tore his gaze back to face her.

Her expression said it all. She had caught him appraising her. Carefully placing her whistle on the ground beside her, she leaned down toward his face. Her hand moved to his chest. He pulled her gently down to accept his kiss. Timid at first, she soon relaxed her mouth and her lips parted. He deepened the kiss, nibbling her lip, stroking it with his tongue before plundering the depths of her mouth. He worked his fingers into her hair, its softness falling around him, enveloping their kiss within its tresses. When he would have pushed his advantage, his mind going over every part of her he longed to touch in vivid detail, he realized the Monk's pepper was working. There was no responsive hardening in his groin.

She pulled back slightly and opened her eyes. She smiled. A smile that spoke of a thousand longings. Longings never realized. Longings that result in a lifetime of regret. Longings tucked deep inside the heart. "Now I will go into the Priory with the knowledge of a man's lips against mine, a very handsome man. A man I could have loved. And every time I sneak away to play my whistle, I will remember this night. I will remember you."

Collecting the whistle, she rose and headed back the way they'd come. Peter followed her back. There was nothing left to be said.

CHAPTER 16

$\mathcal{B}$y mid-day they were walking again. After waiting most of the morning for the man with the carriage to get underway, they were only slightly closer to the Priory. They probably could have walked that far if they'd left when Peter had wanted to. Mort resumed his idle chatter no doubt to try and initiate a conversation. The lack of response appeared not to affect him at all. His constant talking only increased Peter's irritation.

"Enough, Mort," Peter finally bellowed. "There is nothing wrong with walking in silence. You do not need to keep up that incessant babbling. Please!"

"Why, I never bab—"

An object whistled by the man's head. An arrow. He ducked for cover. Peter grabbed Brighit and veered into the gully beside the road. He landed with her safely beneath him.

Mort dragged himself by his elbows to where Peter lay.

"Where did it come from?" Peter asked.

"I saw nothing, my lord."

"And I heard nothing." Peter's irritation was not well checked, inwardly cursing Mort's non-stop talk. It made awareness of his surroundings near impossible.

Mort jerked his head toward him. "Since when is a warrior not able to hear his enemy?"

"When there is too much noise around him. You are never quiet."

"I am not to blame. You had other things crowding your mind."

"I'm having trouble breathing." Brighit's muffled voice interrupted the squabble.

Peter looked beneath him and into her wide, brown eyes. He shifted just enough that she could take a breath, still using his body to shield her.

"Thank you." She shoved her hair out of her face.

Peter had taken her down pretty hard. "Are you hurt?"

"I'm fine."

Her expression betrayed her fears despite the brave words.

"And I plan to keep it that way," Peter said.

Mort lifted his head just over the rise. Another arrow flew past, landing just beyond them. Peter grabbed it, bringing it close to his face. "It's not well made."

"It didn't miss my head by that much, my lord." Mort had pulled his hat off. His feather drooped awkwardly. Its quill sliced in two. "Not much at all."

"They can't be soldiers. Or they'd have shown themselves by now."

Mort lifted his hat above the rise as bait. Another arrow hit with deadly accuracy, ripping it from his hand. It landed to the other side of Mort.

"What type of feather is that?"

"OH! It looks like a parrot feather," Brighit said.

Both men turned and looked at her.

"See the green here?" She pointed at the line of solid green mixed in with the brown along the flat end of the arrow.

"I'd say there are at least two with bows. One shooting from the left. One from the right. Maybe three feet between them."

"Who's to say there are not more?"

Peter raised a finger to his lips. In the silence was the distinct sound of approaching horses.

"More back up arriving?"

Another arrow landed just short of where they lay hidden behind a slight rise in the ground.

"If they move in any closer, we will be at their mercy," Peter said.

Mort rolled onto his back. "So what do we do?"

A high screech pierced the air just ahead of the horses' arrival. Dirt sprayed them from the road where at least one horse was pulled up short not far from them. Other horses could be heard from further away. Peter readied his sword and braced himself for the attack. It was never good to go in with brandished swords when the number of attackers was unknown, but he had no choice.

"Ready?" Peter asked Mort.

Brighit cowered beneath him. Another high screech pierced the air. Her eyes widening with the sound.

"I will protect you."

"Sir Peter," a familiar voice called to him. "Reveal yourself."

"Is that—"

The war cry erupted again and it seemed to be coming from the same area as the arrows had. Mort dragged himself in the direction of the sound and snuck a peak above the hill.

"Ha!" Mort turned to Peter and smiled. He stood up before Peter could stop him.

"What are you doing?" Peter spoke with a clenched jaw.

Instead of being pierced, Mort waved then turned and smiled at him. "It's our Scottish friends."

"Your attackers have been disarmed," the voice he now recognized as Niall called to him again.

"Do you think I can get up now?"

Peter immediately released her and stood, pulling her up behind him until he could assess the situation. Aldred and Lachlann had their swords trained on Brighit's would-be protectors as they forced them to their knees. Their poorly made bows on the ground.

"Methinks you were under attack," Niall offered from where he stepped to stand beside his horse, a grin across his young face.

Peter pressed his lips together. He was in his debt. "Yes. So you've saved us."

"Give me any reason." His voice was low and menacing.

"It appears I have," Niall said to Peter. He raised one eyebrow in a questioning what-are-you-going-to-give-me-for-it look.

"My thanks." Peter tried for finality in the statement.

Apparently Niall missed it since he was now focused on Brighit.

"And how are you, fair lady?" The redhead bestowed what was more than likely his most charming smile and bowed deeply, as if he were greeting the Queen.

Brighit shifted her dress back into proper place and pushed her hair over her shoulders before answering. "I am well. Thank you for your assistance."

Lachlann made quick work of tying Cole and Andrew's hands. They jerked their arms as if to pull away but Aldred adjusted his blade closer to their throats.

"How did you happen upon us? Is this just a coincidence?" Peter asked.

"You are a suspicious one. Of course this was not planned." Niall tipped his head toward his friend. "Aldred, go get the man his horse."

Lachlann held his blade against Ivan's throat, a murderous glint in his eye. Aldred disappeared into the woods.

"My horse?"

Aldred quickly returned with Roman, handling him by his lead.

"Yes, we came upon him in the woods a day ago. Still saddled—" Niall explained. "We searched for any signs of you but found nothing. The palfrey was nowhere to be found either. I've never met a warrior yet who would willingly part with his mount."

"And you still haven't." The horse snorted in recognition. Peter stroked his warm, soft nose. The rest of his items seemed intact. "Look at you. Did you try to find me?"

It had crossed Peter's mind that Cole and Andrew's horse abilities must be great. Anyone able to stop his horse from retuning must have good horse skills.

"Not a chance he could have returned." Aldred pulled a black cloth from his belt. "He had this over his head."

Snatching the black sack, Peter stalked past Aldred and shoved it in Ivan's face. "Is this what you did to keep him from returning to me?"

Peter grabbed him by the tunic. Ivan turned his head, straining against Peter's unyielding grip.

"You son of a whore. You bully women and animals?" Peter pulled back his fist, landed it squarely on the man's jaw, and released his hold. Ivan fell on his arse with the force of the movement. "You're a sorry excuse for a man."

Aldred smiled. He shifted Ivan to his knees and grabbed back his hands to tie him up.

Peter returned to stand beside Niall. His anger still simmering.

"So what will we do with them now?" Lachlann glanced at Niall.

"Whatever the Norman says to do with them."

The three Scots turned toward Peter.

His anger was still simmering. He moved around the men now kneeling before him. "Have you any defense for attacking us?"

"Taking back my property," Ivan scowled at Brighit.

Peter tensed. He would enjoy breaking the man's nose with his fist. He glanced toward Brighit not doubting she felt the same.

"What say you, Lady Brighit? What will we do with them?"

She gritted her teeth and walked up to the man. With an open hand, she slapped the little man so hard he tipped over. Unable to right himself, they all watched Ivan struggle and sputter incoherent threats.

Her determination gave her a fierce forced-to-be-reckoned-with look and a great sense of satisfaction swelled inside Peter. He crossed his arms about his chest. Brighit had stood up for herself and her anger did not seem assuaged yet.

"Who do you think you are to speak of me as your property?"

Ivan had managed to sit upright. He glared at her but refused to answer.

"Have you received satisfaction?" Peter addressed Brighit. The small group waited on her command. It was that revelation, no doubt, that put a huge smile on her face and a twinkle in her eye.

"I have. If he is imprisoned, I will have even greater satisfaction."

Peter fought to keep a straight face. "Unfortunately, there is a definite lack of laws as well as prisons in the area." He took Brighit's place in front of Ivan. It was time to see this matter dealt with. "I'm still waiting to hear an answer."

"So you'll beat an unarmed man?" Ivan sneered.

"Man?" Peter spit on the ground.

Cole finally spoke up. "I have no grievance with you, my lord."

"Oh, my lord, now?"

Cole had the grace to look embarrassed. "My lord, my friend and I are simple men for hire. We have no grievance with you and will be happy to allow you to pass without further incident, with or without the young lady."

"Allow him?" Niall's voice cracked. "Ha! You are in no position to be allowing anyone to do anything."

Andrew looked away tight lipped.

"So you wish us to let you go? And you'll just go about your life as if this never happened?" Lachlann asked.

"Yes!" Andrew's quick answer was accompanied by an ever-so-hopeful expression.

Cole rolled his eyes, shaking his head as if to say his friend was an idiot.

"No, that's not going to happen," Peter said. "Niall, can we speak?"

"Keep your eyes on these three," Niall directed Lachlann and Aldred then followed Peter a short distance away.

"What are you thinking?" Niall asked, speaking in conspiratorial tones.

Peter smiled. "I am in no position to enforce anything. It will be up to you to see these men get what they deserve."

"Do you know of any reason they would be attacking you? Is it really because of the girl?" Niall let his gaze wander over Brighit.

Peter clenched his hand into a fist at his side. "She may be part of some bigger plan."

"She is well worth the trouble." Niall stroked his bottom lip with his thumb.

Peter grasped him by the tunic and jerked his face in close. "Do not speak so of the lady. I have a very long memory and you do not want me as your enemy. Do you understand?"

Niall quickly hid his alarm with a smirk. "I believe I understand completely." When Peter released him, he adjusted his tunic, and glanced at the others. "Luck was with you that my friends didn't notice you handling me so... or surely they'd have ripped your balls off. No harm. But I believe we do have an understanding. A Norman as an ally may work out well for me if I ever again travel too far south."

Peter clenched his teeth but he nodded.

"Good. So perhaps we should see our slimy friends back to the coast and give them a shove off?"

Peter relaxed and smiled. "I think that sounds about right. Any sign of the carriage?"

"We caught sight of those three as they were coming from the market. They stood out because they weren't on the path, they cut right across the glen and into the woods on foot." He pointed to the trees. "You are actually lucky we kept our horses hidden. If we'd walked, we'd never have been here in time to save the day."

Niall's eyes twinkled with mischief. Peter refused to drop his stoic stance. The mild cocker already had one up on him. He didn't need to confirm that he liked the lad.

"So how will we do this? I have three people but only one horse now."

The redhead paused and rubbed his thumb along his lip. When he turned on him with wide-eyed enthusiasm, Peter knew he was not going to like his answer. "I'll go with you and we'll both take a rider. Lachlann and Aldred will have to walk the prisoners back to their horses."

"That will work. Mort and Brighit," Peter said, walking toward his horse, "we're continuing on to the Priory."

Niall trotted into the woods, returning after a short time with the Scots horses. He mounted his black horse in one easy sweep of his leg and urged it toward Brighit. He bent over and reached his arm out to her. "Might I give you a hand up?"

"What?" Brighit's confusion was evident. "What are we doing?"

Peter sighed and closed the distance between them. "They're bringing your 'guardians' back to the coast. We need one of them to ride with us so we can have two to a horse."

He glanced over at Niall's cocky smirk and his blood boiled.

"Lachlann! Your horse looks sturdier, what say you come with us and let your leader... lead."

Niall caught his jaw before it dropped to his chest then smiled. "As you wish, Sir Peter."

Lachlann led his horse to the little group, stopping in front of Peter.

"You take Mort."

"What? No! You take Mort."

Mort shifted his feet beside Peter.

"It will be better if he is with you."

"If you wish me to be of assistance, then I will gladly accept Brighit on my horse. She is smaller."

Peter glanced at Mort who was shooting daggers. "Very well. Get up here, Mort."

Peter soothed his mount and tried not to notice the way Lachlann leaned his strong arm toward Brighit. Or the way she grabbed it and was pulled effortlessly to sit sideways in front of him.

An arm on either side of her, Lachlann pulled his reins to catch up with Peter. After seeing Brighit wrapping her arm around the man's side and the man's grin of satisfaction, Peter refused to look again. When Mort started to wrap his arms around Peter's middle from where he sat behind him, Peter swatted at his arms.

"Use your legs man!"

"As you wish, my lord."

Peter would not have believed his irritation could get any worse until this moment. He felt ready to burst. A jiggling movement behind him that felt suspiciously like suppressed laughter gave him an ideal outlet for his anger.

"Enough." The command came in a menacingly low tone. "I see no humor in this situation."

A few minutes later, it started again. Peter pulled up his horse and jumped to the ground. He pierced Mort with his look then crossed over to Lachlann and Brighit. The man had moved his reins to one hand so his other arm could wrap around Brighit's waist. Peter closed the distance and reached up to remove a startled Brighit.

"Lachlann, can you see that your friends have everything in hand?"

A questioning frown crossed the man's face before he said, "Aye."

Peter fought for composure before facing Brighit. Her concern was apparent. Mort stood a few feet away, shaking his head.

"Can you give us a moment?"

Mort's shocked look gave Peter pause. To hell with the man. He wanted to speak to Brighit alone. He waited until Mort withdrew to the forest edge.

"What is wrong? You seem very upset. Did you get hurt by the arrows?"

"What? Certainly not." He took her hands lightly in his, rubbing his thumb across the soft flesh of her palms. They were warm and he had the urge to place one against his cheek. He dropped her hand and took a step back. "I wanted to be sure you were not overwrought by having to ride with Lachlann."

"Why—oh, because of the earlier situation? That was all Ivan. They all flirted with me—mercilessly—but Lachlann was nothing but sweet."

Sweet? Another screw turned into the pit of his stomach. "So you have no qualms?"

"It was Niall that Ivan offered to sell me to. That's preposterous. The lad knows you can't buy a woman. If he had said yes..."

She would not be with him now. The screw turned tighter.

"They were not proper with you."

Brighit tipped her head as if considering his words. "You are right but Lachlann was the least improper. He reminds me of the lads who courted me at home."

His gut wrenched and his breath ceased. "But that is not who he is."

"You are correct. And this is not home."

Her fleeting sadness shoved against his tension. He hadn't meant to make her sad. "You will probably arrive at your destination this very night."

A horse came up behind him but Peter ignored Lachlann, his eyes intent on Brighit.

"Yes. My new life." She looked down, avoiding his gaze. "A new adventure?" She faced him. "Do you think?"

Peter exhaled slowly and allowed himself to trace the side of her face with his fingertips. So soft. So lovely. Such a waste to be locked up in a convent with no hope for a future or a family. "Will all be well with you, sweet Brighit?"

"I pray it will be." Her voice was quiet. "Will you pray for me as well?"

Peter couldn't speak. He nodded. He took her hand, led her to Lachlann's horse, then allowed the lad to pull her back up in front of him. "Let me know if you need to rest."

"I will."

A sudden tightness settled into his chest as he mounted. He grabbed Mort's arm and pulled him up behind him. He gave the horse his lead. She would soon be left behind with her life and he would need to go on with his. He just wished he had more of a life to get back to.

CHAPTER 17

The sun was low in the sky when they crested the last hill and the Priory finally came into sight. It was smaller than Peter expected. It appeared to be under construction by the amount of small rocks piled at the gate. From the flourishing tall grass and wild heather that grew around it, however, he'd say nothing had been done recently. Narrow arrow slits along the top of the building seemed to be the only source of light, giving the building an overall dark and forbidding appearance.

He spotted four, heavily robed women working in the field, one of which was very pregnant. Peter remembered how he had thought perhaps Brighit was with child and that might be the reason she was being brought to the Priory. When did he begin to see her differently? When he'd kissed her? When Ivan cowered her in front of him? When he'd gazed upon her naked loveliness which showed no visible signs of being with child?

The closer they got to the gate, the slower they all moved. Even Mort ceased his talking as if the atmosphere required a reverent silence. A lump rose in Peter's throat. A tightness in his chest as if bound by a heavy cord that, with each breath, drew more taut. He did not want to leave her here with no one to look after her. Her life would now become all about her vows, her orders, her devotion. Brighit the woman would all but disappear. And she would be completely alone.

They halted their horses but no one moved to get down. When Brighit caught him watching her, she offered a reassuring smile that didn't reach her eyes.

"I will be well," she spoke the words aloud before turning to Lachlann. "Can you help me down?"

Peter was there before the Scot's foot touched the ground, spreading his hands about her small middle and lifting her down. She weighed next to nothing. He didn't immediately release her. She stood close enough to feel her warmth. She was close enough to kiss. She was close enough to still press against him.

"Lachlann, can you get the horses some water?" Peter asked, his eyes remaining on Brighit.

Lachlann moved in close. He glanced at Peter. Then at Brighit. He sighed as if in resignation then led both horses down the little hill. From the opposite direction came the women that were in the field.

"I will take you away from here if that is your desire," Peter spoke in a hushed tone, for her ears only. "You need only say the word."

Her rounded eyes were sad but she held his gaze. "I do what I must."

"Greetings," Mort called from behind Peter, his voice retreating as he no doubt approached the women. "Good day to you all."

Brighit took a deep breath, straightened her shoulders, and looked deeply into Peter's eyes. And waited. He fought down the ridiculous urge to throw her onto his horse, move up close behind her, and take her away despite what she said. He released his hands.

"Are you the MacNaughton?" A woman's voice came from behind them.

Brighit dipped her head, darting a glance at Peter, and approached the women. "That I am."

"Well, 'tis a great blessing to have you join us," the pregnant woman offered and took her hand. "We expected you to be later than this."

"Later?" Brighit asked.

Peter waited for more information, fighting the uneasy feeling Brighit's one word question stirred in him. She hadn't understood the woman's statement either. The Priory had no way of knowing when she would get here.

"We received word that you would be delayed," a shriveled woman of over fifty years spoke, then eyed each of the men as if they'd been the reason for her delay. "You're here now and that is what matters most."

"Who brought such word?" Brighit asked.

The woman was fixed on Peter, peered closer into his face, then withdrew. She appeared disgruntled as if she were far too important to deal with him right before she gave him her back.

"I couldn't say for sure," the pregnant woman offered.

"Ah, quiet now, Ruth. They have no right to question us."

"They're just curious. It is right to answer them."

"It is not right to be questioned, so the answering is also not right."

Ruth rolled her eyes then smiled at Brighit as if this bickering was something that happened quite often.

The older woman said, "We are glad you made it here unharmed."

The two other nuns joined them. Closing in around her on all sides, the women moved as one toward the entrance. The realization that they were taking her away caused Peter to go into full-blown panic. It was suddenly difficult to breathe. His heart raced.

"Wait!"

The women stopped.

"We have traveled far with little to eat or drink in order to see her safely here. Have you nothing to quench our thirst from our weary travel?"

The four exchanged quizzical glances as if making a decision was a difficult thing. The elderly woman raised her shoulders for a moment and then dropped them.

It was Ruth who finally spoke up. "Forgive us. We are very excited to have her with us. My name is Sister Ruth. This is Sister Martha," she indicated the older woman, "Sister Hannah and Sister Elizabeth."

The other two women nodded.

"Please! Come into the courtyard where you can partake of food and drink before you depart."

Within the high-walled bailey was a wooden table carved with rough-hewn wood and benches scattered around. Martha indicated the men needed to remain there then they all disappeared inside the stone structure. When Brighit was no longer in his sight, Peter paced the small area.

"Surely, she is safe here," Mort said.

Peter continued his walking.

"There is nothing more for us to do."

Stopping suddenly, Peter gave Mort a wide smile. "I believe I need to meet with the head of the Priory."

Mort mirrored his expression. "That seems reasonable."

The two jumped up and nearly ran to knock on the wooden door set within the small entrance. No answer.

Mort glanced nervously toward Peter, his small hands rubbing together. He knocked again, louder. No answer.

"Perhaps they are out of earshot?" he asked.

Peter looked around the small area. "It doesn't look big enough to ever be beyond earshot."

He went as far as he could within the bailey. The building had thick, impenetrable walls and small towers at every advantage point. There was a long building, just visible that connected to the back.

"This place is built to resist attack," Peter said.

"Many Priories and Monasteries are."

Frowning, Peter gave an irritated look to the little man who then raised his hands as if in surrender. "I'm just saying it is not unusual for them to be well fortified."

"It would be near impossible to break through the wall without a battering ram."

"Are you making plans to attack, my lord?"

Peter blew an exasperated sigh then retraced his steps. They seemed to be taking an awfully long time. He settled himself on the bench and counted to ten.

"I think I hear someone," Mort said from where he had his ear to the wooden door.

He quickly shifted away. Peter stood alongside him.

The door opened just enough to reveal Martha's face. "I'm sorry you can't be entering."

"I need to speak with the Prioress."

"The who?"

Peter's throat went dry. "The Prior?" He searched beyond the head of the little woman but could only make out a darkened hall behind her.

"Oh, you mean Father Tinsley? He is not here now. He won't be back until later."

His body tensed. His fingers flexed. "Then I would speak to Brighit."

Certainly she wouldn't wish to be left here without all the details worked out. Peter didn't know any of the details but until she indicated to him that all was well, he would prefer to stay near.

"Can't."

Peter leveled his gaze at the woman, his jaw clenched. Mort pushed in a little closer and Peter gave him room. Martha, however, resisted the slight push he gave against the door. "Please. We would like to see Lady Brighit to know what she wants us to do."

"She wants you to leave."

"NO!" Peter didn't regret his forceful tone. He was about ready to rip the door down. The four straps holding the door in place appeared quite sliceable. Not very good planning on their part. "I will see Lady Brighit."

The woman shoved the door against his boot when he started to slip it inside. Pain shot up his leg.

"Lady Brighit is no longer here."

"WHAT?" his voice boomed. His fingers gripped the width of the wooden door, preparing to pull it lose.

"She has a new name within these walls."

Peter's face reddened. He released the door. She was referring to the vow taking, not that she was no longer within. He breathed a grateful sigh.

"I wish to speak to her, whatever you may choose to call her—now."

Someone spoke behind the woman and she glanced back.

"No. Please, Sister Martha." It was Ruth speaking.

"You can't let them inside." Martha's words carried over her shoulder.

As they bickered back and forth, Peter fought to remain composed. He would not be leaving without seeing *Brighit* regardless of who won the argument.

Ruth elbowed her way past the older woman. With a huff, Martha opened the door wider, allowing the pregnant woman to step through and for Peter to see down the hall straight ahead and a door to the right just inside.

Ruth smiled. She carried a tray of hard bread and cheese, a pitcher, and mugs to the table. "I have brought you what you requested. Come. Please."

He glanced at Ruth, then at Martha who glowered at him.

Mort remained where he was. Peter acquiesced and walked to the table, accepting the cup offered him.

"Forgive, Sister Martha, we do not have many visitors here," Ruth said. Her tone dropped when she added, "and she trusts no one."

Peter couldn't care less what Martha thought. He was going to see Brighit. Out here or in there but he would be taking his leave only after she presented her reassurances.

"She will be here anon," she said as if reading his mind, then poured a cup for Mort.

"Thank you, Sister Ruth," Mort said as he took the cup.

"How long will we have to wait for Brighit?" Peter regretted demonstrating his extreme impatience with the situation but refused to back down.

"I believe they are just showing her where she will sleep."

He reached to the sack that hung from his belt, assuring him that the flute he bought her was still inside. Perhaps she'd be allowed to play quietly here.

"Is it her own area?" Mort said, always so adept at idle chatter.

Ruth took a sip of her drink, her hand resting on the bulge where her child lay, and smiled. "It is very small, but yes, it is her own."

Peter ground his teeth. How long would they keep Brighit?

"How long have you been here?" Mort appeared to be trying to ease the tension. Peter was fine with the amount of tension.

"About a year."

Peter stilled.

Mort nodded and sipped his drink then glanced around. "It is lovely here. Do you tend all these gardens?"

Peter wanted to pulverize the man for interrupting. A year? She's been here a year and she's pregnant? He began to count to ten but stopped at three.

"Were you not with child when you arrived?"

Ruth lips parted slighted but then she smiled, her nose wrinkling with the gesture. "Of course. I am past my time to give birth."

The chords in Peter's neck tightened. She would have a child here? The macabre sense that they would not survive wormed into his gut. He put down his cup and returned to pacing.

Mort demonstrated a spark of wisdom by deciding to cease the idle conversation.

"Let me see what is keeping Sister Mary."

"Sister Mary?" Peter bellowed then clamped his mouth, trying to check his irritation. "It is not Sister Mary we care about. We wish to see our ward, Brighit."

"I will see what is taking so long."

Once alone, Mort turned on Peter. "My lord, Sister Mary must be her name now."

Peter threw his arms up to the heavens. "She has barely arrived. How can she already have a different name? She is not a different person!"

"Please try to calm yourself—"

The door opened and Peter gasped at the sight of Brighit covered in several layers of rough linen, from the tip of her head to the bottom of her feet. If not for the expressive, brown eyes, he would recognize anywhere, he wouldn't have known her.

"Forgive me for taking so long. I didn't mean to worry you," she said.

He recognized the voice as well and relief swept over him. He stepped toward her. Martha and Ruth, who were right on her heels, moved to stand on either side of her. They halted his approach with a look.

"May we speak in private?" He refused to hide his hostility.

"NO!" Martha used the same tone he had earlier. He reddened again.

"My apologies for my earlier surliness. Her safety has been my concern of late... it is hard to let go."

Martha nearly *harrumphed* her irritation. "No. You may no longer spend time with her alone."

"Then just a few feet away? Within your sight? Just so I can be sure she is well?" It galled him to ask for their permission. He'd noticed Brighit's fearful expression at his earlier outburst. It was out of concern for her that he attempted to quell his resentment now.

"No. You may speak to her in front of us."

Peter ground his teeth again. Focusing on Brighit's face, the little he could see, he took a slow breath, then smiled. "How does it seem? Will all be well?"

She gave a half-hearted smile. "I will adjust. Do not fash yourself. I will be fine."

He began to nod. "Oh." Peter reached into his sack and pulled out her flute. "I didn't want you to forget this."

Martha would have grabbed it but Ruth stilled her hand and said, "We do not have music at this time. Perhaps we can let Father Tinsley care for it?"

Brighit allowed the younger woman to take the flute. Peter was enraged but cooled his ire. Upsetting Brighit further was not his intent.

"So you wish to stay? Even now?"

Despite the confusion that passed between the other two women, Peter knew Brighit understood his question. Without her music, would she be able to get by?

"Yes."

An awkward silence covered them like a heavy blanket. Suffocating. Peter struggled with what to say. This felt wrong to just leave her here. Mort moved in close, took her hand to his lips and bestowed a feather-light kiss.

"All the best for you, Lady Brighit."

Martha inhaled sharply in protest but Ruth put her hand on her arm.

He stepped back, retreating to the horse. Brighit searched Peter's face and waited.

"You are very good at practicing patience." He spoke in quiet tones. "You wish for me to leave you here? Would you prefer that I stay longer?"

"You may leave me here."

Peter took her hand as Mort had and pressed his fingers into her warm palm as he brought it to his lips. He held her gaze. Her brown eyes bright but clear, then kissed her knuckles.

"All the best indeed."

Slowly he released her hand and stepped back. He glanced between the other women but they paid him no heed. They were too interested in quickly turning Brighit back toward the entrance. Peter refused to look away. He would watch her safely enter that door. What happened beyond that, he would never know. At least he would be assured he saw her cross the threshold.

"Goodbye dear Brighit." His voice was barely a whisper for no one else's ears but his own. The door thudded closed and the unmistakable sound of the bar being lowered echoed in the courtyard. His face tightened. He could still manage to bust the door down. That gave him great comfort.

Peter turned quickly, nearly colliding with Lachlann who was out of breath.

"Did I miss the goodbyes?"

"You have." Brighit had not looked for him either which gave Peter great satisfaction. "They were rather quick to snatch her up and hide her away."

The young man's crestfallen look was genuine. Peter patted his back. "She knew you wished her well."

Peter turned toward his horse, taking the reins as he mounted in front of Mort who was already mounted. "I'm damn sick of riding with you in case you wondered."

"But now there is no one else you'd throw me over for so I believe I'm safe."

Peter snorted a quiet laugh then added. "Really? You believe I would throw you over? Never. Your golden tongue alone is worth... something, I'm sure."

Mort crossed his arms, effectively poking Peter in the back with the movement.

"We need to head back to York," Peter said with as much

determination as he could muster. "The King will want to hear from us on the situation rather than waste the trip north."

Mort did not respond. Peter glanced back to witness the expression of a very irritated man.

"Yes, my lord," Mort said with very little deference.

CHAPTER 18

The establishment was one big room with several trestles and benches neatly arranged for visitors. It was warm enough. Peter was satisfied. They'd made it by nightfall. However, he had no appetite. Mort, on the other hand, ate like a horse and was licking his fingertips with a lot of ceremony. Fastidious was the only word to describe him. No. Obnoxious worked, too.

"So?" Peter's voice was flat.

Mort stopped mid-lick and stared back. "So? So what?"

"What did you learn?"

Mort finished his last lick before continuing. "Well, our newly departed dinner companions were happy to chat and assured me that the castle has not been under siege. Recently." His face showed that was something.

Peter did not feel it was much. "And?"

"And…it will still be closed to you."

Peter slammed his fist on the worn table. "Damn me."

No one dare look his way as he was the only knight present. He was probably the only knight for miles. These were the wilds of England. Respect was the very least accorded to him even in this establishment. He couldn't really call it an inn although they'd given him a bed for the night. He had to share it with Mort and two others but it would be dry.

"Did you expect other news?" Mort's question intruded on his thoughts. "It is the same Baron in control now as before we were .. sidetracked."

"I'd hoped."

Mort's impertinence was becoming tiring. It worked its way under his skin like a burr. Nearly as bad as—no he would not even mention her name. She was safely delivered. Set in her little cocoon. Closely guarded by all. Her virginity sacrificed on the very altar of their Lord and Savior. So why was he still thinking on her? Why could he not remove her from his mind? Be done with it.

"Based on what?" Mort's stare pierced his. "What is wrong with you?"

"We'll have a fight on our hands after we arrive."

"You're a soldier."

"And?"

"It's what you do," Mort said it emphatically as if that was all there was to it. Of course he was correct. So why did he feel so cross about the whole ordeal?

Peter stood abruptly. He needed to clear his head. "I'm going for a walk."

Mort stood to accompany him but Peter shoved him back down onto the bench. "No. I will go alone."

"But, my lord," Mort glanced at the few men close enough to overhear and lowered his voice to a whisper. "We are not known here. You are a...target."

"Have someone try and capture me for ransom. They'll soon find they have more than they can handle." Now why did that statement bring her upturned face to his memory? Her lips parted invitingly, slightly pink from their first passionate kiss.

"Damn me," he cursed under his breath and headed out the door.

The brisk air was refreshing, but the cold lingered. Winter hung in the mist. The naked trees seemed strange and mystical, silhouetted in the moonlight. An owl voiced its objection to his presence.

"To hell with you, too," Peter answered. The door opened behind him and he stepped into the shadow of the necessary. The scent of excrement drifted to him. A man stumbled across the stone walk and headed toward the main road. In the direction of the Priory.

Must every thought and feeling that he have somehow evolve around her? Is there nothing else down that road except the Priory? He exhaled noisily and rubbed his hands against the dropping temperature. Mort came through the door and sat on the little bench beside it. He took his clay whistle from his bag and began to play a quiet tune. Peter recognized it as the one Brighit had played that first night.

"Must you haunt me as well?"

Mort stopped playing. He put his pipe in his lap and leaned his head against the straw structure. "Is that what's bothering you so?"

Peter shook his head. Mort had no idea.

"You're missing the lass already?"

"Like I'd miss the plague." Peter's voice sounded overly loud and defensive. "Another duty seen to. No more. It's best not to get attached."

He tried to settle his anger but it had taken up residence in the pit of his stomach.

"Maybe," Peter said, his voice quieter now.

"She was certainly a beauty."

"Beauty is fragile. I had a beauty and she wasn't safe with me. My loving killed her. No woman is safe with me. I'm cursed." Pain shot through him like an arrow to the heart. "I never even said those words to her. I never said my goodbyes either."

"Aw. I see. You have regrets."

Mort was quiet and Peter thought perhaps he'd fallen asleep until he spoke again. "The pain of your loss is very deep."

The evenness of his tone was calming. And the calming made Peter start to remember. It made him feel again the excruciating pain of the loss. He had been so happy to be home, so looking forward to being with Jeanette. He shook his head to clear it of the memories.

"Loving someone doesn't always cause pain," Mort said.

"What do you know of love?" Venom coated every word.

"My lord, you have never asked of my situation and I would not burden you now but I do know of love. I have a wife."

Peter turned toward him. "And children?"

Mort's teeth were visible when he smiled. "Aye, hardy boys. She bore them all with no help from me... well except for the making of them. And that I verily enjoyed."

"So many women die giving birth. Were you not afeared it would be so?"

"Yes. I worried about it but I had to obey the King's orders. She knew that. As did your Jeanette."

Peter swallowed hard. *Jeanette*. The child probably would have had her green eyes. Beguiling all she met just like her mother.

"Not every woman who becomes pregnant dies in childbirth, Peter."

"No. Not all women. I need only know two to know it is not worth the risk."

"Two?"

"My own mother died delivering me. My father never missed a day reminding me of that."

"But surely you know that it was not your fault your mother died."

"That mattered little to my father. He would have chosen her life over mine and told me as much. Repeatedly."

"That is cruel."

"Yes. My father was certainly that."

"So to live your life alone is the course you will take? You, my lord? You? A man of great passion and caring? You would choose a life of what? Of soldiering? Of no one to return home to?" Mort laughed quietly. "No, my lord, that is not the life for you."

"Enough of this prattle." Peter moved into the moonlight once again fully under control. "You're like an old woman."

He jerked the door open, intent on making his way to the little room without talking to anyone. He'd had enough talk for today. A woman with long, black hair had other ideas. She threw herself in front of him, leaning her body against him for emphasis. "Where are you going in such haste, my lord?"

The woman's eyes were hooded and there was no question of her occupation.

"Waiting for me?" Peter asked. He did not need this now.

She let go a throaty laugh and tossed her hair over her shoulder. Peter recognized the little act for what it was but she was only doing her job. He decided to play along then let her down easy. "And where should I be going?"

She twisted toward him, rubbing up the length of him.

The men around them were enjoying the display, murmuring their encouragement. He just wasn't sure if the encouragement was meant for him or her.

"She'd take care of you." One grizzly man smiled a toothless grin, lifting his mug toward them.

"She don't charge much either," a skinny, young man behind him added. He couldn't have been more than fifteen.

Peter looked at the two of them. "And has she taken care of you?"

"Not a few minutes before you and your man came in," Grizzly responded, his laugh more of a gasping chuckle.

The woman smiled provocatively. "It can be as long or as short as you want it."

She moved in closer, her lips hovering near his own, surrounding him with the scent of rotted teeth and barley soup. He wouldn't have touched this woman for all the power in the world.

He pulled back. "Well, I don't doubt you but I've no need of you tonight."

The instant silence in the room was the first clue. Mort had come in quietly and stood by the only exit, no doubt watching the scene unfold.

"You too good for our Cinda?" The gauntlet had been effectively dropped. The grizzly man stood from the bench, hitching his pants up as he swayed.

Skinny beside him was not as drunk. He stood beside the man, his chest puffed out. They presented an intoxicated, unified front. Father and son? Perhaps.

"I'm afraid it's the 'our Cinda' that I find objectionable." Peter's hand was itching to draw his sword. These two seemed ready for a fight. Let them start something. He knew it wouldn't be a fair fight but that release was much more to his liking. He smiled his apologies at the woman. "I'm sure you understand."

"I'm good enough for the priest but not good enough for you?" She spit in his face. It dribbled down his cheek.

Peter wiped his face. Mort came closer, his sword drawn. "That's no way to treat a representative from the crown."

"King William?" She spit on the ground.

Grizzly and Skinny pushed her behind them, their daggers poised for defense.

Peter turned toward Mort and started to laugh. He couldn't believe the temerity of the wench. When he started to laugh, he realized he couldn't stop. It felt good to laugh. Too good. It felt better than...damn was he hysterical then? Mort had a concerned look on his face. Peter fought to get himself under control and finally coughed his way to silence.

"Shall I see to these two, my lord?" Mort was serious. He could certainly handle them both and the innkeeper, if he felt so inclined as to get involved. Peter wasn't worried about that but something she'd said alarmed him. The priest? His body tensed in response to the sudden threat. Did she mean the one at the Priory?

Peter yanked her toward him by the front of her dress. He pulled her close to his face. Mort held the two men at bay with his blade. "What are you saying? What priest?"

He saw her start gathering spit again, so he squeezed her gown tighter in his hand. "Don't try it again." His tone was menacing. Her eyes widened in response. "Give me an answer."

"The priest from the Priory. Father Tinsley."

That couldn't be. They were celibate. That would be the only way they could be locked up with all those young women and not be taking advantage—Damn. He shoved her away from him and gave his orders. "She's in danger. Stay here."

Mort moved toward the outraged men, ready to make quick work of them. Peter could not wait and headed out the door. He just hoped he would not be too late.

～

The sweat dripped down the side of Brighit's face. It was stifling hot in the kitchen with the enormous fire. Heavy, iron pots were arranged both in the ash and hanging from a pole. Keeping the soup from burning despite its closeness to the huge flames was her job.

"Are you sure we couldn't raise the pot a little higher?" Brighit asked for the third time.

Martha smiled. "Just keep to your job, Mary."

The transformation of this woman had been like night and day. As soon as the men were gone, she relaxed into easy conversation with Brighit, content to answer her many questions.

This job seemed to be a sort of test of her obedience. No one else in the room was required to remain so near the heat as her. Perhaps they waited to see if she ignited into flames. She wiped her dampened sleeve across her cheek. The soup should be nearly ready.

"Would you care to taste the soup?"

Martha paused and came nearer to her. "Hot work?"

Brighit fought the urge to roll her eyes. "A bit."

"Then it's not quite done yet."

That observation made no sense but the woman moved away before Brighit could question her further. A door slammed in the distance. The other women in the room jumped at the sound. All except Ruth who continued to chop the root vegetables in front of her. Martha glanced between the two.

"Will you see to her?" Martha wiped her hands on a cloth and directed the question to Ruth. The younger woman glanced up, smiled, and nodded.

Martha led the rest of the women out the door in a single file. They moved as if approaching a death sentence. There were seven women in all at the Priory. Brighit had met them. Martha was the oldest. Ruth was the only one who was with child.

"Was that Father Tinsley we heard come in?"

Ruth rubbed her swollen stomach with long, gentle strokes. "Yes. He has returned."

Brighit stepped away from the fire. She expected to be brought to him as soon as he arrived. The few comments she's heard assured her he was very particular about where the women were and what they were doing.

"Do you think I should meet with him now?"

Ruth looked up, a surprised expression. "Dear Mary," Brighit cringed at the name she'd been given, "*he* will come and find *you* when he is ready."

Brighit returned to stirring the soup. It certainly sounded ominous. Fear was making its way into its favorite spot in her stomach. Swallowing became difficult.

"I was surprised he did not make it to vespers."

Ruth's brows darted down. "It's best if you keep to your work and not worry yourself about Father's whereabouts. You won't be able to avoid him if he's searching you out." She changed the direction of the circles she rubbed along her abdomen. "Prayer is always a safe endeavor."

Brighit opened her mouth to ask what she was talking about but the door to the kitchen burst open. A tiny, young woman, Esther, stood in the doorway. She had wide set eyes that made her constantly look as if she were petrified.

"Father Tinsley wants to meet you," Esther said.

Ruth stilled her hand. Her lips took on the shape of an "oh" but she said nothing. No one moved.

"Do I—I just go?" Brighit finally asked.

"I'll help you." Esther reached toward her. "Best not to keep him waiting."

Ruth was quiet but kept her eyes on Brighit.

Brighit followed Esther down the hall that led to the back of the Priory. They turned right at the entrance to the chapel. A huge door at the end of the hall was shut. That was the Great Hall. Small alcoves built into the stone ran along the wall to her right. Heavy curtains that would close off the rooms for warmth at night were all pushed aside now. Each one identical to the next. Trepidation joined fear and her stomach gurgled.

"Why do we go this way? Where will I be meeting Father Tinsley."

Esther did not answer. She turned back at Brighit, those wide eyes sending her heart into a faster pace. They stopped beside the alcove Brighit had been given as her own.

"Here? He will meet me here?"

It was barely big enough for the pallet that lay on the floor. It would be a tight squeeze to have someone else in there with her.

"Yes. You'd best spend your time in prayer as you wait."

"What?" Brighit's heart leapt into her throat until she remembered prayer was what they did here. "Oh, yes."

"Repentance for sin will come after he leaves," Esther said then retreated back the way they'd come.

Brighit's sense of foreboding increased three-fold with that cryptic statement. She looked around the tiny area. Too small to even pace in. The single candle that burned in the blackened holder on the wall cast the room in flickering shadows. She smoothed the stiff material of her new clothes. It crinkled beneath her fingers. Her hand paused at the slight bulge of her knife still tucked beneath her robes. The security it gave her was not something she was willing to part with just yet.

A distant clicking sound drifted to her from the direction of the chapel. Its rhythmic *tap* getting louder as it moved closer. She felt a sudden urge to run. The clicking was nearly to her room. Perhaps it wasn't Father Tinsley. Perhaps it would pass by.

Brighit backed against the wall. She took a deep breath and held it before blowing it out in a whoosh. This was ridiculous. If it was the priest, no doubt he'd come to welcome her and see that she had everything she needed. The heavy curtain was being pulled back. She glanced around for anything to hold on to. There was nothing.

A man with slightly graying black hair stood in the opening, a kind smile on his face.

"Welcome, Sister Mary. How wonderful to finally meet you."

He didn't take the few steps into the room. Brighit forced herself away from the wall and curtsied. "Thank you, Father."

"Come nearer to me." He motioned her closer with spotless hands and neatly trimmed fingernails.

She knew her own were stained with carrots and beet juice and hid them behind her as she stepped in front of him.

"I am Father Tinsley."

Brighit dipped her head. "Father Tinsley."

He placed his hand on her cheek. His hand was like ice. "You are a lovely woman."

She couldn't control the shiver that went through her body.

"Are you cold?" he asked.

"Forgive me, I was—"

"Ah," he interrupted her with the raise of his finger. "Forgiveness actually means something here. It is not to be given lightly."

She flashed him an awkward smile then started again. "It was very warm in the kitchens. I was sweating." She attempted to smile again but it felt like a grimace.

Father Tinsley's eyes closed slightly. "Ah, yes. Soup duty. The other women are working the devil out of you."

"What?"

His eyes widened. "The devil? Have you never heard of him?"

Brighit laughed nervously. "Yes, of course, but I didn't und—"

"Hope you don't know him too well." The priest must have seen her confusion. "The devil. I hope you don't know him too well."

"Oh, no, Father. I do not know the devil well." Brighit didn't know what he wanted her to say. Judging by his expression, she was very near to condemning herself to hell.

"Are you a virgin?"

Brighit gasped. It didn't seem like an appropriate question and she was suddenly very afraid of this man. The clicking started again and she noticed the black stick he held in his hand for the first time. He tapped it up and down.

"Yes." Heat flooded her cheeks and the closeness of the room made it hard to take a deep breath.

"Ah, but you've thought about fornication."

Her cheeks were burning. She shook her head, afraid to speak.

"Yes. It is clearly on your face. In your eyes." He glanced over her gown. "Remove your clothing."

Brighit backed away and he stepped closer. "No."

"You will do as you're told."

"No." She backed against the cold, hard wall. It sucked all the heat from her body. Her palm scraped against the rough stone behind her.

Realization hit her like a slap across the face. Even if she could make it past him, she had nowhere to run. "I will not reveal myself to you."

"It is not for me but for all of us who live under God's law here. I will be sure there is no mark of the devil on your flesh. NOW!"

Father Tinsley's face showed no sign of distress. He hadn't looked at her with lust. Perhaps this was the normal procedure.

Brighit reached with trembling fingers to the ties at the side of her robes.

"No." Father Tinsley stilled her hand. His palms were wet now. "Your hair first."

Without pausing, she ripped the wimple from her head. Her hair cascaded around her. His eyes followed her hair, taking in all of her body. The look of appreciation that crossed the priest's face could not be denied. This man was not chaste.

His pupils dilated as he kept his eyes on hers now. As if he could see into her very soul.

"Paul says it is vanity to have hair as glorious as yours. Do you take pride in your hair."

"I do not." Her tone was flat.

Father Tinsley slipped a wayward strand behind her ear. She stiffened. His eyes narrowed and he searched her face.

"I find that hard to believe." His voice was low.

She dare not breathe or she would be sick.

"Take off the gown." He used a commanding tone now and looked a bit rattled.

Brighit noticed the change in his breathing. He scratched at his crotch. "I prefer to have another woman present."

"This is not a matter for the others. If you have any sign that the devil has touched you, I will need to take care of it. They will not be able to help you." He pierced her through with his look. "I am the only one who can cleanse you from Satan."

There was not a chance in hell.

"Do as I say!" He slapped her across the face with a stiff hand.

She gasped, holding her hand to her face.

"Now!"

Brighit bent forward and grabbed the hem of her dress. Tears slipped up her face, onto the floor. They were tears of pain and humiliation. She refused to watch him as she dragged the material up her legs, exposing her thin chemise. Perhaps he would be satisfied with seeing her thus. That was quite bad enough. She crunched the stiff material in her hands and pulled it over her head. It scratched against her cheek.

The sounds of his appreciation filled the space. She refused to look at him but she knew what she would see. He was not seeing her as a nun but as a woman. She kept the gown in her hand, tucked close to her waist. Bile rose in her throat. She was going to throw up.

Peter dropped from his horse before approaching the high, wooden fence surrounding the Priory. The moon was just about to disappear behind the stone tower, giving him an opportunity to get his bearings if he needed to. He did not. From the moment he'd helped Brighit off the horse, he'd been studying the place as if a battle were about to ensue. The need to protect her had wrapped itself around his heart. He realized he was not able to let it go. Doing so would surely cause his own heart to stop beating. Her safety had become tantamount to his own survival.

When the path to the door fell into shadow, Peter eased up to the fence. There were no guards he had to contend with so he made little work of forcing the door. Crossing the bailey, he used his knife on the leather supporting the door then reached in to lift the wooden bar holding it in place. The sound of it falling to the ground was loud. He held his breath. Waited. No movement within. No doubt all were asleep at this hour.

Was Father Tinsley within even now? Peter cursed himself for barreling to Brighit's rescue rather than ascertain the exact time the priest had been there with *Cinda*. Perhaps that's where he'd been earlier. If he'd had a chance to see the man, could he have sensed his lecherous nature? No doubt he used his position here to his full advantage. Brighit's beauty would be difficult for any man to overlook. She'd lose her virginity in no time, especially with no one to see to her protection.

He made his way inside. A footfall in the distance and he flattened against the wall to the right of the door. A dim light flickered at the far end of the hall. Someone was awake. He waited but it didn't get any closer. All he wanted was to find Brighit and get her out of here.

He continued down the hall, his sword drawn, toward the faint glow. The fresh rushes beneath his feet crackled with each step. The scent of sage and lilacs drifted to him. He turned to the left. The chapel doors were wide open. A single candle sputtered from the altar a few feet inside. It seemed strange to have an empty room with a candle burning in it. Too late, he realized it was not empty.

The pregnant woman from earlier kneeled near a bench in the darkness, her head bowed in prayer. Sister Ruth.

"If you hurry you may be of some assistance." She did not look up.

"I've come for Brighit."

"I know." Picking her head up, she crossed herself then stood, grabbing at the altar for assistance. "Go quickly. Hers is the second room on the right. Hurry."

The woman's voice held not the slightest surprise or hint of concern or warning.

"Did you know I would come?" Peter said.

"I knew you would realize she was in danger."

Peter backed out of the room despite wanting to question her cryptic message. Brighit was his first concern. He hurried toward the second alcove. The sound of a struggle carried to him.

"Brighit." Peter knew better than to give warning of his presence but the need to hear her voice overran his better judgment.

There was no response. His legs trembled beneath him as he covered the last few feet. As if moving in a dream, the sight of a prone body filled his senses. The mud on the bottom of the calf-skinned boots, the smell of urine and excrement, the blood pooling on the ground. He swept his eyes along the darkly-robed body up to Brighit's face as pale as the moon. One hand clasped against breast, fisting the top of her chemise to hold it in place. Her other hand covered in blood, the small knife falling to the cold, stone floor with a loud clatter. Her wail of terror shoved him forward. He stumbled over the body on the floor, took her in his arms.

"My sweet Brighit. What did he do to you?"

Her mouth worked but no decipherable sounds came out.

"Did he touch you?"

"NO!" Brighit's voice echoed in the small room. *"I would not let him touch me."*

Her emphatic tone touched his heart. Her bravery surpassed many men he'd fought beside. A red welt showed on her hand where she clutched her chemise to hold it up. A black stick lay on the ground.

He lightly touched her hand. "Did he strike you?"

He tried to keep his voice calm but she seemed to sense his alarm and clutched him tighter. "He hit me and hit me. He insisted I obey him. That I bare my body to him."

Peter glanced to the ground, the pilfered knife from the inn lay on the floor. "I suppose that knife was big enough then."

She covered her mouth, smothering the laugh. She pulled away, her eyes widened. "Oh, Peter, that is not.... I killed a man."

"You defended yourself."

By the blood spreading from beneath the body, soaking across to the mattress, Peter knew he was indeed dead. He shoved him over with the toe of his shoe. The slice of the blade between the ribs was very small but deep. She must have cut right into his heart.

"Is this Father Tinsley?"

The man was indeed dead. Peter closed the unseeing eyes and retrieved the knife. She trembled beside him and eventually nodded.

"Did he rip your clothing, too?"

"He insisted he needed to check for the mark of the devil on me. He ordered me to remove my gown. Then he—he jerked me closer and ripped it." She covered her eyes as if to block out the memory. "The look on his face. He was about to force himself on me."

Peter took her into his arms. Stiff at first, she finally relaxed and began to sob in earnest. He tried to reassure her, caressing her hair, and led her into the hall.

"Is he finally dead?" Ruth asked from the doorway of the chapel. Her voice emotionless.

Brighit jerked away from Peter and moved toward the other woman. "I didn't mean to."

She sounded close to hysteria but Ruth quickly gathered her into her arms in a most maternal way and led her into the next chamber, sitting her gently on a wooden stool. It occurred to Peter that although the child was not yet born, it would be well cared for by this woman. If she survived.

"Shh, now. Hush. It's over now." With tears shimmering on her own lashes, she stroked Brighit's hair where her head rested lightly against her. "Did he touch you?"

The words fell like an axe at a beheading and the silence that was left was deafening. Brighit shook her head, slowly at first, then with more determination. Peter exhaled the breath he didn't realize he was holding. The overwhelming relief made him lightheaded. He stroked Brighit's hair and she turned her face into his palm before looking up at him.

"Then it is truly finished," Ruth spoke with great solemnity.

"I didn't mean to do it." Brighit's repeated words were muffled.

"You do not need to defend yourself to me. You need to repent."

Brighit went rigid before his eyes.

"He's like no other priest I've ever met." Ruth didn't seem to notice. She rubbed at her belly. "I was a virgin when I came here."

Peter's irritation with this woman was great but this shocking revelation knocked the air right out of him. He paused to gather his wits. "Are you telling us that is *his* child growing inside of you?"

The woman gave him a sad smile. "Yes. He forced himself on me... on all of us. Used us for his own pleasure."

"And yet you believe Brighit has sinned and needs to repent because she protected herself?"

"Murder is always a sin. That doesn't mean God will not forgive her." She turned back to Brighit. "Thank you for ridding us all of the curse of that man. I first came here expecting to find the Prioress. I never expected my life given to Christ would be so violated. It was certainly not God's will."

Brighit sniffled then swallowed, struggling to regain her composure. "Did you know the Prioress?"

"No. I just heard stories of her great faith. I'd hoped to learn from her. When I got here, she had already passed. I stayed because I didn't know where else to go."

"Nor do I."

Peter's heart squeezed tight.

"Is there someone else who can take over?" Peter's question sounded like a demand.

"Oh, yes. Martha was the Prioress's helper. She could become Prioress once the Bishop confirms her. That was what she was doing before Father Tinsley moved in. There had been no advanced edict that she knew of for his arrival."

When Ruth turned to him, the encouraging smile she'd had for Brighit vanished. It was replaced by a frown almost as if she sensed his deepest desire—to remove Brighit from this place immediately. She stood abruptly.

"Let me get you something to change into... and some warm water."

After Ruth left, Peter hunkered down beside Brighit, pushing her hair away from her face. "She is right. You did not have to submit yourself to this man. If he demanded that you do, you have every right to stop him... however you needed to."

Brighit took a shaky breath then exhaled one slow, steady *whoosh* of air. "Are you certain he is dead?"

Her upset was speaking now. Peter spent a lot of time with men in battle that fought most bravely and then refused to accept the death of those around them. When he took her hands, they were cold as snow.

"Yes. He is dead. He cannot hurt you again."

The bright, red welt on her hand had doubled in size. She inspected it. "My own father never used a cane on me." She pushed against the skin and wiggled her fingers. "It hurts."

Ruth returned with a basin of water and a sack hanging from her arm. She stood tall and faced Peter. "You must leave now."

Peter stood.

"I'm not leaving her." He crossed his arms about his chest. If he'd followed his own inclinations earlier and not left here, Brighit would not have been subjected to this.

A slight smile softened her face. "Just stand outside so that I can assist her with changing and properly washing her."

Brighit's color was beginning to return but her eyes were still wide with fear. Peter was not convinced he should obey this woman. "Do you want me to leave?"

"It's just for a moment," Ruth said.

Brighit looked from one then the other. "Yes."

Ruth smiled as if she had won the keys to the King's store rooms. Peter returned to Brighit's room to drag the body out and away from the chapel. He would need to bury the man but there was no reason any type of inquest needed to be done. Ruth said the man used the girls. Good riddance. He would be respectful but not overly so.

"I have something wonderful for you to wear."

Ruth chattered on as she worked but Brighit paid her little attention, removing herself from the ministrations. She needed a chance to settle herself. Inside. She'd never come so close to being violated. Not even with Ivan and his men. They talked of things—inappropriate things—but no one ever touched her. Ivan slapping her bottom at the inn was the only time he'd actually laid hands on her. That priest had been a vile man.

The gown dropping over her head brought Brighit back to reality. Ruth bent to urge it over her legs and shook it out around her.

"What? No. I can't wear this." It was the beautiful dress from the market. "I'm to be a nun."

Ruth stood before her, a smile so big she had a dimple on each cheek. "I think you were not meant to be a nun."

"You are wrong."

"Martha and I discussed it. We believe you were intended for marriage and children and love."

Brighit nibbled at her finger then removed it. "How do you know that?"

The other woman looked at her as if she could see right into her heart. "A woman knows these things."

Brighit was afraid to ask. Then she couldn't stop herself. "What things?"

"You are a woman in love."

Her gasp couldn't be contained.

"Is there aught amiss, ladies?" Peter's muffled voice came to them from the hall.

Brighit covered her mouth.

"No. We're fine," Ruth said.

"How can you know such a thing?" Brighit lowered her voice this time.

"The way your face lights up every time he looks at you."

Peter's smile did make her feel warm inside.

"And your wistful expression whenever he's near you."

She clasped her hands together. It was true that his touch gave flight to the butterflies in her stomach. And in his arms, she'd felt... alive.

"See! I can tell you're thinking of him. Also," Ruth's voice dropped, "you became so sad after he left."

It had felt as if her heart had been ripped right out through her throat when he was gone. She kept wanting to tell him things but he wasn't there.

"But my life has been decided by others. That is not what my life is to be."

"Who says such a thing? That to be truly loved and cherished is not to be your life."

Thoughts and feelings jumbled up inside her so she couldn't form a sentence in response. Finally saying the truth from her heart, "How I feel matters little."

"Oh, no!" Ruth shook her head as if Brighit had been caught in a lie. "How you feel matters the most."

"Are you about changed?" Peter asked.

Both women turned toward the door.

"One more moment, please," Ruth said. "Now gather your wits about you and keep this between us. You will see that I know of what I speak."

She jerked the door open, smiled up at Peter, and continued back toward the chapel.

Peter searched Brighit's face. "Have you stopped your tears? Dare I suspect you may even have been smiling?"

She dipped her head to her chest so he couldn't see her joyful expression.

Keep this between us.

Hiding her emotions, she faced him. "Yes, Sir Peter. I will be fine."

He offered her a reassuring smile along with his arm. She hesitated but a moment before placing her hand there. Her butterflies took flight.

"Let us go offer our repentance to the Lord together," he said.

"What do you have to repent for?"

"I was ready to split the priest in two when I realized what he did here. Does it not say in the Holy words that evil thoughts are the same as evil acts?"

Peter's brown eyes rounded in anticipation, a light growth of hair on his chin giving him an unkempt look. His soft touch on her hand sent ripples of pleasure through her. He was a handsome man and his undivided attention was on her. Surely there would be no harm in appreciating that for these few moments. To stand alongside him in the chapel as if her destiny had been shifted from a solitary life to one filled with marriage and family.

Brighit turned aside, hiding her face and the smile threatening to erupt at any moment. She pressed her lips together before answering him. "Yes, let us go to the chapel together."

CHAPTER 19

Screams erupted from the hall when Brighit and Peter left the chapel. It sounded like Ruth, but surely she was abed by now.

"What is that God-awful sound?" Peter reddened, perhaps at his choice of words.

"It sounds like Ru—the baby!" Excitement danced along her arms. Ruth had told her she was due any time and surely this was the time.

Brighit ran toward Ruth's room. She passed as the curtain where Martha slept was pushed aside. They exchanged knowing smiles.

"It sounds like her babe is ready to be born," Martha said.

When they entered Ruth's room, the sight before them was of her sitting up on her pallet, her gown pulled up to her bent knees, sweat dampening her nightgown, her face reddened from the exertion.

Martha checked the progress of the babe.

Brighit went to stand beside the laboring woman. "Your time has come?"

Ruth's body went rigid. Her face scrunched up in pain, as bright as an apple, but she nodded with quite a bit of enthusiasm.

Brighit brushed the hair away from her face. "We are here, my dear."

"This babe is coming fast." Martha's head was obscured by Ruth's knees. "Yes, that's the head. This child has no patience."

The pain subsiding, Ruth took a deep gasp and smiled. "That is true enough. I awoke in a puddle and sharp pain. I tried not to awaken everyone."

"It will not be long," Martha said.

Ruth's smile shifted to a grimace as she tightened up again. "Sorry about the scream." It came out in a whoosh.

"You could have just called us, though." Martha smiled at her own cleverness.

Brighit took Ruth's hand that was fisting into the straw mattress beneath her. "You can squeeze my hand. That is my usual role in a birthing."

She bobbed her head and started panting.

"Now, don't be panting so hard. We don't need you weakened."

"It hurts."

Martha gave her a do-you-actually-plan-on-arguing-with-me-now look. Brighit ducked to hide her smile.

"I'll try not to."

"Oh, dear, this babe wants out."

"All is well?" Brighit asked.

Martha looked up and smiled. "We just need some blankets to swaddle the babe in."

"Where are they?"

"Behind the altar."

Brighit nodded. When Ruth finally released her hand, Brighit ran through the curtained doorway and stopped. Peter stood rigid, his back to her, a few feet away.

"Peter, we need blankets." Brighit could barely breathe in her excitement. "Quickly."

He didn't respond. She moved to take his arm. He grabbed it out of her hand. Turning toward her, he looked livid.

"What?" he barked the question at her as if she were some lackey bothering him.

She frowned. "Why are you yelling at me?"

Peter's features softened. "You startled me." His eyes darted about the hall before piercing her though. "Is the woman dying?"

Brighit gasped. "No! She is having a baby. 'Tis all."

"Brighit? The blankets," Martha called from within sounding a little desperate.

"Maybe I should ju—" Brighit said.

Peter grabbed her arm then loosened his hold. "Please, what do you need me to get? Blankets? Where will I find them."

He sounded more himself but Brighit was suddenly frightened of this man. His strength. His size. His determination. His rounded eyes begged for... for what? She couldn't name it but backed away before she answered.

"They are behind the altar in the chapel."

Peter trotted down toward the open doors.

"*Argh.*" Ruth sounded exhausted. Poor thing. It may be happening with great speed but it was still difficult work.

Brighit smiled and ran into the room. The little round head was just poking its way out. Tears sprang to her eyes and she went to clasp Ruth's sweat drenched hand.

"Push the little one out now, Ruthie."

"Your labor is near over," Brighit said. She stroked her brow.

Ruth gasped for breath. "Yes."

"This will be it." Martha nodded and smiled.

Peter stopped at the entrance and all color drained from his face. Brighit went to him, afeared he may fall to the ground. "What is amiss?"

He shoved the course cloth toward her and backed out. Surely it wasn't the emerging babe, since Martha was blocking the view.

Brighit turned back to see Ruth's own surprised expression right before she clenched with the pain again.

"There." Martha accepted the blankets. "Push now."

Brighit grabbed Ruth's hand, steeling herself for the pain that always came at the end. Mothers had an excruciating grip at the end. She'd almost had her hand broken a time or two. Seeing the newborn was a wonderful reward.

The baby's cry filled the cramped space.

"It is a girl," Martha said, as if she were making a royal proclamation.

Peter's head appeared in the doorway. His eyes wide with surprise.

"Come," Ruth called to him, adjusting her gown. "It won't bite you. I won't bite you."

She laughed and Brighit joined in. "Just do not allow her to take your hand. You'll ner get it back."

Peter stepped into the room as if any sudden movement might cause the ceiling to fall on their heads. He screwed up his face in confusion at their comments and stood far to the side of the bed.

"You two are silly." Martha wiped the child dry then wrapped it in the blanket. "Here you go, my lady." The babe cried out. "Oh my, she's a hungry thing."

Peter's eyes remained on the small bundle as it went from Martha to Brighit to Ruth, whose face glowed with her happiness.

"Oh, my lovely, little girl." Ruth kissed the tiny head. "You are a beautiful, little thing. Such a blessing."

"A blessing?" Peter's voice was loud with accusation. "How can it be a blessing when your innocence was taken from you? When you were raped?"

The only sound in the room was the babe's breathing as it worked itself into a hungry wail. Brighit helped Ruth to bare her breast so the child could nurse. With practiced deliberation, Brighit supported the tiny head, shifting until its small mouth rooted solidly onto the nipple. The women gave a collective sigh. If a child was unable to suck, its hopes for survival were very small.

With the babe's head now cradled in the crook of Ruth's arm, she leaned back against the wall and looked at Peter. "How is it a blessing? God alone is good. He can make good out of any circumstance."

Brighit tipped her head. Such wonderful words. Ruth had great faith. She'd said she'd hoped to learn from the Prioress. Perhaps even as Brighit's own mother had learned from her. A lump swelled in her throat that made it hard to swallow.

If she stayed here and did her father's bidding, she would never know intimate love or have a family of her own. Was it his place to make this choice for her? No. She should be able to decide for herself. Tears slid down her face. She also loved her father and would honor his wishes.

"Is there no longer fear that Ruth will die now?"

Ruth's head jerked up. The child was undisturbed by the movement, asleep in its mother's arms. Her tiny mouth grew lax and she released the nipple with a quiet *pop*.

"Of course I will live."

"Why would you ask such a thing?" Brighit swiped the tears from her cheeks and turned on him.

Ruth laid a gentle hand on Brighit's arm and shook her head. Addressing Peter, she said, "Why would you believe I would die?"

He paused before answering. "No, I don't suppose you will die. You had these women with you as well. They helped you birth the child."

Ruth shook her head adamantly. "My lord, I am sorry, but they did not help me birth this child. I did it quite by myself. I assure you."

"So they were of little use? You could have done this all alone?"

"Women birth their children alone all the time," Martha said.

Peter's expression turned hard. Brighit didn't recognize him. In all the time she'd spent with him, all the things they'd shared, she'd never witnessed this side of him. He seemed a stranger suddenly.

"Well, I'll certainly have none of that. Life is precarious enough without adding the threat of imminent death with every birthing. Fate will not decide for me again."

A knife to her gut could not have pained her more. This valiant man, so powerful and strong, just announced he had no need of intimacy. The flash of a memory flooded her like she was drowning in it—his firm lips pressing against her own, his gentle hands grasping her flesh, coaxing her, flooding her with heat, his eyes hooded with his passion and desire. It was not to be. It was never to be. It was a cruel joke. A joke that she was bearing the brunt of.

Peter rubbed his horse down in the shadow of the Priory. He was glad to be away from the women.

"So happy to have you back, my friend." The crisp air turned both his and the horse's breath to vapor. "We've quite a trek ahead of us. 'War have you waged, so on to war proceed.' What say you?"

"Are you expecting the horse to answer?"

Peter jumped at Brighit's question. He turned and faced her, the horse forgotten at the sight of her wrapped in a heavy, woolen cloak. "Are you going somewhere?"

"I must impose on you again, Sir Knight. Will you bring me to the inn down the road?"

Her words sounded like she offered a death sentence. He wasn't sure why he felt a sudden chasm breaking out between them. "Is aught amiss?"

"I must send word to the Bishop. Martha has asked if you could take me there."

"I would gladly do it but why would Martha need to ask? I would do it for you." He moved closer to her.

"It was her idea. Not mine." Her voice sounded flat.

In closer proximity, her wide, brown eyes hid their innocent spark and he wondered why that would be. "Are you distraught about the Priest? It was not your doing."

Confusion covered her face before irritation set in. "Nor did I say that it was. Will you bring me? We need to leave anon."

Peter opened one arm, directing her to his mount. "I am ready now, my lady."

Brighit walked with stiff legs to the side of the horse. Peter mounted then offered his arm. She grasped it and was lifted onto his lap with little effort. She sat with a stiff back, refusing to lean against him for support and turned awkwardly to look ahead of them. Something was amiss but Peter refused to question her further. It was just as well. He would see her to the inn and return her. That would be the end of it. His time with this lovely lady would come to an end.

An arm on either side of her stiff body, he held the reins in his open palm and waited. She did not appear inclined to even brush against him. And certainly not to wrap her arm around his side as she had with Lachlann. So be it.

With a flick of his wrist and *click* of his tongue, the horse darted forward. Brighit slammed into him, then nearly became unseated as the awkward gait made sitting erect nearly impossible. She wrapped an arm around his side and glanced up at him shyly. After a few more jostling moments, she relaxed and leaned against his chest. Peter smiled.

A light snow began to fall, covering the ground, as they moved down the path to the inn. The moon now hidden by the heavy clouds. One knee bent slightly forward, her bottom rested on his thigh. Firm and warm. His hips rocking with the movement of the horse, settled her over his growing hardness as she moved against him. He jerked his cloak tighter between them but it did little to remove his awareness of her breast pressing into his chest and the wiggle of her bottom every time she moved to secure her seat.

Peter took a deep breath and felt her do the same. Out of desperation, he shifted her bottom away from the heightened attentiveness of his male member. He settled his thighs more firmly against the beast and urged it into a gallop. They could not arrive at the inn quick enough.

Unfortunately the motion only increased his attentiveness to every nuance of her enticing form moving against him. From the scent of her long hair wafting to him as it slapped against his cheek, to her bottom's rise up and down against his hardened shaft with the motion of the horse, his desire increased. Every breath that escaped her. Every touch that reached him. He thanked God the horse needed little guidance because his total attention was on her. He closed his eyes, struggling for composure, and opened them to the view of the small house he'd noticed as a blur on his way to the Priory. He reined the horse with a sudden movement. He jumped down off the horse, setting her on her feet, and quickly moved away from his all-encompassing passenger.

"We need to stop here. The snow is getting too difficult for my tired horse."

"Can we go back then?"

"When the snow lightens up."

He walked quickly to rap against the little, wooden door. These must be farmers but nothing nearby signified they worked for themselves. No place to store any grain or supplies. No animals to yoke or provide food. No answer to his knock. He repeated with more urgency. Brighit came up beside him without a sound. The snow covered her cloak and a few flakes were captured by her lashes.

"Is no one home?"

Damn. She may be correct in that. On further inspection, the little hut seemed to have been empty for a while. He glanced up at the heavy flakes falling from the sky and wondered when it had stopped being a light snowfall. Glancing at the cause of his lack of attention, he refused to ask and pushed the door open.

"Is anyone here?" he called out to an empty room.

It seemed as if the occupants had just up and left. A small stool waited beside the cold hearth, a stiff mat of straw covered with a woolen blanket lay against the wall, and an iron pot sat beside the door.

Brighit covered the space in a few steps then turned toward him. "There does not appear to be anyone here."

He looked out the open door. The snow was falling so fast that the horse was no longer visible even from a few feet away.

"Perhaps he can come in with us?" Brighit asked.

Peter smiled at her hopeful expression. She no longer seemed vexed with him. The urge to bring her toward him and feel her full length pressed against him was strong. The memory of the way she'd felt increased his desire and he took a step closer to her. He gingerly stroked her cheek. Her eyes no longer appeared indifferent. Perhaps their closeness on the horse had affected her as well.

Her skin was cold against the heat of his palm. "You're cold."

He removed his cloak and wrapped it around her, breathing in her scent as he pulled it together. Her head just below his chin, he could swear he smelled her arousal. He held his breath to cut off the groan threatening to escape.

When he should have stepped away, he slid his arm along her back. She trembled. She didn't move away. His breath quickened.

"I should start a fire for you."

He grasped her shoulder then rubbed her arm lightly as if for warmth, still not putting any distance between them. She yielded to him, adjusting herself to be more fully within the circle of his arms. Her other arm brushed against his chest. Surely she could feel the racing of his heart. He was ready to burst.

With the lightest touch, he tipped her chin up so he could see into her eyes. He tugged her hood back with his other hand and lowered his lips to hers. Watching for any sign of resistance, there was none. Her lips yielded to gentle pressure, parting to allow him full access. His tongue darted along hers, enticing a response, which was quick in coming. She moaned into his mouth. He placed his hands on either side of her face and deepened the kiss. Then slipping a hand beneath her cloaks, he pulled her against him. His eager manhood pressed toward her softness. When she reached her arm around him to pull him closer still, he fought against the desire to drop her to the pallet. His body begged to have its way with her, responding to this unrelenting need to take her.

Instead he stroked her back with long, gentle caresses. Caresses became firmer strokes, moving lower and lower along her back. When he grasped her firm bottom and pressed her closer still, he rubbed his rigid shaft against her. She cantered her hips in response as if in encouragement. His own moan startled him. He moved his lips along her jaw, drawn to the crook of her neck, nuzzling her. He cupped both cheeks and undulated against her in a mock display of what his body was so eager for.

"I want to be inside you." His whispered words were tight.

"Please." Her plea sounded desperate.

When he pulled away, her flushed face revealed her own desire. Her eyes were closed, her lips loosely parted, her tongue darting out to wet its pink length.

"I fear I am not able to stop. I could ravish you."

"I wish to ravished by you." Her words came on a moan, sweeping him along with her passion.

Grasping handfuls of her gown, he dragged it up and out of his way, until he could touch her bare skin. Soft as the finest silk. His manhood pushed against her. With open palms, he fondled her with increasing urgency. Finally cupping her fine arse again, he lifted her against him. He pressed himself against her needing the release.

Dragging the tip of his tongue along the ridge of her collarbone, he dipped down to the swell of her breasts. He released one lovely round cheek to follow along the curve of her side up to the swell of her luscious breasts. Firm and full and overflowing in his hand. With great deliberation he brought his mouth down, capturing the hardened nipple, sucking it even through the material. She moaned and rocked her hips against him.

Kissing her again, he shoved the cloaks over her shoulder and slipped his fingers inside the neck of her gown, slipping the one sleeve down to bare a breast. Feasting on the sight before him, covering it with his palm. He tugged her hardened nipple, damp from his assault. He crushed her against him.

"I need to be inside you, Brighit." He whispered the words, watching her reaction. He took a shaky breath. "I need it more than my next breath."

She dragged his hand under her gown, parting her legs for his touch.

He worked his fingers into her soft, drenched flesh. "As do you."

Her moan resonated from deep inside.

Nothing could stop him from slaking himself on this woman. Repeatedly. And the fates be damned.

CHAPTER 20

The wind howled against the primitive shelter that offered little more than a stool and the possibility of a fire. Peter's scent enveloped her, adding to her overwhelming desire. His fingers stroked her, rubbing her sensitive flesh, sending ripples of pleasure through her core.

"Have your way with me," Brighit said. Her plea came from deep inside. Her deepest longing. Her body ached to feel him more intimately. His mouth on every inch of her. His hands igniting everywhere he touched.

"Now, Peter."

Brighit's sudden urgency was not having the desired effect. He should have lowered her to the pallet. Covered her body with his.

Instead he withdrew and took a deep, shaky breath. Still within his arms, she opened her eyes to find him surveying her face, her body, as if he had received a precious gift and he wasn't quite sure what to do with it.

"Do not stop."

He finally looked her in the eye. "I do not want to stop."

"Then why are you?"

"This doesn't seem—"

"I need you... inside me."

His eyes rounded. "Brighit, I don't want it to be like this for you."

She glanced around, noticed the cold air against her skin where he had pulled away, the dirt floor, the darkened corners. For the first time she wondered if there were rats seeking shelter nearby as well. Suddenly embarrassed, not because of the location, but because she had been so swept away by her passion. She backed out of his arms, adjusting her dress, and pulling the cloak back in place, allowing his to drop to the floor. Her face reddened with shame. She wanted him to make love to her. Still wanted it.

She walked about the room, rubbing her arms, and felt his eyes on her. She wanted him to take her in his arms, put his hand between her legs, and stroke her again. The dampness there was near impossible to ignore. Just to have him love her one time. To know the feel of him. Like a treasured memory she could hold on to. Now she would never have that. He was correct. This was no place for them to be together.

"Will you build us a fire?" She sounded much more in control than she felt, almost demanding. Finally she turned to face him.

"Is that what you would have me do?" he asked. Deep lines creased his forehead.

"No. I told you what I wanted."

He picked his cloak off the floor, shook it, and put it on. He moved toward her. "Brighit, I didn't me—"

She raised her hand.

"No. Do not touch me again. You are correct. This is not the best place." She turned away. "Please just make the fire if you would. It's bitter cold in here."

The door shut behind her and she fell to her knees on the straw pallet. She'd acted like a wanton woman and her unquenched desire still held her in its grip. He had clarity even in his passion and she showed none.

The scrape of his footfall at the door had her sitting on the pallet. He came in covered with snow and carrying a pile of small twigs in his arms.

"I found a shelter almost big enough for my horse and a pile of dry kindling." She saw his glance but she refused to look at him. "I'll take care of him after I get the fire going."

He dropped the twigs into the open hearth, striking the flint by the hearth, and waited for it to catch a flame.

"I need to bring in more wood." He stood beside her. ""Brighit, I want to te—"

"Do not. It is done. When the snow stops, we continue to the inn and get word to the Bishop as I have been asked to do. If you could please return me to the Priory, you can be about your duties."

"That is not my want." He stared at her until she relented and turned to him. "I want you still. I did not want this," he gestured to their surroundings, "to be the memory of our love making."

"Yes. I see you are concerned for me." Her nostrils flared but she swallowed down the tears. "I understand also that I will not have another chance for such a memory."

"So I am to give you your memory? And then be done?" he asked.

Her composure slipped but she refused to respond.

"That is not to my liking either." He left, pulling the door tightly behind him.

"But that is the way it must be." She rolled over, pulled the cloak tightly around her and rocked herself to sleep.

A short time later, Peter awoke her by gathering her into his arms.

"Hush. You sleep. Just let me hold you." He kissed her lightly on the head.

It felt so right in his arms. He was warm and smelled of horses and smoke. She snuggled into his chest and struggled to make words then drifted off again.

The wind busting the door open jerked Brighit upright and out of Peter's embrace. He slept with his back against the wall. She had been against his chest. Snow blurred her vision but there appeared to be a man standing in the doorway. She shook Peter.

"Peter! I think someone is here."

"What the hell are you doing with my sister!"

Peter pulled himself to standing, the tip of a sword pointed at his chest.

"Answer me or I'll run you through."

Brighit stood as well. "Sister?"

Covered from head to toe with a thick coating of snow, Brighit could not make out the man. The voice was familiar.

Peter raised his hands. "Do you know this man, Brighit?"

"Do not be disrespectful to my sister by using her given name."

Brighit got up close to peer through the single opening around his face which revealed the brown eyes she knew so well. "Tadhg! What are you doing here?"

She reached around to hug him but he refused to lower his sword. She moved to shut the door and cut off the heavy snow. It left a coating everywhere and threatened to smother the fire struggling to survive.

"What are you doing here?" she asked again.

"Perhaps you could tell him that you know who I am," Peter said, his eyes on the unwavering blade.

"Tadhg, I do know him."

"Yes. I could see that you *know* him. I want to know why that is and what is going on here."

Standing akimbo, she stared him down. How dare he insinuate anything about a situation of which he knew nothing. She didn't *know* him, even if that was her deepest desire and she would never deny it.

"Please lower your sword." Her voice was low and menacing. "This is the man that offered me his protection."

Tadhg snorted. "Protection? He appears to have taken full advantage, dear sister."

Brighit fumed. "And you do not know of what you speak. That slippery uncle of ours put me in harm's way and Pet—Sir Peter saw me to the Priory."

She hoped he hadn't heard her slip.

Tadhg lowered his sword, suspicion still etched on his face. "Yes. I found our uncle was not true to his word when I found him at the O'Brien's."

"You went to the O'Brien?" Her voice rounded in sympathy. "Oh, Tadhg, why would you do such a thing?"

Peter did not wait for the sword to drop completely before shoving Tadhg against the wall and using the same weapon against him. "Explain yourself."

"Peter!" She yanked on his arm where it held the sword against Tadhg's throat. "Do not kill my brother."

"Did you not hear him? He insults you!"

She threw her arms in exaggeration and half turned before stomping her foot. "Please! Desist!"

With Tadhg's sword grasped firmly in his hand, Peter jerked away. A stern visage. A man of duty. "Reveal yourself."

Standing as stiffly as a man about to be given his last rights, Tadhg yanked his hood off.

Peter narrowed his eyes and peered closely as if he could decipher for himself the truth of the statement. Brighit waited, nibbling the inside of her cheek. He finally turned toward her. "I see a resemblance. Not much."

Peter felt an overwhelming need to deck this *brother*. The first words out of his mouth had been an insult to Brighit.

"So you've finally shown up?" Peter crossed his arms. The sword in his grip hung like an unvoiced threat.

This other man was no bigger than he. He could easily best him, he felt certain.

"I've come to get my sister."

All sound ceased. Peter dare not breathe. This man could take her away from him.

"Get her and take her where?" Peter could gut the man right here. He glanced at Brighit. She probably would not appreciate it.

"Back to Ireland where she belongs."

Peter tucked in his chin for his best over-my-dead-body look. "I do not believe that is going to happen."

"You have no say in the matter." Tadhg's eyes narrowed.

"I have every say in the matter."

"By what right do you—"

"The right as her protector. While you left her in harm's way, I saw her saf—"

"I did not know of the dang—"

"Stop! Allow me to speak." She faced both men in turn before proceeding. "Tadhg, of what do you speak? I am bound for the Priory as father—how is he?"

"He passed before you had even crossed the sea."

Her expression showed her deep despair and Peter longed to take her in his arms. His own father's death had created little loss in his life. He had stronger feelings of pain from the strike of the man's hand.

"I am sorry for your loss, sweet Brighit." He gently stroked her cheek but kept his distance otherwise.

Her brother shifted.

Peter ignored the other man. "Was he ill?"

"He was gravely ill but he feared for my safety and sent me away." She faced her brother. "I understand you came when you realized our uncle was a rat, but I am safe now. Pet—Sir Peter came to rescue me."

The man with the face of an angel crossed his own arms and turned to Peter. "Oh did he?"

"Yes."

"And was some payment exchanged for his *rescue?*" The man's gaze did not waver.

Brighit's face reddened. "Of course not."

Tadhg pressed his lips into a narrow line.

Peter was hard pressed to observe Brighit's request for his silence. Ire was working up from the depths of his gut, itching to be released. With word. With deed. With finality. Finality that would shut this man's mouth.

"And yet here you are. The two of you. Alone."

"The snow was impassable. We came in for shelter," Brighit said.

Peter merely cocked an eyebrow in answer.

Brighit glanced between the two of them, shaking her head as if searching for an adequate response. Nothing would satisfy this man. Her brother. He intended to take her away from Peter. There was only one way Peter could stop him from doing the unthinkable.

She rubbed her hands together, her mouth moving like a fish out of water. When she looked at him with pleading eyes, Peter accepted the silent request for his assistance at last.

"You've sincerely no need to defend your sister's honor."

Tadhg's mouth tightened perceptibly. "I'm sure you can understand my own misgivings about believing you in this instance."

"Of course." Peter glanced at Brighit. She was about to become very angry with him, but he saw no other recourse. "If I had trusted my sister's protection to a relative who cared so little about her welfare, I'm sure I would be defensive as well."

Tadhg's face turned darker and darker red with each word Peter spoke.

"A relative that would allow her to be insulted and mistreated."

Tadhg's eyes bore into Brighit who stood rigid between them. "Of what does he speak?"

Brighit glared at Peter before answering her brother. "Fear not. Sir Peter protected me. I was not harmed or molested."

"What have you been subjected to? Who insulted you? I came as soon as I realized how false Ronan was."

"Uncle Ronan's lackey—Ivan."

Tadhg took her in his arms. "Tell me he didn't touch you." His whispered words were spoken in sincere desperation.

"He did not." Peter didn't flinch under the man's scrutiny. "I found an innocent woman in the care of a lecherous whoreson and his men. She was an innocent who needed protection from those men. I rectified the situation."

Brighit looked into Tadhg's face. "He speaks the truth. Sir Peter vowed to get me to the Priory unharmed. He never broke that vow."

"Did you learn why our uncle abandoned you?"

Brighit shrugged. "No. He must have had other plans. He met with a man at the inn while we waited for the curragh to bring us over. Uncle Ronan was arguing with him, assuring him I wouldn't be a problem. The man hid his face from me."

"You? He said *you* wouldn't be a problem?" Peter asked. She had not been so certain earlier.

"Well he said 'she will not be a problem' so I assumed it was me. I think he called him Leo-something."

Peter's mind reeled, every one of his senses alert. "Leofrid?"

Brighit lit up as if he'd guessed the right answer in some game. "Yes! That was it."

Peter raked his hand through his hair. Leofrid Godwinson was connected to their uncle? He'd actually met with him?

Peter's closest friend, John, had exiled the man to Ireland against the King's expressed orders that if Leofrid were found to still be alive, he was to be put to death. The man was cousin to John's wife, Rowena. Her entire family had been defeated and killed when William, Duke of Normandy, was crowned as King of England. John didn't want to increase her loss. He'd sent him to Ireland with another thorn in his side, Abigail, a mad woman from John's past, who was obsessed with him. They'd all believed that would be torturous enough.

Surely Leofrid was not so well connected that he could seek support against King William in Ireland.

"And your uncle's man was looking for Tostig's soldiers. I believe that is Leofrid's father. What do you know of this uncle."

"Very little," Tadhg answered for the both of them. "I don't think my father cared for him overmuch but when he needed to get Brighit safely out of harm's way, he called on him."

"And he abandoned you at first chance," Peter said to Brighit.

Tadhg rubbed his lower lip. "Ronan had been the one to bring our mother to the Priory. That was where my father met her. I think our mother's clan had bad feelings with my father from that time on. She never spoke much of them even though she was Celtic royalty."

Peter could definitely see Brighit as royalty. It fit her.

There were many powerful families across Ireland. If their uncle was one of the forces in Ireland still working to overthrow King William, that could pose quite a problem. A problem for Peter. A problem for Tadhg. A problem for John who had allowed him to live.

"Did your father ever speak of the Normans or King William?"

Tadhg smiled. "Yes! Keep them far from here! That was his most fervent wish."

"Do you believe he would fight against the Normans?"

"We prefer peace but we have ties to other clans that we must support.'

"And you said you saw Ronan with the O'Brien?" Brighit asked.

"Yes. They were quite friendly. Roland called him a powerful man of great influence. When I realized he had abandoned you, I could not speak a single word to even question him. I left immediately. Please forgive me, sister."

Brighit hugged her brother in a tight embrace. "It is forgiven. You were weighted down with many things."

"If he is in collusion with the Godwinson, I'd venture his deception is quite good," Peter said.

Tadhg dropped his head as if in preparation of something unpleasant. Peter braced himself. He could not allow Tadhg to take Brighit from him. Not now.

"Unfortunately, Sir Peter, I cannot overlook what I saw when I came in here. You were clearly abed with my sister."

"Oh, Tadhg, not as you make it sound. Look at me! I am fully clothed." She gestured to Peter. "He is fully clothed. What has happened here changes nothing in our lives. Please let it pass."

Tadhg faced her. One eyebrow went up. Then the other. Raising one, long finger, he pointed to an area of Brighit's chest. She dropped her head to see at the same time Peter turned to look. The sight of one very round, very wet spot, the size of Peter's mouth and then some, revealed the outline of her dark areola. The spot of Peter's attentions had yet to dry with the lack of heat in the room.

Peter expected it should be guilt that coursed through his veins at being found out but it was the tantalizing memory of that pearled nipple rubbing against his tongue that assaulted him. Desire shot to his groin.

Brighit's eyes met his.

Neither spoke.

In a different place, he would have taken her. He would have loved her the way she deserved to be loved. To worship her body—a splendid body that roused him beyond anything he'd ever known. He would have lavished his love on her until they lay sated in each other's arms, still refusing to let go. Ever. The tightness in his groin became unbearable.

"No defense?" Tadhg asked.

Peter knew that tone very well. He used it himself quite often. The one where you've caught someone in the act and there is no denying the facts. Although it wasn't true in this instance, the cost of denying the facts was too great. Intimate details were not to be shared. Intimate details that were certainly not regretted. Intimate details he planned to repeat at the first available moment with a much more satisfying conclusion. Why deny facts that would get him exactly what he wanted.

"There is no need for defense." Peter glanced toward her hoping she would sense his next words for her as well. "We've done nothing to be ashamed of. We've done nothing that needs to be defended."

She looked lost, her eyes rounding in desperation. His heart hurt for her. "Please, sweet Brighit."

When the tears welled, he was lost. He gathered her into his arms where she fit perfectly.

"There will be no more inappropriate behavior toward my sister."

Tadhg's grabbing at Peter's arms to loosen his hold of her, got him a hard elbow in the ribs that resulted in a loud *umph.*

Peter moved quickly, lowering his lips to hers in a passionate lovers kiss she couldn't resist, much to his relief. He leaned her forward to press her chest into his.

"Enough!"

When she worked her fingers into his hair, Peter fought for composure.

Tadhg looked ready to attack. His feet firmly planted. His body rigid. And across his face, the stoic look of murder. Peter still held his sword, however, which would make any move against him a foolish endeavor. Peter stepped away from Brighit but didn't release her until she had found her footing. The kiss had ignited more quickly that he had anticipated. They were still smoldering with their unquenched desire.

"And if I had any reservations, I do not after that little display," Tadhg said. "Thank you, Sir Peter, for clearing up any doubts I'd had."

Peter smiled. Tadhg's eyes narrowed.

"Whatever I can do to help the situation along."

Brighit turned to face Peter. "What situation? What have you done?"

Emotions flitted across her face at the realization of what just happened. That Peter had all but admitted to Tadhg they'd indeed been intimate. A gasp of disbelief. Tight-lipped murderous rage. Outrage at his action? Oh yes. That expression he remembered quite vividly. The same one she had worn right before she slapped him across the face for intentionally revealing her nakedness. That had been misplaced outrage as she discovered that Peter had, in fact, not done it intentionally. This, however, was very well place. He knew exactly what he was doing.

He narrowed his eyes in warning. Perhaps she would remember what he said about her trying to slap him again. Brother or no, he would happily take her over his knee as promised.

It was indeed this fiery nature that first drew his attention to her. What he found so very appealing. He perused the rest of her. That and her enticingly delectable body.

"Well?" Tadhg asked.

Peter had to drag his gaze away from her.

"Well?" Peter responded in kind.

"Do you deny you have compromised my sister?"

"You found us here in a compromising situation. Did you not?"

"You know that I did."

"Then how could I deny what you saw with your own eyes?"

Tadhg looked slightly irritated. "You could perhaps explain how I was wrong."

"Yes, you could do that. Peter?" Brighit's sweet mouth parted as if she could somehow get the words she wanted him to say to come out if she just willed it.

He searched her face. She was not yet aware of how well they were matched. That had to be the reason she resisted. Showing her would be his greatest delight.

"Alas, I cannot."

Indignation swept across Brighit's face, her eyebrows raised in pleading. "No?"

"I am an honorable man as I'm certain you will learn soon enough," Peter said to Tadhg.

Brighit froze. She stared at Peter.

"I do not believe an honorable man would have compromised such innocence in the first place."

Peter's mouth dropped open to defend himself before he realized the man was baiting him. The look of irritation had shifted into the sly look of someone testing his mettle. He tipped his head in acknowledgment but refused to agree.

The silence seemed to drag on forever as Tadhg awaited his response. Then finally he asked, "So you will do the honorable thing?"

"I always do the honorable thing."

"And in this instance?"

"I will marry this woman if that is what you are asking."

Brighit's mouth gaped open. "No, Peter, do not let him force you."

"Now how could anyone force me to do anything?" Peter said.

Peter bowed slightly. Brighit was beside herself, pulling on her brother's arm. "Please do not make him do this! Nothing happened."

"Is this true, Sir Peter? Brighit says nothing happened."

When she turned toward him, Peter had the slightest inkling that she would perhaps never be satisfied with him if he was forced to marry her.

"You saw it with your own eyes," Peter said then turned toward Brighit. "He can make me do nothing against my will. Never believe it."

Confusion clouded her beautiful face. Brighit filled her lungs and backed away from them both. "And when exactly will this happen?"

"I will see you wed this very day. We leave at once for the Priory."

"It's not safe to go now, you imbecile," Brighit said.

"Brighit, do not belittle me in front of my new brother. Surely you could have some compassion for me."

"Never!" She took the few steps to drop onto the pallet. She was shooting arrows at both of them.

"Come, Peter, let us prepare the horses."

Peter secured his cloak and followed the man outside. The snow had let up slightly but it would still be a long ride back to the Priory.

Tadhg stopped beside the horse to gaze off into the distance. He pulled his leather gloves up tight and turned toward Peter.

"I fear I may have been played in there."

"I've no idea of what you speak."

"It baffles me to think that a man would allow himself to be forced into marriage rather than just asking for the lady's hand."

"But if a lady had as strong a sense of honor as some I've recently met, she would never choose her own happiness over that honor."

"Yes. Honor runs deeply in some," Tadhg agreed. "And deeper in others," he continued. "I am aware of the ploy you just used in there. Well played, my friend."

Peter stared at him. He believed Tadhg did have his sister's best interests at heart. However, he did not need Brighit's suspicions to be confirmed about his own willingness to marry her. It was best if she remained uncertain. At least for the time being.

"You've insulted my betrothed. You've interrupted our time together. You've decided you need to drag us out into this storm. Do not be so quick to call me friend."

"Our time together? I believed you called yourself an honorable man."

"And so I am. I'm just not going to take the chance of losing something precious to me."

Peter took the man's mount to the little shelter his own horse occupied. He was certain the man must look smug at having seen through Peter's ploy to force their marriage.

"The passing will be difficult now."

Tadhg seemed to be measuring his worth, watching Peter as he saw to the horses. A sudden nervousness he hadn't experienced since he was a lowly squire overtook Peter. The sudden need for approval. He was overwhelmed with the reality that he could mess things up. With a single word from this man, Brighit would be unavailable to him. He could still take her away from Peter. If Tadhg made that decision, Peter would have no honorable recourse. She was under her brother's protection now.

The idea of sweeping her onto his horse and riding off brought a smile to his lips. He needed to relax. What fault could Tadhg find with him? They would be wed before long. She would be his. Forever.

"It would not be amiss to wait it out a bit longer."

Peter ceased his actions. Tadhg said it as if sensing Peter's sudden unease.

Turning toward him, Tadhg had a smile Peter had not witnessed before. "I've decided we will wait until the storm has passed to see this done. Mid-day will be soon enough."

Peter flashed an insincere smile and turned back to the cottage. It was going to be a very long morning.

CHAPTER 21

As the only building of authority in the area, they returned to the Priory as soon as the storm let up. It was there that the marriage would take place. The bright sun glared off the huge piles of windblown snow. The storm had subsided but it was with a great sense of dread that they made the trip back. Dread that had little to do with the weather.

Tadhg had explained that he and his men had traveled without delay when he learned of Uncle Ronan's betrayal. They had been to the Priory and met the sisters. Welcomed as travelers in the storm, they'd been given food and drink. Peter found it hard to believe they'd been so welcoming. Tadhg insisted they were very well received even before they were acknowledged as Brighit's clan. However, by the time he learned Brighit was no longer within, it was too dark and the snow was falling too hard to head back out. He'd left at dawn by himself rather than disturb his exhausted men.

"It was fortunate indeed," Tadhg said, "that I spotted the faint tracks heading off the road."

Peter rolled his eyes and turned away. It wasn't the first time her brother had mentioned that fact.

"I could not have ensured Peter's safety had my men witnessed what I did when I arrived to find you in the cozy setting."

"To get out of the storm." Peter's voice was laced with resentment. "I was not about to let her freeze in the snow."

Tadhg glanced Peter's way. Brighit wrapped her arm tightly around her brother. She would have liked to punch him instead. These constant taunts were becoming unbearable. Peter's stern look had gotten more stoic with each taunting remark. She knew Peter did not want to marry her. He'd said as much at the Priory. With a decidedly loud and determined voice.

"Well, I'll certainly have none of that. Life is precarious enough without adding the threat of imminent death with every birthing. Fate will not decide for me."

And here they were. Fate had indeed decided for the man.

She had no idea why he had insisted on kissing her so passionately. As soon as his lips had touched hers, she'd been lost. He'd stirred up all her longings and desires again. But it was as if Peter thought it was some farce. How will he feel when he finds himself strapped with her for the rest of his life?

Dismounting, Tadhg was quick to help her get down, glaring at Peter. As they walked toward the door, Peter allowed Tadhg to lead the way. Peter grabbed hold of her hand with a firm grip. Tadhg knocked loudly, glancing toward her. They waited for the Priory door to be opened. No one spoke. This situation way intolerable.

"So my men will be happy to see you, Brighit." Tadhg smiled at her, then included Peter, "They've missed her sorely. My father's decision to send her away was not well received. That was the first thing Sean said to me after father was buried."

Brighit frowned. "What did Sean say?"

"To go and get you back."

Peter stood at attention beside her. He looked neither left nor right.

"I explained father had chosen the Priory rather than him which he did not take kindly. Understandably."

Peter growled low in his chest. Tadhg and Brighit glanced toward him.

Tadhg moved in close, looking into Peter's eyes.

"I do not believe it is necessary to keep her attached to your side." Tadhg indicated the tight hold he had of her hand.

Peter merely glanced back at the man.

"Sir Peter, please release my sister."

Immediately her hand was let go.

"Whatever you say, *Tadhg*." Peter pronounced her brother's name incorrectly again. He did it no matter how many times she corrected him. She stopped correcting him. "Just as she was not allowed to ride with me here, or sit next to me when we broke our fast, or stand too close now."

"I said nothing about how close you were standing. But come to think of it, you should take a step away."

Peter made that same low sound. The door jerked open.

"Greetings. Tadhg!" Martha exclaimed, pulling Tadhg in by the shoulder. "Come in from the cold."

They followed her inside, stomping and shaking to remove the snow as they did.

"I see you've found your wayward sister."

"Martha!" Brighit stilled her movements to glower at the woman. "I was certainly not wayward. You sent me to get the Bishop and Peter—Sir Peter was kind enough to take me."

Tadhg offered his hand to the older woman as they led the way down the hall. "Yes. I have found my wayward sister. And how have my men been treating you?"

Peter and Brighit followed behind. He took her hand in his again and smiled.

"They have been entertaining us with tales of Ireland. What a wonderful place you come from Brighit."

When they both turned toward them, Tadhg grabbed Brighit's hand out of Peter's and took it for himself, resting it in the crook of his arm. "Wait until you see who has come with me."

Peter gave Martha a tight smile. She did not smile back. She averted his gaze and ceased her talking. She appeared quite taken with Brighit's brother. He wondered why.

"Sean has come with you?" Brighit's tight voice caught his attention.

"He could not be kept away. When he heard you may be in danger, he dropped everything to be here."

Peter's jaw tightened. Tadhg turned to smile at him. "Sean was to be her betrothed."

"No—" Brighit began.

"Oh, I doubt he cares one way or another," Tadhg said.

Peter would like to throttle the man.

"He pines over you." Tadhg was enjoying this.

"Stop, Tadhg. You're being silly."

Just as they walked into the Great Hall, some of the nuns came forward as did a few men Peter assumed were Tadhg's men. They were about the same size as Tadhg. They rushed toward her. One by one they embraced her as if she'd been gone for years. With each exchange, Peter felt his blood boiling that much higher. She smiled in return, hugging them just as tight. He was about to ask which one was Sean when a golden-haired man entered.

He was slightly taller than Peter with long hair, tied at the back. He had a full beard, slightly darker than the color of his hair. He walked with purpose. Swagger. Like a warrior. His eyes stopped on Brighit. Peter recognized the look. Desire. No doubt this was Sean.

The man halted. His expressive blue eyes surveyed every inch of Peter's wife to be. She beamed. Even giggled at his slow nod of apparent approval.

"My love, you are a sight for these tired eyes."

Love?

She ran into his arms. Peter didn't realize he'd moved toward them until Tadhg yanked him back.

"Keep your place, Peter. She doesn't come to you without a long list of suitors that would gladly be where you are, receiving her as your wife," he turned to face him and continued, "to have and to hold. That alone would make any one of these men slit your throat if they'd a mind to. And with my blessing. You should realize the worth of the treasure you are stealing from Ireland."

"I realize her worth." Peter spoke in a low tone, his body tense, allowing the man to keep hold of his arm.

"Oh do you? We shall see."

Peter yanked his arm away.

"Can we get on with this?" Peter's surliness was not well received by any but it was Brighit who looked hurt. He was sorry for that. She'd looked unhappy ever since the marriage was agreed to. "My apologies, my lady. I am anxious to see this thing done."

Sean frowned as if he'd spotted a fly on his food. He pressed his way in front of Brighit, blocking her as effectively as a shield from Peter. "And what is this *thing* you wish to see done?"

Peter had never needed to look up to any man before. It was a bit disconcerting. With his hands fisted at his side, he had an overwhelming need to feel the man's bones slam against his knuckles as he smashed his fist into the man's face.

"They are to be wed," Tadhg answered.

The responses in the room varied from gasps, to murmurs of confusion, to loudly voiced objections.

"Settle down. Settle. I've no choice in the matter. I *must* see this done," Tadhg said.

The Irish group's demeanor shifted from bewilderment, no doubt due to his choice of words, to the sudden desire for bloodshed in the blink of his eye as they realized what Tadhg's words meant.

"Ah, now they've seen the truth of it," Tadhg announced amicably.

Peter turned to the man. "My thanks for that."

Tadhg smiled and took a protective step toward Brighit.

The men encircled Peter. He mentally shifted to a defensive position. When Brighit would have moved toward him, Tadhg held her fast.

They moved with slow deliberation. Assessing everything about him, their eyes missing nothing. He now understood what a horse at auction felt like but these men were not interested buyers. These were men intent on finding him lacking. He would never be found good enough for *their* Brighit.

"Gentlemen, I am Sir Peter of Normandy. I come on behalf of King William—"

"Are you marrying a King then, Brig?" The red-haired man with a long, auburn beard guffawed at his own joke.

The others joined in. Peter waited somewhat patiently, joining his hands behind his back.

"You'd be a Queen then!" Another one offered, which set them into yet another round of unbridled mirth.

His patience was waning.

After the forth comment, he'd had enough.

Peter glared at Tadhg. "Are you satisfied with your attempts at mocking me? I am happy to oblige any of your *men* that may care to test my strength."

Tadhg *tsked*. "Sir Peter. The weather would not allow for such sport. Are we to tear down the Sisters' home to accommodate your desire to prove yourself worthy? A proof that would never be forthcoming?"

Peter did not respond. He searched out Brighit to find her in deep conversation with Sean, their heads close together. Peter didn't need to be outside and he wouldn't call it any kind of sport. He covered the distance in two steps and grabbed the man by the front of his tunic.

"What do you find so interesting to say to my betrothed that you need to speak in whispers?"

"Peter," Brighit said. "You're being silly. Sean is like a brother to me."

He glanced at the man with narrowed eyes before turning back to her. "Hear me. He is not thinking of you as a sister."

Sean took a hard swing at the side of Peter's head which he dodged with little difficulty. Peter shoved him away.

Sean barely lost his footing, straightened his tunic, then laughed. "Beware, Brighit. I think you may be marrying an animal rather than a man."

"Enough!" Peter's voice boomed. His patience was gone.

"This one seems a little short-tempered, Brig. Are you sure you haven't made a mistake with him?"

When she glanced Peter's way, he clearly read the message that she wondered the same thing. He swallowed hard.

Red moved closer to her, lowering his gaze. "Any one of us would gladly accept you to wife regardless of... of any situation you may be in."

"That's true enough." Sean slipped his arm around her shoulder. When they started to lead her to the door at the far end of the hall, Peter decided he could take no more.

"Tadhg! Either call off your lackeys or I will take them down myself. I am taking Brighit to wife and your men will not change that." Peter glanced at the other men as he spoke. "I will not allow that."

Sean crossed his arms. "You? *You* will not allow that? Are you daft? It's her choice, man. None of us would gainsay our sweet Brighit's decision." His expression softened when he turned to her. "Whatever you say, we'll abide by it."

Brighit looked lost. Ruth came in, her babe tightly held in her arms. "I hope we are not too late to join in the blessing."

Martha's eyes crinkled at the corner with her smile as she joined her. "Oh. Wonderful." She turned toward Brighit. "Ruth and I were just discussing the great plans God has for you."

All fell silent. Peter had pushed his way to Brighit's side. He refused to leave it. Her warm hand, so small in his own, trembled at his touch. No matter what was pronounced as God's plans, he would be taking her to wife—and his bed—anon.

"Good to see you again, Sir Peter," Ruth said. She tipped her head toward Brighit. "Have you won over our fair lady?"

Relieved to have a possible ally, Peter smiled. "I'm afraid her clan wishes she would choose another."

She handed her babe to Brighit. They exchanged smiles. Ruth approached the men and curtsied. "I am glad you are all here for this auspicious occasion. A wedding is not often seen at a place where nuns dwell. Will you be joining us in the blessing? I believe it will be at the chapel."

"No!" Sean spoke up. "She'll not be marrying him until she tells us it is what she chooses."

Peter knew there was no choice here. Tadhg was forcing her to marry Peter. Could she now have an opening to break it off? Fear slithered through his gut. Fear of losing what he'd only recently realized he wanted. He wanted it more than he had ever wanted anything. Yes, he'd deeply cared for Jeanette. He'd thought it was love but this was different. He wanted to protect Brighit, to please her, to make her smile. To grow old with her. And children? Yes. He wanted her to birth his children and he would pray every day—every minute —that it would not kill her. He wanted to take the leap of faith required to take this woman as his wife. To make her the mother of his children.

He waited for her answer, praying that, even though she didn't love him, barely even knew him, she would honor her brother. Honor him as determinedly as she had honored her father.

CHAPTER 22

$\mathcal{T}$he tension was thick and the babe began to cry in response. Its strong voice filling the space.

Brighit quickly offered her back to her mother. "I believe she wants something from you."

Ruth accepted the bundle. "Oh, but I want to be at the chapel with you." She snuggled the babe close. It immediately quieted down.

Brighit glanced at her brother and clan members, her face tight with concern. "I'm not—"

Peter moved nearer to her. "Please, Brighit." His voice was quiet. "Let it stand."

Ruth and Martha shifted uncomfortably as if a fight was ensuing that they preferred not to be a part of. A marital argument. Brighit nearly gasped at the idea.

"No."

Sean's face lit up. "No? You don't wish to be wed to this Norman?"

"This is not right," Brighit said.

Tadhg came alongside her. "It is not up for discussion." He glanced toward Sean. "You've had your say. She doesn't have a choice. She'll obey as she always does."

Brighit's teeth ground against each other. It was always the way of it.

She was a good daughter. A good sister. She would do as she was told. A fuss was never stirred by her. She was obedient. Her jaw ached with the tension.

The other men were glancing toward each other. Toward Tadhg. Peter's eyes were on her alone. Unwavering. Searching her face as if he could know what was in her mind. The inner corners of his eyebrows raised as if in sympathy. Almost as if he'd discovered her well-hidden anger and resentment. Warmth radiated through her chest. He recognized she was angry enough to spit.

When he dipped his head, she felt the loss of his sympathy. She'd felt less alone when she thought he understood.

He turned to Tadhg. "Would you give us a moment to speak alone?"

A loud eruption of objections bounced against the walls and the babe wailed again.

"He shouldn't be alone with her."

"She doesn't know her own mind."

"How can you think to force her into marriage?"

Without saying a word, Tadhg raised his hand and the hall full of men fell silent save for the child.

Ruth bounced the babe trying to quiet her down then with a shrug and a smile, she said. "I will go see to her."

Tadhg watched her and the child leave before turning back to Peter. "We will remove ourselves so that you may speak."

Objections arose again but Tadhg strode with purpose to the far side of the hall and his men followed.

Peter turned her to him. He was all she could see. He pulled her in close.

"None of that!" Sean said from the across the room.

Peter withdrew slightly but kept his hand at her waist, out of sight within her cloak.

"What vexes you so? That I will do this? Or that it comes from your brother rather than from me?"

The strike of a hammer on an anvil seemed to ring in her ears. He knew. He knew just how she was feeling. He knew exactly what bothered her.

"My lord," Brighit said but he placed his warm hand against her cheek, immediately disorienting her.

Her eyes closed unbidden. His touch sent heat to every part of her. She opened her eyes. His smile was no less than the sunshine on her face. She sighed in defeat.

"Why do you not just tell them nothing happened?"

"They would not believe me. And something did happen. You know that."

And if what they had both wanted had happened, if he had been less of a gentleman, they would be going through this anyway.

"Methinks this is unfair." He should not be forced to marry when he did not want that.

If he was willing to do this, who was she to say no? No to a chance to love him truly? No to the fulfillment of a dream? No when she knew in her heart that she loved this man?

It felt as if he had always held a secret place in her heart. The secret place needing only to be awakened by him. By his touch. By his smile. His arrival in her life had been planned long ago.

If she were completely honest with herself, she would admit she wanted to be married to him. She wanted to bear his children. She wanted to make him as happy as his mere smile did for her.

Brighit sighed in defeat. "As you wish, my lord."

He placed a gentle kiss on her cheek before brushing her lips with his own.

"We'll have no more of that." This time it was Tadhg's voice that carried across the hall. "I believe that's what has gotten you into this predicament to begin with."

Peter winked, a mischievous look on his face. He took her hand and tucked it into the crook of his arm, then turned to face his future brother-in-law. "Let us proceed."

The walk to the chapel seemed to take an eternity. The sounds around Brighit became muffled. The faces of the smiling sisters around them seemed distant even as they surrounded her, guiding her to a little room behind the altar. It was tiny with just enough room for three of them. Ruth had returned and, with Martha, pulled off Brighit's dress. The touch of the cold air on her skin seemed as if it were happening to someone else. Martha pushing down a chemise that smelled of lilacs. Its flimsy material confusing Brighit. When she looked down at herself, it was as if she wore nothing at all.

The thought of protesting vanished when the softest material she'd ever felt was being pulled over her head. Its blue color was the same as a robin's eggs. It slipped over her hips, just touching the tips of her feet. Martha helped her into doeskin slippers.

"You look lovely." Their exclamations seemed a step behind their jubilant expressions.

Brighit rubbed her eyes. Their laughter erupted in the small chamber.

Ruth was brushing her hair. Martha was using a cloth on her face.

"You're pale. Do not worry so." The older woman moved close to her ear. "I know Peter will be kind to you."

The reality of what she implied was like a slap in the face. "You know?"

"What do you speak of?"

"That the deed has not been done?"

Martha tipped her head with that knowing smile.

Then Ruth stood beside her with that same smile. "It is as I said."

"And I still should go through with this?"

Ruth hugged her close. "Yes."

The door opened and she stepped into the dimly lit room. Peter sat over a small table topped with quill and ink. Tadhg bent over to watch him as he signed the document then rocked a small, curved board over the vellum. When he stood, he clasped hands with her brother. Peter smiled and surveyed the document as if surveying a great deed he had accomplished.

"Sister. You look lovely." Tadhg's familiar voice seemed to break the spell. He stepped forward and took her hands. He kissed her lightly on the cheek as he had before she departed from Ireland. That seemed like years ago. So much had transpired.

Peter surveyed her. His chest seeming to fill then bashfully took one hand. "May we partake of the Lord's supper to seal our bond?"

"Who will serve—?"

"I have it prepared." Martha stepped forward. "God's blessing will be upon this marriage."

Tadhg put his arm around his sister opposite Peter and stepped with them to the small altar. A single candle flickered. Martha came forward for the blessing, broke the bread and blessed the cup, then offered it to all present. Her Latin was impeccable. She would be a splendid Prioress.

Then with the Holy Scriptures in her hands, she tipped her head and smiled. "Where two or more are gathered in His name, His holy presence is assured. Let us speak the prayer Jesus taught us."

Fæder ure þu þe eart on heofonum
*   Si þin nama gehalgod*
*   to becume þin rice*
*   gewurþe ðin willa*
*   on eorðan swa swa on heofonum.*
*   urne gedæghwamlican hlaf syle us todæg*
*   and forgyf us ure gyltas*
*   swa swa we forgyfað urum gyltendum*
*   and ne gelæd þu us on costnunge*
*   ac alys us of yfele soþlice*

"Amen."

They all raised their heads and glanced at each other, not quite certain what should happen next.

"May God add His blessing on this marriage," Martha said, her voice as confident as any Priest's blessing. She turned first to Brighit. "You may kiss your husband." Then to Peter. "And you may kiss your wife."

Tadhg stepped away from the couple as a symbol of his acceptance of the joining. He stood beside the Nuns, glancing between them with a smile.

Peter wrapped his arms around Brighit and pulled her against him with great reverence. He searched her face, then lowered his lips to hers.

She closed her eyes and allowed the touch of her husband's lips, with its radiant heat, to spread throughout her body.

When he released her, Brighit's eyes fluttered open and she smiled. "I love you."

Those around them erupted into cheering but the look of shock on Peter's face made her breath catch. When she'd closed her eyes, she decided she would tell him how she felt. She expected nothing in return but wanted there to be truth in their marriage.

"The feast awaits," Martha announced then led the way out of the chapel.

The others surrounded Brighit and Peter, ushering them into the Great Hall which had been transformed. Its high ceiling was decorated with the greens of the forest. The trestle tables covered with fall leaves of every hue. The table that ran along one side was near to overflowing with a roasted pig, a pheasant stuffed with a chicken which was stuffed with a smaller hen, and three different salted fish. Along with orange, green, and red fruits which they must have stolen from their winter stores, and winter vegetables of every shape and size. Sweets lined one end with liquid libations of mead, beer, and cider lining the other.

At the head table, which was covered with a white linen cloth, sat a great pot set right in the middle, still steaming.

"How did you possibly manage all this?" Brighit couldn't believe what she saw around her.

"You helped." Martha smiled.

"When did I help?"

Martha walked her to the head table so she could look inside the heavy pot.

"Soup!" Brighit cried out then hugged Martha tightly.

"It had been so long that we had anything to celebrate here that we started it all upon your arrival. It was only readied this morning." Martha said.

Brighit turned to Peter, beaming. "This soup was my first duty here."

"And the last," Ruth offered.

The sudden tightness in Brighit's chest felt like she'd had too many frights. One gasp followed by another, followed by another, and she couldn't exhale.

"Greetings."

Mort stood in the doorway dressed for battle. Chain mail covered his body. A helmet tucked under his arm. A look of confusion flashed across his face and then his eyes met Peter's. He lifted a hand then crossed the room with great comportment, his sword hanging from his waist, a dagger tucked into his leather gauntlet.

Peter perused his attire, a horn of mead in his grip. "Mort, why the change in clothing? Hopefully you haven't dressed so on our account. Although the gesture is certainly appreciated."

"Are they celebrating our Brighit's taking her vows so soon?"

"Not even close," Sean said. He stood beside the table passing cups of beer around.

"We've seen her wed." Tadhg lifted his cup, the other men did the same before emptying their cups.

"Wed?" Mort screwed his face up in confusion. "How can a nun get married?"

"When she doesn't take her vows but gets married instead," Sean said and refilled their cups. He lifted one toward Mort who waved his hand to decline.

"I abstain when preparing for battle."

"Battle?" Peter's enjoyment was replaced by serious concern.

Mort tipped his head to the side. "Alas, my friend, I didn't happen upon this celebration but have come to retrieve you. Lord John arrived at the inn and wishes to see you immediately."

"John is here?" Peter's cup nearly dropped from his hand. "He wants to see me—now?"

Brighit warmed at the thought of him not wanting to leave her so soon. Now? Her heart dropped to her stomach.

Mort reached toward them both, as if wavering between which arm to reassure. "Please. No. I am certain he would not want to take you away from... he would not interrupt... he does not know of this turn of events."

Peter placed the cup on the table behind him. "When did he arrive?"

"It was two days ago."

"Yes. When we were snowed in."

"It was the night you left for the Priory. He actually arrived ahead of his men—"

"He has brought his men?"

"Yes, my lord, he has come to support you in your siege against the castle. King William could wait no longer for information. We are to lay siege immediately."

Peter sighed and Brighit could feel his tension rising. Her own hope was quickly evaporating.

"Very good timing I must say."

"How so?" Peter's voice indicated his own disagreement with Mort's statement.

"He arrived at the inn just as our local ruffians had reinforcements."

"Reinforcements? I had no idea. I'm sure you were handling them well enough on your own."

Mort reddened slightly. "Well, yes, my lord, I had them well in hand but I have to say it was a much more enjoyable encounter with John present. We made quick work of them."

Peter laughed. "I imagine you did. And what word is there now?"

The two walked toward the door leaving Brighit quite bereft. Mayhap Peter was going to continue out that door at this very moment with ner a glance back or another thought for his *bride*.

Ruth came alongside and extended her sleeping bundle. "I've named her Brighit so that I will never forget you."

She was the slightest, little thing, weighing next to nothing. Brighit smiled. "That is very kind of you." She glanced toward Peter's disappearing figure. "I may not be needing to be remembered."

Ruth glanced toward the empty doorway. "I do not understand."

She shook her head before smiling at the baby, moving in close to her face. "You are so sweet." Little Brighit's lip moved up and down as if nursing in her sleep. "She is truly beautiful."

Ruth placed her head alongside Brighit's for the same angle. "She is, isn't she? My sweet, little bundle."

"Please, friends and sisters. Thank you for coming and enjoy the feast

but I believe we have duties to see to first. Namely - the marriage bed must be assessed. Follow my friends."

Martha swept her hand over her head and all followed. Brighit was taken aback at the announcement but Ruth pulled her forward.

"I believe I'm needing to make this trip with my husband." Her voice sounded as small as she felt.

"Here I am." Peter stepped up as they walked through the open doors.

Mort waited for the group to pass by, giving her a kind smile as she went.

With great care, he took the bundle from Brighit's arms and handed the babe back to its mother.

The cheering erupted around them once the group passed Ruth with her child. Bald comments come to them from the men and the women giggled and rolled their eyes.

Brighit felt her face grow hotter with every step down the hallway and not knowing exactly where this "bedding" was to take place. She looked at Peter whose eyes were steadily glancing between where they were being led and her face. Did he measure her trepidation? His sudden responsibility? Or how long it would take before he could go to see John?

She swallowed the fear that swamped at the reality of having just made the biggest error in judgment of her short life. A fool's error. She had allowed herself to believe that somehow this was a good thing but it was truly a farce. She was not compromised. She was not taken advantage of. Yet she was wed.

Just as she readied herself to halt right there and proclaim this marriage nothing more than a big lie, they reached an oak door. Martha pushed it open to reveal a huge chamber of exquisite elegance. Brighit's mouth dropped open. It was a chamber fit for the King with a huge platform in the middle of the room which held a bed like none she'd ever seen before. Long drapes hung around the posts supporting the bed. A gentle fire burned to the far side of the room that was big enough to heat the entire Great Hall.

"What is this place?" Brighit asked.

"Martha told me this is the Bishop's private chambers." Peter looked around him, a slight nod to his head as if assessing something that has met approval. "I believe Odo will not mind if we use his chamber in this instance."

He turned back at her with a knowing look. Her heart dropped to her stomach.

"Our marriage bed will be the bed of the King's half-brother?"

"Hmm, I'm surprised you know that."

The clamor interrupted their discussion. Peter smiled and turned toward the smiling faces that pushed against them in their eagerness to get inside of the room.

"It is not with great reluctance that we bid you goodbye. You may not be entering nor witnessing the bedding. As you believe the bedding has already taken place." He shrugged his shoulders and pulled the door closed.

Peter closed his eyes, leaned back against the door, and blew out a breath. His irritation quite apparent and Brighit felt the tears at the back of her throat. The sound from the crowd outside diminished as they returned to the feast.

He suddenly opened his eyes and pierced her with his look. "Ah, my lovely Brighit. I could eat you up!"

Brighit's eyes widened.

"Do not be afraid. And I promise to make it a pleasurable experience."

CHAPTER 23

$\mathcal{P}$eter pushed away from the door and walked toward Brighit. The look of fear on her face surprised him. She had shown herself to be quite passionate. He glanced around the room. All had been provided for them. Food. Drink. Water. Bed. A fire that could easily make the room extremely warm... for anyone who was dressed. Brighit would need to lose the dress. He pressed his lips together, remembering what was hidden beneath. Libations may be the best approach.

"Come." He took her cold hand. The room was expansive and he led her to the bench. "Sit."

The mead warmed beside the fire and he offered her a cup before sitting beside her. Taking a sip himself, he said, "Mead always tastes best at the Monasteries and Priories."

She brought the cup to her mouth, a slight tremble in her hand. "This is the only one I've been to but I would agree it is good."

No one would be interrupting them this time and he had time to ease any nervousness. He also knew no one would ever know what they did or didn't do.

"They think we have already done the deed."

"That is true enough," Brighit said.

"If we choose to consummate this tonight or not, it is our decision alone."

He dare not breathe. He wasn't sure what he would do if she decided she required more time.

Brighit thoughtfully sipped her drink before answering. "Waiting creates more jitters. Fear of the unknown."

She searched his face and swallowed down her mead, returning it to him for more.

"I prefer not to wait," she said.

He exhaled his relief, refilling her mead. He'd prefer she not become drunk. Making love was not usually an event requiring drunkenness.

"Are you afeared now?" He traced his finger along the side of her face. "I would die before I ever hurt you."

She took the last swallow. He took her empty cup then placed his hand against her flushed cheek.

Brighit turned her face into his palm, closing her eyes. Her skin was as soft as he remembered. All her skin was soft. He pulled her face toward him. Her lips were soft and inviting and tasted of mead. She placed one hand against his chest and returned the kiss. He traced his tongue along the seam of her tightened lips.

"Open your mouth to me," he whispered the words.

After the slightest hesitation, she did, shifting closer to accommodate him. The honey sweetness coated her tongue. The warmth of the mead spread through him as he was sure it was her. She wrapped one hand tentatively around his neck, still reaching her head toward him. He needed her much closer. Pulling his head away, he let his gaze sweep over her body. He lightly traced the outline of one breast with his fingertip, running along the nipple when it pearled in response to his touch, then around again as his tongue longed to do.

"I remember these beautiful breasts." His voice was quiet. He glanced at her when her breath quickened. "Reveal yourself to me." In his mind he saw her naked again and he needed to touch her. He looked into her eyes. "Let me touch you."

She searched his face before standing in front of him. With crossed hands, she pulled the material up with what he'd swear was slow deliberation. He dare not breathe. His eyes remained fixed on her rising hem as each part was revealed to him. Dainty ankles and graceful knees followed by lovely thighs that he longed to drag his hands along, ending with his fingers buried between them.

He glanced at her face again. Her eyes were hooded, her breath shallow. She may be nervous but she was enjoying this. When she pulled the gown over her head, her breasts were caught by the chemise and they shook with the movement, nearly setting him off. Out of sheer desperation, he stood and grasped the under curve of each delectable swell, cupping their heaviness, kneading them against his hand.

"I've dreamed of doing this."

Her nipples were hard against his palm. Her eyes fluttered shut in response. He dropped his mouth and suckled her. Sliding one hand lower, he slipped it between her legs. He caressed her with light strokes. She relaxed against him, her hands moving around his head, pulling him more fully against her.

He placed a hand on either hip and took her mouth in a passionate kiss. Turning her away from him, he ran his hands along every inch of her, getting her accustomed to his touch. With one hand grasping her breast, his other hand slid over her lovely derriere.

"You've a mouth-watering arse," he whispered into her ear.

He felt her shiver and he pulled her back against him. He wanted to be driving into her now. To hear her panting in his ear as he thrust into her. To get his release. He steadied himself. When she rubbed against his hardness, he was lost. He turned her in his arms.

"I need to take you. Now." His hands grasped and pulled her closer.

Brighit reached down to cover his manhood with her palm, grasping as he had her. He pulled her hand away, struggling for composure.

"No. It's your turn to be touched and I'm not nearly finished touching you," he said.

He lowered her across the bed then followed. With slow deliberation, he released the material tied back at the four posts of the bed. One by one, the outside world was closed off, leaving them in a haven of solitude.

With his lips on her mouth, he worshipped her body with his hands. Caressing. Fondling. Tugging. She opened her mouth to him as she did her body. He ravaged both. When he slid his hand down her stomach toward the apex of her legs, she hesitated only slightly before parting her knees to grant him access.

"Ah, woman, you're going to be the death of me."

With gentle strokes he touched her lightly at first but dipping into her wetness, his breath hitched. He wanted to go slow but he was not a saint. He stood to remove the rest of his clothing but her intent gaze made him wonder about his own ability to pleasure her first. Covering her with his body, he slipped between her legs. His hardened shaft eagerly pushing against her slick surface.

"Sweet Lord."

"I need... more." She sounded breathless.

That was all he needed to hear. With one firm thrust, he entered here. A gentle burst of air was the only sound she made as her maidenhead was breached. He stopped to kiss her deeply. She kissed him back.

"You're mine now."

"I've been yours forever."

At a different time or place, Peter would have wondered about that cryptic message but his body had other ideas. Slowly he began to move in the sweetest tightness he'd ever experienced, gently rocking in and out until his body demanded more. To his surprise, she moved against him, spreading her legs, deepening his thrust.

"We fit perfectly," he whispered, his mouth against her ear.

He slid his hands beneath her and took her arse in both hands, lifting her. She made pleasurable noises deep in her throat.

"Can you feel? We are one."

She nodded. Then her muscles pulsed against him, a needy sound from her lips. He moved with long, slow strokes prolonging her pleasure until he could wait no longer. She held him tight, accepting each thrust until his seed was spilled. He dropped alongside her, panting. They were covered with sweat. He pulled the blanket over them both, tucking her close against him. Brighit sighed as if she'd just seen paradise. Kissing her lightly on the head, he'd have to agree.

Brighit awoke to her husband's lips on her neck. His tongue stroking against her ear.

"Are you awake yet?"

She turned into his arms. "I am."

He had loved her again last night then took great care to help her wash. His gentle ministrations turned into another opportunity for him to bring her body to life. She was enthralled by his ability to give her so much pleasure. And he had assured her his own pleasure was being satisfied as well.

He positioned himself between her legs and looked down at her, brushing her hair away from her face. "You look well-ravished."

"Oh, I have been that."

"Mayhap I can do better." His crooked smile sent her stomach into quivers of excitement with the promise of even more.

He positioned one breast to his mouth, suckling it into a firm bud and sending scorching heat to her core. She closed her eyes.

"You are unquenchable," she said.

He ran his hands along her sides sending ripples of pleasure through her exhausted limbs. When he slid his hands beneath her bottom, she spread her legs to him.

"I am," he said then turned his attention to her other breast. "Would you have me cease?"

She opened her eyes. He was watching her while the tip of his tongue licked at her nipple. Her breath quickened. He sucked it into his mouth and she arched her back, pushing her breast more fully into his warm mouth.

"No." Her word was more of a groan.

He continued his assault, moving down to the flat of her stomach. The rough hair on his face sending shivers over her skin. She squirmed beneath him.

"My love you are going the wrong way."

"No, I do not believe that I am." He slipped his finger into her wetness, stroking her. "Or is this more to your liking."

Her eyes were closed again, experiencing sweet sensation after sensation. She felt his eyes on her. Watching her seemed to give him great enjoyment. She'd have preferred to be beneath the covers and unseen. He told her he wanted to see her pleasure. When he slipped his finger into her tightness, she gasped at the exquisite pressure. She cantered her hips toward him, giving him better access.

He dipped his tongue into her naval, keeping the same rhythm as his finger burying deep within her. She giggled.

Peter lifted his head, a frown creasing his forehead. "I make love to my wife and she laughs?"

She struggled to keep focused on his face when his hand was demanding her total attention. "No. I won't laugh."

He licked her abdomen with long, searing strokes of his tongue, moving ever closer to where his hand was giving her such pleasure.

"I'm sure your mouth is going the wrong way, my love." She pointed to her lips. "I want your lips on mine."

She gasped at the sensation when his mouth found its target, her eyes flying open. When she reached to pull him away from her, he held her hand. His passion-filled eyes watching her over her dark mound of hair and he dragged his tongue through her most intimate space. He stroked with insistent pressure that sent ripples of sensations through her. Her hips began to move against him almost of their own accord. His finger was joined by another and she was racing toward her release.

The groan exploded from deep in her throat. He moved up to cover her and entered her with one swift stroke. Ever so slowly, he moved with long, deep strokes, pausing before withdrawing. When her climax came again, he lifted her legs and buried himself deep inside, thrusting harder and harder. She gasped and moaned. She was unable to hold back. The feelings washing over her, through her, were overwhelming her. She called his name.

When he stilled inside her, she opened her eyes to a look of pure ecstasy on his face. He collapsed on her.

Their breathing was labored and he gave a little laugh. "We are well suited."

"Mmm." She nodded, exhausted. Caressing the soft hair covering his chest, she waited for her breathing to ease.

He blew out a breath then pulled her close. "Rest. It's almost daybreak."

She stilled her hand. "What will happen at daybreak?"

He kissed her head. "Rest."

CHAPTER 24

*A*s they walked down the narrow hallway, Peter felt near to bursting with pride, the hand of his beautiful bride resting lightly on his arm. He glanced at her and she returned his gaze. Her look was one of a woman well-cherished. Or was it well-bedded?

"How do you feel?"

"A little sore."

That wasn't the answer he'd expected.

"Did I wear you out?"

She looked at him sheepishly. "I would say not."

"You have been well-loved." He stopped to kiss her on the nose before taking her again in his arms. She fit so perfectly against him as if her body were made for his.

"I believe this is what pushed me to the sore stage," Brighit whispered against his chest then lightly nuzzled against him. "Are we returning to the room again, my lord?"

Her eyes were closed. Her body yielding against him. She was certainly willing.

"Perhaps—"

"Peter!" John's loud voice boomed through the quiet hall.

Brighit tensed, her eyes flew open and she jerked away. Peter kept hold of her elbow so she was not able to completely detach from him. His eyes stayed on hers.

"Fear not. We are allowed to touch each other. We are married."

A deep blush covered her features and she glanced away.

Peter turned his irritation on his good friend. "John! Could you not wait until I came to you?"

John struggled to keep from smiling, nodding his head. He glanced at Brighit then back at Peter.

"I understand you've been wed?"

Peter wrapped a loving arm around Brighit but not too tightly. If she was uncomfortable with him touching her in public, he could cool his ardor. Her responsiveness in bed was more important and he wanted to do nothing to jeopardize that pleasure.

"So Mort has explained it to you?"

John pulled back in surprise. "You appear nettled with me."

Peter gave a deep sigh. "No, John, but I was on my way to the hall. Methinks it would be best to keep my wife well nourished."

John dropped his gaze to Brighit. "An honor to meet you, Lady Brighit."

She curtsied. "My pleasure."

John looked back at Peter. "She doesn't have three heads."

"Who said that she did?"

"Then why would you keep her holed up with you? I assumed she'd be hideously disfigured. She's lovely."

Peter's irritation was rising in direct proportion to the tightness he could feel in Brighit's body. "Have a care, John. My lady is not use to your insensible comments."

"My insensible comments? Never!" John turned to Brighit, took her hand to his lips for a light kiss, then asked, "May I have a word with your husband?"

"We're headed for the hall and breaking our fast, John. Allow us to proceed."

"Am I such a bore as to stop you?" John effectively blocked the way.

He seemed unaware of that fact. Peter waited. Brighit cleared her throat.

"Oh, yes, allow me." John took Brighit's other hand and tucked it in the crook of his arm. "I'm not sure how this all transpired but you have my deepest sympathy for the situation you now find yourself in."

Brighit gasped, her mouth hanging open, her eyes wide.

"John! Desist with your teasing. She does not know you as of yet." Peter stopped and took both her hands. "My apologies, sweet Brighit. My friend has no manners at all. He is a complete idiot and I should have warned you about him. Please forgive me. Would you have me return you to our room and bring you food there?"

Brighit narrowed her eyes and pressed her lips together. She glanced between the two. "I believe this is your idea of humor. You belittling the man who you have great respect for? And in front of me?" She shook her head. "You two deserve each other. I can proceed to the hall without you."

She strode down the hall but when she turned the corner to the main hall, she looked back and winked at them.

"Oh my, she is quite charming isn't she?" John questioned.

"She has so much more than charm, my friend."

John searched his friend's face. "I can see that. You are besotted with her."

"She is a precious gem I was blessed to find."

"And was that the reason for the hurried marriage?"

"I refused to be parted from her. Her brother would have taken her from me. I had to act quickly."

John looked down at his hands before facing Peter. "You do know we have orders to lay siege to the castle at York?"

Peter became serious. "Yes, my lord, I have been informed of the King's orders. The Earl there must be an impudent dog. His name?"

"Earl de Gael."

"The old man Emma FitzOsbern was wed to? He really is impudent. A woman half his age and he dare defy the King who gave them his blessing?"

"Ah, but William's sudden refusal to bless Emma's marriage to Ralph de Gael was quite the turn of events."

"Why the change of heart?"

John shrugged. "Perhaps William did not trust him. Rumors abound regarding the discontentment of the Earls."

"Had her father arranged the marriage before his death without the King's approval?"

"I'm not sure if it was FitzOsbern or the King who arranged it but this resulting uprising against the King appears to confirm the King's distrust. It also seems to be the collapse of the bridge. The King will take no more impudence. Even this far north."

"When would you have us depart?"

"I've sent the army ahead with Mort. Their travel will be slow. We will join them before they make the castle."

John stood there, his hands at his hips and a far off look in his eyes. Peter knew he was seeing the harsh winter and hardships they would have to face if they were unable to convince the Earl to open his gates. Sieges were always difficult but more difficult for those inside.

"Let us set aside these concerns for now. I would like to get to know this *wife* of yours. My Rowena will be overjoyed that you have taken a wife. She worried over you."

"Lady Rowena is very special to me as well." He smiled with relief that he would not be leaving his bride immediately. "I would like you to get to know Brighit as well."

They walked without talking until they were right outside the Great Hall, the doors stood open. Brighit was inside and surrounded by the men of her clan. The smile she bestowed on each of them bristled Peter's pride but John grabbed his arm before he could approach her.

"Wait. No doubt she is only happy to be with someone from home."

Peter's eyes widened. "You know about them, too?"

"Mort loves to talk."

"A truer statement I've never heard."

"He has mastered the ability to get information from his seemingly idle chatter."

They paused and watched the exchange. Brighit's coloring spoke volumes about her spirited responses.

"Do you fear she may return with them?"

Peter's heart leapt in his chest. "No! She would never—" he turned back toward her. "I do not believe she would want to leave me."

"Peter." John's tone was suddenly serious. "I do have news regarding Jeanette."

Peter flinched inside. He hadn't thought of her in days. Guilt swept over him and he looked away.

"It won't be easy to hear what I have to tell you."

Peter shoved down the mix of emotions swamping him. Guilt. Fear. Happiness. "Tell me."

"Jeanette's brother was not truthful with you."

It was worse than he'd feared.

"She died more recently than he professed to you."

Confusion added to the mix churning in the pit of his stomach. "What are you saying? I have been away since the fall. How..."

John searched his features. Reality ran over him like a stampede of horses. "It wasn't my child she carried. She had been with another?"

"Peter, she had been with many others."

The urge to punch his best friend in the mouth was overpowering. "Why demean her with such words?"

John grabbed on to his clenched fist. "So that you could allow yourself to grieve over the loss of your lover without the guilt of believing your murdered her. She did not carry your child. She died delivering another's child."

Betrayal was hard to swallow. In all the time he'd spent separated from Jeanette, he'd never considered coupling with another. Peter and John were alike in that way. They would prefer to abstain than be rutting like pigs. John, not even knowing who his sire was, convinced him to always see the act resulting in a possible birth. He could never do that to his child. Many of the soldiers thought it their right to take from the women they came across even if they were unwilling. Regardless of the outcome.

It was a difficult choice to make. Battle often left Peter with a raging need for release. Sometimes release came by his own hand but it wasn't satisfying. It was merely to lessen the tension. When he matured, he learned better ways than physical manipulation to overcome his roaring desires. He chose to be loyal to Jeanette alone.

"There never were any promises between us." Peter could see her face before him. "I lusted after her and she took me into her bed. She made herself available whenever I returned to court. I suppose I knew deep inside that she would find another in my absence."

Peter rubbed his thumb along his bottom lip. Jeanette had not died because he loved her. Cursed? Perhaps he was not. Hope sparked inside and he felt like the night watchmen just as the promise of dawn spread light across the horizon. Dare he believe the darkness in him was lifting?

"Do you remember my sire?" He glanced at John. Peter's father had been a powerful leader for King William when he was still a duke, always able to subdue the enemy.

"He was a great warrior. I served him as squire for a short time and know he was a hard man," John said.

Peter's derisive snort was met with a slow nod from John. "He was a cruel bastard."

"And you are nothing like him, Peter. I never knew who my father was. Once William took me in, no one raised a hand to me."

"I envied you for that."

"No one raising a hand to me?"

"Not knowing who your father was. It must have been a blessing."

John didn't respond immediately. "A father should not beat his son although some believe differently. He also should not subject him to cruel taunts and make him afraid. I never imagined that my father would be like that. I'd have to disagree about not knowing being a blessing."

"I know how much you wish to know where you came from. I'm sorry," Peter said.

"William never allowed a hand to be raised against you either."

"I'd been told so many times that I was worthless, that it was my fault my mother was dead, that I was a curse upon humanity."

"Your sire told you those lies?"

"Repeatedly. Fear had been instilled in me. I believe I deserved every beating my father gave me. Any of those knights knew that just by looking at me. I had not the makings of a good soldier. All they needed was to take one threatening step toward me and they would have me cowering."

John put a hand on his shoulder. "I did not realize that was how it was for you. Is that why you preferred to squire for FitzOsbern?"

"That one never obeyed William. He cuffed me several times and I felt we were a good match. I knew what to expect. As I grew, he taught me to subdue my fear. To use it as a weapon. Turn it against the enemy. He turned me into the soldier I am."

John squeezed his shoulder. "Should I have kept the truth from you about Jeanette?"

"Never."

John pulled him into the Great Hall. "Come. Let us interrupt the eager pups circling your wife."

Peter sneered. "With great pleasure, my lord."

Brighit glanced toward the two knights in the doorway for the hundredth time. They were in deep conversation and it did not bode well for her. Barely a bride for an entire day and her husband appeared ready to ride off to battle.

"Do you wish to remain here?" Sean's audacious question sent a new ripple of laughter through the men surrounding her.

Brighit gave him her most tolerant smile. "I am well married now. Enough with your foolishness."

Sean stepped closer, looking down into her face. His own eyes twinkling with the mischief he intentionally ignited. "It would have been good with us, Brig."

His impassioned words sent a shiver of repulsion down her spine. She could never have submitted to this man. Not like she willingly gave to Peter. She glanced toward the tall, blond Norman making his way toward her. True, she'd had a glimpse of what was hidden beneath his tunic and hose before her wedding night but the reality was far different. The touch of him, like solid rock, made her innards turn to mush. And those hands—what his hands could ignite inside her. His mouth mesmerized and enticed.

"You're bright as a cardinal, Brighit! Are you thinking about us?"

Her mouth fell open. "Never in your wildest imagination! You are like my brother. I could never allow you to touch me—"

"Mhwah, look at her! She's besotted by the Norman."

Brighit realized it was her expression from the glance toward Peter and the longing her thoughts had stirred they were commenting on. She pressed her lips together.

"Enough with your silliness. I am a married woman and I'll have no more of your teasing."

Peter was close behind her. She could feel him. His all-encompassing heat. He laid not a single finger on her but he was requiring all her attention with his mere presence.

"Is aught amiss?" He kissed her lightly on the cheek. "Are these lads bothering you?"

Sean's nostrils flared like a mad bull. Bracing himself as if ready for battle, he confronted Peter. "Hurt our Brighit and I'll come back and drive a dagger straight through your heart."

Peter's relaxed stance never wavered, even as he broke into a huge smile. A smile that seemed to say he had won and he knew it. He allowed the threat to pass. The tension Sean's earlier words had coiled in her stomach lessened. There was no way to let Sean down easy. It was true. She was totally besotted by her handsome Norman.

"So will you be going back to Ireland now?" she said.

"I believe we will. Do you think you will ever return?" Sean asked.

Brighit glanced at Peter. It would be his decision to make now. Where she would go and where she would live.

Peter smiled back at her. "Perhaps. We will have to discuss these things."

"Truly?" she asked.

Peter didn't turn the idea down out of hand as she'd expected him to.

Impulsively, she reached up to offer him a passionate kiss then said, 'I do love you so."

She quickly turned away so he couldn't see the blush of her cheeks. Tadhg, entering the hall, gave her the perfect reason to retreat from her unwise revelation about her feelings. She couldn't stop herself. He was so kind to her. So patient. So loving. Never could she have imagined being married to someone like him.

"Sister. You look... refreshed." Tadhg kissed her lightly on the cheek, pausing beside her ear, "See what happens when you keep your deepest desires close?"

"I do," she said in a whisper then returned his kiss.

"Ah, Sir Peter." Tadhg took the other man's hand. "My sister seems to have survived an entire night with you."

Brighit's cheeks heated. She turned away. Perhaps they would refrain from any more comments if they did not notice her embarrassment.

"She's besotted with him. Although I see no reason for that to be the case." Sean's attempt at humor ended in a disgruntled tone. He glanced at Peter. "I will see that the horses are properly cared for."

Tadhg watched him until he left the hall then turned back to Brighit. "Mayhap he did pine after you."

"That's ridiculous. He is like one of my brothers."

"There was that time I caught you in the field with him and ner a stitch of clothing on either of you."

Her eyes widened. When she glanced at Peter's shocked expression, she wanted to rip her brother's tongue out. "We were four!"

Peter laughed.

"I didn't say how old you were."

"You implied—oh stop." She rolled her eyes.

Peter wrapped his strong arms about her shoulders and pulled her back against him. He kissed her lightly on the top of the head. "You were a spirited one even then."

"Well, when he mentioned—oh never mind."

"Enough, Tadhg. I will not have even you embarrassing my sweet wife."

A lump grew in her throat, making it hard to swallow. Peter spoke of her with such endearments. She held his arm where it crossed just above her breasts. She felt protected and loved... but she knew he did not feel that way. He'd declared he wanted none of that.

He'd not even questioned her after her impulsive declaration of love after they were wed. Perhaps dismissing it as an impulsive response, without foundation. Or not feeling it was necessary to respond when he would be leaving. Now that she'd repeated the declaration, she wasn't sure if he would broach the subject with her.

Although he had seemed quite pleased with her in bed and had said as much. She felt the same. They were indeed well suited. Even now the solid wall of his body against her back, made her knees weak. As if sensing that, he pulled her tighter still. Then brought his lips to her ear.

"Shall we see to that voracious appetite of yours now?"

She gasped.

"Not that appetite."

Turning to face him, she saw the sly smile. He kissed her with more passion this time. "I promise to see to that after we have sustenance."

Although Peter's words were for her ears only, Tadhg's unwavering smile caused her already heated face to grow even hotter.

"Well, as long as someone will still be embarrassing her," Tadhg said.

He turned toward the table of food, leaving Peter and Brighit alone.

"Your emotions are easy to see," Peter said. He pulled her in for another kiss. "Is it because I am so enthralled by this luscious body?"

"I verily hope so, my lord."

He offered his arm and they followed Tadhg to the food.

CHAPTER 25

*P*eter had followed through with his promise of returning her to bed after they broke their fast. It had been the sweetest coupling. Tears had sprung to her eyes as he held her close. She knew he was saying goodbye.

"I'm sorry to be leaving you so soon." Peter rubbed his lips against the top of her head where she rested against his chest. "I will dream of you being in my arms every night."

Brighit brushed the tear off her cheek before it fell to his bare chest. "You are a soldier, my lord. Your King has sent orders. You need to obey."

He tipped his head to look into her face. "So you believe telling me all the things I know will somehow ease my longing to remain here with you?"

"No." She forced down the lump in her throat. She refused to have him leave with her in tears. "Where has John gone?"

"He returned to the inn to send word to his troops. They will advance to the castle in preparation for the siege."

"A siege?"

"We will ask to enter the castle. If they do not open their gates to us, we will cut off anyone and everything from entering or leaving. We will bombard their walls with our trebuchets until we either break through their walls or they open their gates."

Her sadness turned to fear. He could certainly die if battle ensued. She should have realized that. She could lose him just when she found him.

"What will you do when I leave?"

"I am yours now. What would you have me do?"

He kept his eyes on her. "I do not consider you a possession with no thoughts of your own. What is it you would like to do?"

The tears came anyway. He sat up and gathered her more fully against him. "No. No tears. You will break my will in two. *Shhh.*"

He stroked her hair.

"I will be alone. I know not what I should even want to do."

His body tensed. His hand ceased its movement. "Would you prefer to return with your brother and his men?"

"No! I do not wish to leave... here."

His brown eyes searched her face. He pushed a wayward lock of hair from her face. His smile reached his eyes. "I'm happy to hear you say that.'

"Who are these people that will not open their gates to you? Are they not your King's men?"

He tipped his head, running his thumb along her lip. He kissed her. "The King believed the man inside was loyal. By not opening his gates, he will be showing his defiance of the King's orders."

Her whole body wished for the man to just open his gates so that Peter could come back to her. "Is there any hope that the man will open his gates to you?"

"There seems to be no hope at all."

Peter moved to sit along the side of the bed, pushing the curtain aside. The touch of the cold air against her skin felt like a bad omen. She wrapped the coverings around her. He stood to secure his hose. His tunic was next. She watched until all of his body was covered, hoping to etch him so strongly into her mind that even while he was gone, it might feel as if he were with her still.

"I must meet with John. Did you remember anything else about Ivan and his men? Or your uncle's encounter with Leofrid?"

She shrugged. "I believe I have told you all that I remember. I am sorry there is not more."

"It is enough." He smiled. "I've given orders that you are to use this room as your ow—"

"Peter, I cannot. I am no one of importance. How could I dare?"

His gaze was steady. "Hear me. I *am* of great importance to the King. And the wife of one of the King's most treasured knights *will be* protected. Do you understand? I have yet to find out what Ivan and your uncle are about. I will have you safely within this Priory. This room you will make as your own in my absence. Odo knows me. He would not begrudge you being here. Trust me in this."

A huge rock had been deposited in the pit of her stomach with his declaration. She would prefer to have been near Ruth and the baby or even Martha at night.

"Yes. I will use this room as my own." He opened his arms and she kneeled on the bed beside him. She leaned against his chest.

"Mmm, I will miss how this feels. Our time has been too short."

She nodded against him. When he pulled back, he gently grasped her chin to tip her head back to receive his passionate kiss. His arms wrapped rigidly around her as if to stay his hands from caressing her.

When he loosened his hold to step back, Brighit moved to follow him to the door. He held up his hand.

"Please. Let me leave you here. This is where I want you. And when I return, this is where I want to find you."

Peter backed away three steps before turning to the door, closing it behind him without a glance back.

Brighit lay on the bed and stared at the canopy over her head for a long time. There were no movements outside her door. No one came to knock or check on her. Eventually she turned onto her side. Sleep was long in coming despite the tiredness that filled her. When it did, she had dreams of dark voids and haunting voices that seemed to reassure her she would never see her husband alive again.

~

Peter's gray destrier strained against the tight hold of his reins. He couldn't blame the animal. He, too, wanted to break free and close the distance to the castle at York rather than plodding along at this snail's pace.

"Peter." John's voice sliced through his irritation. "We have time. There is no hurry."

Three days into their ride north and Peter would wholeheartedly disagree with that assessment. He wished to be done with this matter. He wished to return to his wife. The wife he dreamed about even in the light of day.

"My lord, my belief is that if we get there ahead of the trebuchets, perhaps we can persuade the inhabitants to forego the inevitable loss of life that will result from the siege." He turned back to John. "Does that not sound a plausible plan?"

John looked away. Peter could see he was holding his temper.

"Would it not be more amicable to have men show up on horseback than an entire army at your gate?"

Incredulity was etched in the sharp lines of John's face when he finally turned back toward him. "Peter. It's called a show of force. That's how this is done, as well you know. Are you in such a hurry to return to Brighit that you can no longer even think like a solider?"

Peter reined in his horse that snorted loudly. Propping his bent knee across his saddle he faced his friend. "My concern is what the men were doing as they traveled with Brighit. I believe she was their cover. She said they spoke to everyone. Some were responsive while others were not. They were looking for Godwinson supporters."

John crossed his arms. "So how would you have us proceed?"

"Mort is with your soldiers. He knows what he is about. The siege will not wait for either of us. By the slim chance that the gates are opened to him, I'm certain he would send word to us. Could we travel back along the Great North road to measure just how much support there is for Godwinson? Tostig was very powerful in this area."

"As I am well aware. But the King has orders that I must obey. He knows little of how close I have come—several times—to complete disregard for those orders. I prefer to keep it that way."

Peter knew he spoke not only of allowing Leofrid to live but of John's leaving his bride untouched after he was forced to wed the Saxon. That he later found her much to his liking and was more than willing to see to his husbandly duties rectified the situation but he had defied the King nonetheless. A treasonous act.

"Then let us see this done!"

"Ralph de Gael traveled from London to York, raising the hackles of every earl William slighted in his play for absolute control." John's face softened. "I admit I am most concerned for sweet Emma. She is caught in the middle. To know she suffered within the castle would pain me greatly."

"You have always had a soft spot for William FitzOsbern's only daughter."

"True but my feelings for her never ran so deep as my feelings for Rowena. What I thought was love was not. And you said Leofrid was still in Ireland?"

"That he was about a month ago is all I can say."

John nodded. "Then we will proceed with the siege and pray it will end without too much bloodshed. Then I will assess whether I must confess to the King that Leofrid still lives."

"I would prefer you not have to do that, John."

"As would I." John's face was tight with concern. "Once we have the castle, we will deal with this. If we can ascertain for certain that Leofrid remains in Ireland, we will deal with the threat he may become to the King."

"And I pray it will not be too late," Peter said.

CHAPTER 26

The next few months dragged by for Brighit with her constant worrying about Peter and John's condition outside the castle at York. Her own condition became more and more apparent. Her menses had stopped completely. She was with child.

Martha, as the newly appointed Prioress, received word from the King. He considered himself a godly man and expected much from his Priory at the River Aire, such as getting word to his soldiers. Reinforcements and supplies would be late in arriving due to the heavy snows so they would need to make other arrangement. The King had decided to wait until the spring to travel north.

"I've no one to send," Martha said.

"Doesn't the Priory have knights they can dispense?" Tadhg asked right before biting into a biscuit dripping with honey.

She put her hand on her hip, a very annoyed look on her face. "Tadhg, I know about Saint John and Saint Peter, not about warfare. I know there are knights... somewhere... but the previous Prioress really depended on the Bishop to send notices and dispatch them."

He took a deep swallow of mead. "Well, the King's not asking for them to be dispatched. He's requesting a message be sent. I can do that."

"Oh, Tadhg, are you sure you should?" Brighit had no appetite and watching her brother shovel in food as if he may never eat again made her queasy.

He turned to her, a smile playing over his lips. "And you would not be appreciative of some word on Peter's conditions?"

Heat suffused her face. "Of course, I would like to know how he fares but not if it puts you in harm's way."

Tadhg rolled his eyes. "Can you ever be less of a woman?"

Brighit pulled back. "Whatever do you mean? I am a woman."

"I know that. I mean can't you ever just realize I'm a warrior and being near fighting does not put me in harm's way. I can fend for myself in all situations."

She snorted. "I see."

Her brother had remained very tight lipped about the goings on at home and she wondered for the hundredth time if there was something he wasn't telling her. He was not usually so defensive.

"Martha, I can bring the message for you. It may be best to let the others head back to Ireland without me."

Brighit was suddenly swamped with sadness at the idea of losing her connection to Ireland. They had all been very attentive, making it their mission to keep her entertained.

Tadhg, as always, saw her true feelings no matter how she tried to hide them. "I'm sorry, dear sister. We have all stayed longer than we intended. Say your goodbyes. They'll be leaving forthwith."

Within an hour's time, they'd all assembled in the bailey. Each man hugged Brighit in turn and went to his horse. Sean was the only one remaining.

"Head down the hill. I'll be there anon," Sean gave the order to the other men. He'd be in command until Tadhg's return.

He pierced Tadhg with his can-you-please-give-us-a-moment-alone look. Tadhg rolled his eyes. Brighit pretended not to notice the exchange but she was aware that her brother did not wander far.

Sean took her hands in his and gazed into her eyes. "My dear, Brighit." He smiled, tipping his head to one side. "I have long desired to take you as my wife."

"Please! We are too close. Like brother and sister. It would never have worked."

"I kept my distance out of respect for my best friend—your brother."

Tadhg shifted behind them. Brighit knew he heard every word. He was protecting her in Peter's absence even from this man that they'd both known their entire lives.

"He made me promise to never take advantage of your innocence. I fear I took his advice too much to heart in never expressing my feelings for you."

She glanced down, afraid Sean would realize that Tadhg was only doing her bidding. She had never thought of him in a romantic way.

"I hope you will remember me as I will never forget you," he said.

When he closed in on her, she offered her cheek to him. He kissed it lightly.

She attempted to give him a sage expression along with her next words. "There is a wonderful woman out there intended for you alone, dear Sean. Open your heart so that love may find you."

He tipped his head, released her hand and mounted his horse. Gripping the reins in one hand, he turned back to Tadhg who stepped up beside his sister.

"Protect her well so that Peter may return to a healthy babe."

Brighit's jaw dropped. Sean winked and urged his horse to a trot.

"How did he—"

Tadhg kissed her on the other cheek. "Men can tell these things, Brig."

She turned to him. "You know as well?"

"Of course."

Brighit grabbed his arm in a tight hold, her face close to his. "Do. Not. Tell. Peter."

Tadhg's eyes rounded. "Why would I tell him? It is not my place."

She relaxed her grip. "I'm happy to hear you say that."

The nuns put together supplies and Tadhg went off. Brighit believed her brother would be safe. She wanted word of her husband.

~

The land surrounding the motte and bailey structure no longer resembled a field that had ever grown anything. The small amount of tall grass that had begun to grow these many years after the harrowing could not withstand the trampling of soldiers. The thick mud sucked at the hooves of the horses and the boots of the men. Blackened earth mixed with horse excrement and refuse, reeked throughout their camp. The thudding of the trebuchet as it launched sundry items into and over the castle walls was deafening. Hell on earth.

John and Peter sat upwind of the horses and tried to block out their surroundings.

"You talked in your sleep again, Peter. Do I need to give you more work to keep your thoughts from her? We could always use another pit dug."

"My thoughts are always on her. I wake from my dreams raging with need." Peter glanced at his friend. "My apologies for keeping you awake."

"I've never known you to allow a woman to so trouble your dreams."

"Brighit is unlike any woman I have ever met."

John took a sip from the near empty skin. "My impression is that they are not all happy dreams. I hear your distress."

Peter bit into the apple Tadhg had just brought for the troops. The nuns constant supply of fresh food was probably the only thing keeping them from all becoming sick.

"Do not allow her brother to her you." He glanced around until he spotted the man helping to organize the supplies he'd brought. "I am very pleased to be wed to her but I fear I did not handle it well."

"You ask her to marry you. She says yes. You are wed. It is done."

Peter couldn't hold John's gaze. "I fear I did not confess all to you."

"Did you force her to marry you against her wishes? I'd say you have verily turned her wishes then. She is enamored with you."

Peter shook his head, finding it difficult to voice his concerns. She 'd said she loved him. But he was not sure he had ever said it back.

"Tadhg found us... in a compromising situation."

John pulled back, surprise written across his face. "I wouldn't expect that from you."

"It is not as you assume. We became... impassioned and I would have lain with her as was her wont but for the condition of our surroundings. She was a virgin and I did not believe it appropriate—"

"So there was no compromising situation?"

"We were abed when he entered. He made accusations..."

John waited. Peter looked back then shrugged.

"You didn't defend or explain?"

"Why? I realized I was in love with her. She was bound for the Priory. She would never have agreed to marry me. She was a woman with a mission more determined than most men. This way... she had to marry me because her brother said so."

John leaned back and laughed. And laughed. Just when he started to settle down, he looked at Peter and started all over again.

Peter decided he would count to five and if John could not stop finding humor in a situation that was quite disconcerting to him, he would leave. Five. Four. Three—

"Enough, John!" He glanced toward Tadhg who was looking over at them. "I do not need to air this in front of Tadhg again."

"He knows?"

"Of course. He's a smart man. He saw right through my ruse." John chuckled some more.

"I'm in love with her. I don't wish to lose her."

John sobered at his sincere words. "We will offer terms again. See if we can move this along. Get you back to your wife." John then turned his attention to another man. "Philip!"

The tall man Tadhg was speaking to turned toward John. Tadhg followed him over.

"We're going to see if we can end this. They must be suffering within. I don't know why they can be so pig-headed. Emma is surely not so obstinate."

Philip and Peter exchanged glances. John was remembering the girl he grew up with. Not the stubborn woman she turned into. Her father would have all but ignored her if she hadn't made an issue on every little thing. It was the only time she was ever given any attention by William FitzOsbern.

"Surely it is her husband who is pig-headed," Philip offered, trying to be amicable. He knew the truth about Emma, too.

John stood and brushed the dried mud from his mail. "Damn mud. I'll be glad to get out of here and get a bath."

Philip raised his hand to halt the assault of the trebuchet just as it was about to launch the carcass of the cow they'd recently devoured over the castle walls. The cow had come from the farm that should have been replenishing the supplies for the occupants inside the castle. The soldiers signaled their understanding, disarming the large machine.

Philip stood beside Peter and the two followed John, fully covered in mail, as they crossed the field to approach the guard who stood high in the tower beside the front gate.

"Hail," John's voice held a commanding tone.

The man barely stirred. "Yes?"

"We wish to speak to the Earl."

The soldier leaned forward slightly. "Are you leaving?"

John laughed and looked around him, his arms extended. "Why would we need to leave? We have everything we need. We have *your* supplies at our disposal. The Earl!"

The man could be heard yelling down to the other soldiers as the message was relayed across the bailey and within the castle. John turned away, his hands on his hips. "I'm ready to see this end. Let us hope the Earl and his lady feel the same."

A short time later, another message could be heard making its way back to the guard. Lady Emma was coming.

"John! What are you about? King William robs my husband of power and command, puts sheriffs in places of honor, collecting taxes that are rightfully my husband's and he expects we should just open the gate at his orders?"

John looked up at the tower guard who effectively blocked any arrow that may be aimed at the lady. "That is how it is done, Lady Emma."

She pulled at the guard, moving him out of the way so that she could lean over the wall. "John, I must have your reassurance that my men will be allowed to be freed with no repercussion."

"*Your* men?"

Emma's loud sigh could be heard even from that distance. "Yes! They are my men. My husband is not within. He snuck out as soon as he heard of your approach."

"The scoundrel left you here to defend the castle alone?"

She shrugged.

"Why did you not just open the gates?"

"Because, John! King William is... is... a tyrant and well you know."

John refused to respond. Emma waited. They stared at each other. She put her hand to her hip. Not a hair moved on John's head. Emma refused to back down from the statement that may be acceptable in the privacy of a chamber but not here in front of the soldiers that swore allegiance to the man she maligned.

"Lady Emma, will you open the gates to us?" John spoke in a strong voice. Not a trace of emotion or consideration. A commander in complete control.

Emma waited. John counted to ten and turned back toward their camp. Peter and Philip close behind. No one said a word.

"Wait!" Emma's voice held desperation. "Yes. I accept any terms as long as my soldiers and I are not arrested."

John smiled, turned to Philip then Peter and together they walked back to the gate. "Open the gates."

The sound of chains moving within the walls was like the sound of sweet angels singing to Peter's ears. It would not be long now and he would be back with his wife. He just hoped he would find the words she needed to hear to find peace in their marriage.

CHAPTER 27

The snows raged on and Peter had been gone nearly five months. When Tadhg had returned from his last supply trip north, he assured her the siege was at an end. At the first sign of spring, he left to return home.

Brighit felt very alone After many sleepless nights in Bishop Odo's magnificent bed, Brighit moved to the hall with the other nuns. They welcomed her in and she was soon fitting into the rhythm of prayer and work. She even began to wear the nun's robes. It felt good to stay busy. They needed to be ready for planting at the first thaw. She decided to keep the fact that she was with child to herself.

In the quieter times, Brighit wondered at Peter's insistence they marry. She came to realize it was his overwhelming sense of honor that made him do it. Tadhg had been so unyielding about the impropriety of the situation. She should have been more determined. Tadhg would have eventually believed her if she said nothing happened. Peter must have felt he had wronged her with his lustful advances, despite her own willingness. When he believed she would be considered soiled, he did the only honorable thing.

Well, I'll certainly have none of that.

His declaration haunted her dreams. And here she was carrying his child. He would never feel free of his duty to her now. Brighit fought against the overwhelming sadness. She loved Peter. She wanted to be with him but not because of some sense of duty. She wanted him to be happy. Every night she prayed for his safe return. And she prayed he would return before her condition showed. She decided to let him have his life continue as it would have been without her. If he wanted "none of that" then she loved him enough to let him have it.

The smell of rain was in the air. The clouds were dark and threatening. Martha dragged the shovel through the blackened pile of decaying earth. Ruth and Brighit sifted through the dried seeds for planting.

"I don't see how you can tell the good from the bad," Brighit frowned.

Ruth smiled back. "You are too impatient. See." She held one brown seed before Brighit's face. "Is it broken open?"

"No?"

"Brighit, maybe you should just help me." Martha hefted the heavy tool again. "No knowledge needed for this."

"Not in her condition." Ruth's eyes widened.

Brighit froze. Perhaps she hadn't heard her right. She knew she was getting a little bigger around the middle but surely not noticeably so. She glanced over at Martha who had stopped as well. She shrugged at Brighit.

"Sorry. I forgot," Ruth said.

Brighit gave them her most barely-able-to-tolerate-you look. "I do not know of what you speak."

Martha pressed her lips together as if the words would sneak out on their own if she wasn't careful.

Ruth raised her nose in a defiant stance.

"You are with child, Brighit. We both—no—we *all* know it. We just don't understand why you haven't told us yourself."

"You are wrong. I am not with child." Her throat closed off, too tight for her to even swallow.

Ruth's eyes widened. "How can you possibly not know?" She shook her hands in the general direction of Brighit's swelling middle, apparently unable to put words together.

Bright looked to the heaven, her hand on her hip. After a moment, she slid it across her middle rubbing her little babe that she had thought she'd be able to keep secret. "How long have you known?"

"Two months at least." Martha stretched her back and moved to stand beside her. "You've always been well endowed but heavens, it's quite obvious."

Brighit wiped at the tears. "Do you think Peter will know when he sees me?"

Ruth's mouth dropped open and she stared at Martha. Martha's eyes widened. "It's more obvious every day. If he were to return now, he may not. Most men are not so observant. But why would you not want him to know?"

"I love Peter with all my heart but you heard him. He did not want a wife or a family. With me he has both."

"But he loves you, Brighit."

"No. I think he is just an honorable man. He would never leave me in a position where I'd be treated as a fallen woman."

"I think you underestimate Peter." Ruth shook her head. "A knight answers to no one but the King. He would not have married you simply because your brother said he must."

Brighit nibbled at her cheek. "My brother never told him he must marry me. It was all just this and that and nothing really was said right out in the open but the next thing I know, Peter is telling me to let it be and just go through with marrying him. I love him, so I did."

Ruth rubbed her hands together and brushed off her robe. "I think you need a rest. Let us go in before the rain starts and we get drenched."

Martha put an arm around Brighit. "Do not worry about what will happen when Peter returns. I'm sure he will be glad you are with child."

"No!" Brighit halted, pulling against her arm. "You cannot tell him! Please." She glanced between the two women. "Promise me you will not tell him."

"Oh, Brighit, I fear you are making a terrible mistake." Ruth's eyes rounded. "We will not tell him but I pray you will do the right thing by him just as he has done by you."

Martha and Ruth left Brighit to follow behind through the front gates of the Priory. Incessant drumming became a fast-paced horse just coming into view in the distance.

"Peter." Brighit whispered the words. Her heart leapt in her chest. The women watched as the horse and rider came closer.

"Look at you! You're filthy." Martha started her toward the front door.

"Halt!" Peter's order stilled all movement.

Martha and Ruth exchanged glances. "I think we can safely wait within. It is you he wants to see, no doubt."

Brighit felt abandoned and the sound of the horse stopping just inside the gate set her heart to drumming in her ears. She heard him call to her and when she turned, the sun could have been bursting through the clouds with the intense pleasure that filled her.

Peter took her in his arms, tight against his body. "I've dreamed of holding you for the past five months."

Brighit's knees buckled as intense relief swept over her. He pulled her into his arms, right off the ground, then kissed her. Nose to nose, he smiled at her. "Sweet Brighit, I have missed you. I was a man dying of thirst for want of a drink of you."

He kissed her again, more gently this time. She opened her mouth to him and wrapped her arms around his shoulders. She felt like a ship in a storm that had found safe harbor. "I have missed you, too."

A horse approached at a slower pace. He set her down and smiled again. "Mort!"

"Greetings, Brighit! I'm not sure how my friend did not get thrown from his horse with the pace he took getting back to you."

Peter never took his eyes from her. "Mort, enough. See to the horses. I'm busy."

He lifted her in his arms and pushed his way into the Priory. "I've missed you more than I've missed anything in my life." He shifted her head so he could kiss her on the mouth. "You are the sweetest thing I've tasted for months."

Brighit put her hand to his cheek, caressing it tenderly. "Peter, you do look thinner. Have you been eating?"

He nuzzled into her neck as they turned away from the Great Hall. "No. I don't want to talk about that. I'm fine. Let me look into your eyes."

Brighit noticed the direction he was headed and she tensed. He kicked open the door to the Bishop's chamber. He released her legs. She slid down to standing. His eyes closed in pleasure. "Just the touch of you against me renews my spirit."

With a hand on either side of her face, he took her mouth. The touch of his tongue against hers sent sparks straight to her core. Her body turned to mush and she clung to him for dear life. "I have missed you so."

He nibbled at her ear. "I've longed to hold you again."

His hand went to her head and he pulled back. "What?"

He looked at her as if he'd never seen her before and stepped away. "What are you wearing? Why are you—" His eyes took in their surroundings.

When she'd moved into the nun's quarters, they put Bishop Odo's chamber back in order. "Why does this room look like this?"

Peter ran his fingers through his long hair then scratched along his scalp and turned away. "I don't understand..."

He turned back to her. "Have you been sleeping here?"

"No. I was lonely. I missed you. I moved to sleep with the nuns."

He crossed his arms, his eyes ran the length of her nun's clothing, up to the wimple on her head, and back down again before stopping at her face.

"And why are you dressed like that?"

The hard angles of his face matched the anger she saw in his eyes. She looked away. "It seemed easier to dress as the nuns do."

He moved closer. Close enough that she could feel the heat pour off him. Close enough that she could sense the tightly leashed desire within him. Close enough that all she needed to do was move against him and he would take her. He would have her beneath him. He would ravage her. He would make her body sing and she would be lost. She didn't move.

"Has something transpired since I left that I should be told about?" He glanced over her body, pausing at her bosom.

Brighit held her breath. "No, my lord."

"Then I'm not sure why you look like a nun, sleep with the nuns, work with the nuns when I believe you are still my wife."

She looked down and paused before facing him. "We are wed, my lord. Of course. I just had time to think and... well..."

Peter raised his eyebrows as if asking for better clarification. She hadn't thought through what she would say. She hadn't expected him to set off such happiness and longing when he returned. And she hadn't expected him to act like he had missed her just as much.

She gave him her back when her eyes filled. "Um, I just had been thinking—"

He moved in closer to her. Her eyes shut. Her breathing became labored. She wanted him. Peter took a slow, deep breath. He was taking in the scent of her. She imagined he closed his eyes as he did it. Oh, dear God, she had not thought about how hard this would be.

"Tell me, Brighit." He was close enough that his breath brushed against her cheek when he spoke. She would die if she didn't respond to his unspoken desire. The child moved within her, she shifted in surprise, bumping against him.

Peter moaned as he wrapped his arms around her, pulling her tight against him. He rubbed his hardness against her bottom. "I have wanted you, woman."

His words were a hot whisper against her face. He slipped his hand under her wimple and released her hair in one gentle sweep. He nibbled her lobe. "Give me what I've longed for."

She moaned when he reached his hand under the outer robe and fondled her tender breasts. He pressed his mouth against the pulse of her neck, his hands immediately moving more tenderly. With the tip of his tongue, he moved along her neck, releasing her only to turn her toward him.

His eyes were dark pools of deep desire, holding her gaze. He parted her robes, slipping first the gown over her head, then the stark, white chemise. She shivered when the cold touched her heated skin. Then his eyes were on her body. She held her breath. His hands followed the same path and his eyes closed as if overwhelmed by the feel of her under his hands. Pulling her close against him, she could feel his erection pressing into her.

"Take me," she said.

He jerked the covering from the bed, lifted her into his arms, and deposited her with the utmost care onto the middle of the bed. He covered her and stilled. When she moved to touch him, he held her hand.

"No. I've been away too long. I need a moment."

He dipped his head into her neck. His rapid breathing sent ripples of desire through her.

"Please. Do not hold yourself away from me. I am here now."

He leaned on his forearms and searched her face. Reaching beneath his tunic, he yanked down his braies, his throbbing member pressed against her wetness.

Her eyes closed in pleasure and he plunged into her. She exhaled. He braced himself and rode her hard. She welcomed each thrust and was quickly moaning against him. He covered her mouth with his, taking her sounds into himself. His tongue thrusting against her as well. Her passion was peaked. Panting, she cried out his name. Another thrust and he stilled within her, filling her with his seed. He pressed into her again, hard. He looked down at her.

"This is where I belong. Did you have other ideas?"

She looked away, unable to hold his gaze.

He covered her breast with his hand, as if assessing some internal measure of her. She steadied her breath. He couldn't know.

"Any news here? Is there anything you wish to share with me?"

Brighit refused to face him. She shook her head.

Peter was surprised at the overwhelming joy that spread throughout him with the obvious condition of his wife. Brighit was with child. He was sincerely overjoyed. He was also thoroughly confused by her reaction to him.

She snuggled against him where she lay still naked, sleeping beside him. He hugged her closer and kissed the top of her head. Perhaps allowing Tadhg to force him to marry her was not Peter's best idea. Perhaps it left some seed of doubt about his feelings.

When she'd asked him why he didn't just tell them nothing happened, he thought she understood. He'd told her they both knew something happened. He was not willing to let her go. He realized his feelings for her. Feelings that were obvious every time he held her. Every time he kissed her. Every time he loved her.

Brighit made a sound in her sleep and her hand slid over her belly. He wondered if the child could be felt yet.

Despite the exhaustion of his body, his mind raced. The siege had taken much longer than he would have liked. Although it ended with the coming of terms for Emma and the soldiers, Ralph de Gael would be brought to London to face the King. Nothing had been discovered for certain about the Godwinsons. The Earls had lost much when Harold Godwinson was killed. Land. Power. Money. The idea of another Godwinson ruling England could be the impetus for the revolt. No such connection had been discovered for certain.

And why was she wearing the nun's robes? What was Brighit thinking? That she could just continue on with her vows as if he'd never married her? He was not going to let her just walk away. He would rather die than live without her. She'd professed her love to him so why this?

He ran his hand along her side stopping at her belly.

She snuggled closer still.

He slid his hand along the new swell. His lungs expanded. It would be a boy. Or a girl. It mattered little. It would be from her. A pattering against his hand. He flattened his palm. A steady push and a slide.

Brighit mumbled something and rolled away from him. Her full breasts pushing into his hand. He nibbled at her shoulder. Her breasts were heavy. She shifted when his hand brushed her nipple. And sensitive.

"I've missed you so," Peter whispered.

He turned her face toward him and kissed her.

She responded still not quite awake, turning into his arms.

"Do you know how much I've missed you?" he asked.

She shook her head.

"Let me tell you then."

Her eyes opened, still heavy with sleep and unfocused.

"I heard a tune being played from the castle. It was beautiful and reminded me of you. I wanted you to tell me its name."

Fully awake suddenly, there was a wary look in her eyes.

He continued. "I saw a bunch of blue flowers trying to survive beneath a tree where the snow hadn't reached. They reminded me of the one you'd put in your hair. Do you remember?"

She nodded, a frown creasing her brow.

"Everywhere I looked, I saw something that I wanted to share with you." He pushed her hair behind her ear. "And you weren't there with me. I want you with me always, my lovely Brighit."

He lowered his mouth to hers and kissed her deeply. Then pulled away and smiled.

"So how have things been here? You missed me enough to move to the nun's quarters?"

"I did. This room was exceedingly empty without you."

He kissed her again. "I'm sorry I had to leave you so soon. I hope to not leave you again for a very long while."

Her pupils widened.

"How did you spend your days?"

"Well, the nuns work very hard. So I worked very hard."

"Were you careful?"

She narrowed her eyes. "Careful? What do you mean?"

Peter glanced away. "Just were you careful of yourself? Not working too hard?"

"I'm a strong woman. I can work hard."

He turned back to her. "Is there nothing you wish to share with me?"

"No."

He had a hard time hiding his disappointment. A deep sense of loss tripped along his spine. "Is there a reason you're wearing the nun's robes?"

Her throat constricted. "Peter. I wanted you to know—"

No! "I remember something else."

"This is very difficult for m—"

He put his finger to her lips. "Do not."

They stared at each other and he knew she was going to try and send him away. All the clothing, the work, and leaving this room were all in preparation of her telling him goodbye. He had to convince her to change her mind.

"There's one thing you should know for certain. When we were in the shelter to get out of the storm and you offered yourself to me, I realized something that I don't think you understand. Do you know what that is?"

"That we are very well matched in bed."

Peter bit his lip to keep from smiling. "And do you know why that is?"

She lifted a shoulder. "No."

"When you offered yourself to me, I realized you were always mine. I realized how much you meant to me. I realized that I would be lost if I ever had to give you up."

Her eyes widened and she sat up beside him.

"I realized I was in love with you."

"Peter, I—"

"Let me have my say. When your brother would have taken you away from me, I realized I could never let you go. So I played on your brother's anger and sense of honor. By marrying you, I would never have to be without you."

Peter took her hand to his lips, his eyes still on her face, and kissed the palm of her hand. "I love you, Brighit. I should have told you then what you mean to me but you were so determined. I couldn't take the chance of losing you."

Brighit wrapped her arms around his neck and pulled him close against her. "Did you hear me when I told you I loved you? I do, Peter. I love you."

"My heart soared when you spoke those words to me. I vow to never make you regret marrying me."

He leaned up to her and kissed her as he had in the chapel. Then he pulled back. "Is there anything else you wish to tell me?" Peter brushed his knuckles alongside her breast. "I will listen. Anything?"

She flattened his hand over her stomach. "I don't need to tell you what you've already deduced. Do I?"

"Please just say the words."

She took his hand and placed it over her womb then looked at him with an expectant expression. "I am carrying your child."

A small push against his hand.

She smiled. "I believe that may be the babe moving. We'll have to see as it grows."

Peter felt a tug of fear. He rested his head on her breast and spoke without looking at her. "Can we take care that you will deliver without a problem?"

She ran her hand over his head. "Oh, Peter, do you fear that?"

"Woman die in childbirth every day."

"Is that why you seemed so angry when Ruth was in labor? Did you fear she was about to die?"

Peter nodded against her. "And there would have been nothing I could do to save her." He swallowed before he continued. "There was nothing they could do to save my own mother."

"Your mother died in childbirth?"

"Yes. She died delivering me."

Brighit pulled him closer. "That's terrible!"

"And until very shortly, I believed another woman I had been intimate with had died delivering my child. I felt cursed." He exhaled quietly, afraid of her reaction but he wanted to share everything with her. "My father assured me I was indeed cursed."

Brighit tensed beneath him. "How could a man tell that to his child?"

"With the pounding of a fist usually."

"Oh, dear Peter. He beat you?" She held him against her bosom. "That dirty pig!"

"I believed I deserved it. He told me that I did." Peter's voice sounded flat but inside he saw again his father's enraged face. "Over and over, he would hit me. I can't remember how old I was when it started. I don't remember him ever not beating me. I do remember standing at my mother's grave and praying to God to strike me dead."

Brighit's tear hitting his hand brought his mind back to her.

"I'm sorry. I shouldn't have shared that with you."

She shook her head and the tears flowed in earnest. "Peter, that is no way for a man to treat his son." She cupped his cheek. "You are a wonderful, kind man. The gentlest man I know. My heart cries for the little boy you were."

Brighit pulled him close to her. "Let us show our child only love. A gentle hand."

He picked up his head and looked her in the eyes. "I would not want to lose you."

"Peter, I am a strong woman. You will not lose me."

He sat up to lean on his elbow and wiped at her tears. "When John brought news that the other woman had died delivering someone else's child, I felt... relief. Does that not make me cruel?"

"Never. You believed you were cursed. Now you see that you are not. You do see that?"

Peter held her gaze. "I see that I could be immensely happy with you. If you chose to stay with me." He took her hand to his lips and kissed it. "I do love you, Brighit."

"And I love you."

Peter lifted an eyebrow and eased her back to lying in the bed. "Then let us see of this strength of yours. The hour is still early, if you are willing?"

"I'm always willing."

The End

ABOUT THE AUTHOR

Aside from two years spent in the wilds of the Colorado mountains, Ashley York is a proud life-long New Englander and a hardcore romantic. She has an MA in History which brings with it a love for primary documents and the smell of musty old libraries. With her author's imagination, she likes to write about people who could have lived alongside those well-known giants from the past.

Connect with her online at
Website: www.ashleyyorkauthor.com

MORE BOOKS BY ASHLEY YORK

Thanks for reading *The Gentle Knight*. A review would be greatly appreciated since it helps other readers discover the story.

If you enjoy historical romance with a touch of intrigue and adventure, check out these books by Ashley York

The Warrior Kings Series

Curse of the Healer

Eyes of the Seer

Daughter of the Overking

The Norman Conquest Series

The Saxon Bride

The Gentle Knight

The Irish Warrior

The Seventh Son

The Order of the Scottish Thistle

Lachlann's Legacy